PRAISE FOR *THE NATURALIST*

"[A] smoothly written suspense novel from Thriller Award finalist Mayne . . . The action builds to [an] . . . exciting confrontation between Cray and his foe, and scientific detail lends verisimilitude."

—*Publishers Weekly*

"With a strong sense of place and palpable suspense that builds to a violent confrontation and resolution, Mayne's (*Angel Killer*) series debut will satisfy devotees of outdoors mysteries and intriguing characters."

—*Library Journal*

"*The Naturalist* is a suspenseful, tense, and wholly entertaining story . . . Compliments to Andrew Mayne for the brilliant first entry in a fascinating new series."

—*New York Journal of Books*

"An engrossing mix of science, speculation, and suspense, *The Naturalist* will suck you in."

—*Omnivoracious*

"A tour de force of a thriller."

—*Gumshoe Review*

"Mayne is a natural storyteller, and once you start this one, you may find yourself staying up late to finish it . . . It employs everything that makes good thrillers really good . . . The creep factor is high, and the killer, once revealed, will make your skin crawl."

—*Criminal Element*

DARK PATTERN

DARK PATTERN

ANDREW MAYNE

THOMAS & MERCER

Text copyright © 2019 by Andrew Mayne Harter

Published by Thomas & Mercer, Seattle

www.apub.com

Amazon, the Amazon logo, and Thomas & Mercer are trademarks of Amazon.com, Inc., or its affiliates.

ISBN-13: 9781542092562

ISBN-10: 1542092566

Cover design by M. S. Corley

Printed in the United States of America

DARK PATTERN

PROLOGUE

As the aerial tram glided up the hillside to the fortress-like hospital above, Rebecca Graham felt anything but safe. The bearded man at the back of the car was watching her. His eyes were dark, and he clung to the back window as if he were his own shadow.

His jacket was tattered, his hands rough and dirty. Yellow papers with what appeared to be satanic symbols stuck out of his pockets.

This man was clearly nuts. The strange thing was that when she got onto the tram, she hadn't even noticed he was there. Unlike the other homeless she'd encountered working as a nurse in the shelter in the city below, he had no scent. She'd thought she was alone until she glanced at the window in front of her and saw his face reflected from behind her.

She tried to maintain her composure and not show fear. Her left foot trembled, and she braced herself with the overhead handrail. The lights of the hospital were too far away. The tram was moving too slowly.

She was trapped.

She tried to look away from the reflection but was afraid that she'd find his hands around her throat a moment later. And then?

She glanced at the emergency button. Should she push it? Nobody could get to her while she was between stations, but at least help could be waiting on arrival . . .

The tram passed a tower and shook. When she looked in the window again, the man's face was gone. Her heart started racing. Her right hand reached for the red button . . . until she saw his reflection as the tram left the tower's shadow and its interior once again brightened.

He was still behind her. Still staring.

Rebecca Graham scarcely breathed until the tram finally reached the platform. It was the most frightened she'd ever been—and she'd experienced death on a regular basis.

She had no reason to know that their paths would cross again, or that when they did, it would change her fate forever.

CHAPTER ONE
NORA

Nora watched the doorway. This was when the Night Lady usually stopped at her room and stared inside.

The first time she thought she was dreaming. The woman didn't seem real. Her face was blank and without expression.

It reminded Nora of when she woke up in the middle of the night and saw a face in a pile of clothes.

But this woman was real.

At least Nora was certain now.

The Night Lady walked through most nights. But it was only when there were no other adults here that the bad things happened.

Four nights ago, after Nurse Christina had left and the slip-plop of her shoes trailed to the elevator, the Night Lady had gone into Robert's room.

A half hour later, the alarms had gone off and everyone rushed to see Robert.

They didn't say what happened, but the next day when they wheeled all the beds out to watch a movie, his bed wasn't there.

They'd left his toys and shoes in his cubbyhole.

Going away meant going someplace where you didn't need your shoes anymore.

That didn't sound like a good place.

Nora waited to see what room the Night Lady would visit next.

CHAPTER TWO
No-Fly Zone

Under a dull gray sky, the nose cone of the West Air double-decker jetliner is resting inches over the clay shingles of a two-story house in an Austin suburb. Fire-suppressing foam is spilling out from backyards like snow while emergency crews are trying to pump thousands of gallons of jet fuel into two tanker trucks parked in the street. I roll down the window so I can get a better view of the outermost starboard engine, barely visible through a gap between the houses. It looks like a black metal nest ripped apart by the hands of an angry god.

"Amazing that nobody died," says Deputy Reddis from the driver's seat of the SUV, taking me through the disaster zone.

Twenty minutes ago, I'd been lost in my own world—less than eight miles from the crash site—when a loud knock came at the door. I could tell from the staccato rhythm that it was law enforcement. My heart raced as I worried which of my many misdeeds could have finally caught up with me.

"Dr. Cray?" Reddis had asked at the door. My girlfriend, Jillian, was at her bakery café taking care of the influx of Little League baseball teams that flooded in on cupcake Saturdays.

"Yes?" I replied, studying his uniform and wondering if I was about to be served a warrant.

"You're needed at the crash site."

"Crash site?" I'd heard sirens in the distance but hadn't connected them to anything in my world.

"The West Air jumbo jet? It just went down an hour ago." He saw the confusion on my face. "A few miles from here. You're on the list."

"The list?" In my experience there are good lists and bad lists. Being on a list connected with an airplane crash didn't sound like a good thing. My mind raced, and I thought of Jillian. "Where exactly did it crash?"

"Sage Brook."

I exhaled with relief. That was the opposite direction from Jillian.

"The pilot took it down over the conservation land. Nobody was hurt . . . that we know of. Now, if you'll come with me . . ."

I didn't move. "I'm not sure I understand."

"Agent Lowell from the Department of Homeland Security sent me to get you."

I didn't know a Lowell at DHS. "Why?"

Reddis shrugged. It seemed genuine enough. "I was told to bring you to the staging area."

Okay, that was a mild relief. If he'd said the police station or DHS headquarters, I'd expect to be arrested. Still, I hesitated.

Reddis stared at me for a moment. "You really haven't been watching the news?"

"No."

"Every airport in the country is shut down right now. Every airplane is grounded," he explained. He glanced to the side, as if to make sure we were alone, then said in a lower voice, "They think this might be part of a terrorist attack. A big one."

After we'd left my house, I checked the news on my phone and asked Reddis questions as he drove us through traffic with sirens wailing. He didn't know much beyond what I saw on CNN, Fox, and Twitter: way more guesses than facts. Generally, I find it a good idea to wait a day or so before forming an opinion about a crisis, because the first twenty-four hours are usually filled with bullshit speculation by reporters paid by news channels to fill the air with baseless observations while the internet is taken over by people who prefer to speak first and think last.

Our SUV passes the front of the plane and nears the end of the block, where another deputy waves us through a barricade and directs us to a middle school parking lot.

I follow Reddis out of the vehicle and into Eagle Bluff Middle School. The halls are filled with police, federal agents, and every other type of responder you'd expect to find at a disaster like this. Classrooms have been turned into mini command centers as responders deal with the many spin-off crises an event like this creates. Besides the immediate problem of what happened, someone has to figure out where to put the survivors or how to get them home. I can hear a woman on a cell phone asking a hotel how many rooms they have available. Someone else is patiently dealing with a resident yelling at them over the phone about when they can reenter their home. From the barking coming from the cafeteria, I can tell they've already dealt with the four-legged passengers from the cargo hold.

"This way," says Reddis as he directs me to a door protected by two Army National Guardsmen holding M4 rifles. "This is Dr. Cray."

I'm ushered into the gymnasium, where dozens of scattered tables host people working on laptops. I spot FBI, DHS, ATF, and several other three-letter acronym jackets spread around the space. Reddis leads me to a woman with a DHS jacket.

She has dark, curly hair pulled back into a practical ponytail. Suntanned to the point of making her look a few years older than she probably is, she wears an intense expression that I'd hate to have focused on me in anger. Even in a room full of high-testosterone law enforcement males, something tells me she'd be the alpha.

"Cray?" she says, looking up from her laptop.

"Lowell?" I reply.

She gives me a quick nod. I'd bet anything she's ex-military, like Jillian. "One hour and twenty minutes ago, West Air flight 8801 leaving Austin had two engines blow up two minutes after takeoff. We believe shrapnel from the first engine took out the second, forcing an emergency landing. The pilot was able to set it down in the conservation area behind us with minimal injuries. As a precaution, we've grounded all flights in the United States."

"Because you think it might be terrorism?" I ask.

"I don't think anything. I follow protocols and what my bosses tell me. Right now, they want to know if it's safe to reopen air travel."

"You're asking me?"

"You and about five other people here, as well as our experts back in DC. The computer popped your name up as someone in the immediate vicinity with government clearance and experience."

"I'm a biologist . . ."

"A *computational* biologist and the guy that caught the Grizzly Killer and John Christian and helped stop the attempt to sabotage the DoD vaccine supply. You've also worked with counterterrorism operations. I think you'd agree that institutional knowledge only goes so far?"

"Okay. What else do we know?"

"Follow me." Lowell walks quickly to another section of the gym separated by plastic strung over a volleyball net. A group of forensic technicians wearing clean suits and clear face shields are hovering over something on a table.

Lowell hands me a pair of latex gloves and a face shield. "Let Dr. Cray have a look."

A technician holding a camera steps aside, revealing a twisted shape that vaguely resembles a spider. It's about a meter across and has armatures bent at odd angles.

"What's the first question that comes to your mind, Dr. Cray?"

I think back to the sight of the exploded engine. "How did this drone survive the explosion?"

"Exactly," says a man with a gray beard watching from the other side of the table.

"This is Dr. Rossman, formerly of NASA," says Lowell. "He's one of the other brains the computer recommended."

"Take a closer look," says Rossman.

I kneel to get a better view. The body of the drone is made of metal. "Steel?"

Rossman nods. "Yes. Heavier than aluminum or carbon fiber, but likely to do more damage."

"You think this is intentional?" I ask.

"If I had to guess, this is Chinese or Russian made."

"What makes you say that?"

"It's not as sophisticated as some of our technology. But still effective."

"Why Russian or Chinese? Why not a hobbyist?"

He stares at me blankly. "Why go through the effort of a custom build? It'd be much easier to buy one online that could do as much damage."

I glance at Lowell, checking to see if she noticed Rossman backed down in less than ten seconds regarding how much damage a commercial drone could do.

"What exactly did you do at NASA?" I ask.

"Propulsion," he replies.

Okay, he's more qualified to be here than I am.

"We've seen equally sophisticated drones in Syria and Yemen," says a woman standing to my right. "Some were homegrown. Others made by the Chinese." She turns toward me and holds out a hand. "Captain Sarah McCallum, air force, retired." She's tall with short dark hair and a demeanor about as serious as Lowell's.

"Okay," says Lowell, "now that we have you all here, what's the verdict? Onetime event or a master plot? We're getting pressured to open up the skies. What do you say?"

"Well," Rossman starts to say before I cut him off.

"Shut up."

He shoots me an angry look.

I raise my hand. "Hold on. Lowell, before any of us start speaking out of our asses, what exactly is the purpose of the little brain trust here?"

She gives me an impatient glance. "DHS wants outside experts to weigh in on this. We've dealt with criticism in the past for not relying on other expert opinions. You're an advisory panel."

"I've been here fifteen minutes." I glance at the others. "Have any of you had more than twenty minutes here? Have any of you been told anything else?"

Rossman and McCallum shake their heads.

Lowell glares at me. "This is the real world, Dr. Cray—the country is at a standstill. Time is something we don't have."

"Maybe not, but it feels like we're being set up as some kind of scapegoat for you. I seriously doubt the DHS is waiting on our advice. Your bosses just want someone else to share the blame if another attack happens."

"What's he saying?" asks Rossman.

"That this is bullshit," replies McCallum. "If we tell them to open up the skies and another plane falls, it's on us, at least partially."

"Or more precisely, if we come to the same conclusion as her bosses have, then we get the blame if it's a bad idea."

Lowell rolls her eyes. "It's not that difficult. I promise you it's on me. Okay? Lots of other people are weighing in on this. You're not that important."

"Well, that's a relief," I reply. I notice a map spread across a table to the side. I walk away from Lowell and the others to get a closer look.

A red line leads from the airport then deviates into a wide circle where the plane came to rest. An *X* marks the spot on the flight path where the drone presumably hit the engine.

The conservation area is almost the only uninhabited section of the flight path. This could have been bad, very bad.

Rossman joins me. He points to a neighborhood near the impact point. "If it went down here, that would have been real expensive. Some of those homes are worth multiple millions of dollars."

Personally, I'd worry more about a poorer area with a higher population density, but I don't point that out.

"What's the flight radius on a drone like that?" I ask Rossman.

"Average battery? Maybe twenty miles. But with that heavier airframe? I'd say closer to ten."

McCallum comes over to the table to watch. Without seeking permission from Lowell, I grab a ruler and trace a ten-mile circle around the impact point onto the map.

"We already have people doing that," says Lowell. "We just need an answer. Fly or no fly?"

"Science isn't decided like an *American Idol* vote."

"I think they're really trying to decide whether to raise the terror threat level," McCallum says in a hushed tone.

"By asking us?" replies Rossman.

"Not really. We're a kind of a formality," I reply.

Lowell places her fists on the table and growls, "Should I just send you all packing?"

"I have a counteroffer. How about we try to solve this thing?"

She crosses her arms and gives me an incredulous look. "I heard you were an arrogant son of a bitch, but I had no idea how much." She waves her arm at the gymnasium filled with people. "And what do you think these people are doing?"

"Following protocols and their boss's orders. Same as you." I check my watch and then hear my mouth say something that I'm pretty sure is a complete surprise to my brain.

"Give me one hour. Work with me and I promise you that I'll get your biggest lead in that time."

"How?"

"We're about to figure it out." I shrug. "You know me—you know my reputation. Would you really want to bet against me?"

She shakes her head. "Give me a minute to talk it over with my bosses."

Lowell steps aside to make a phone call. McCallum, who's been watching this with some amusement, speaks up. "Do you have any idea what to do?"

"Not a clue."

And I don't. But at least for the next hour or so, I can take my mind off the task that had been my focus before Deputy Reddis's knock at the door.

I'd been seriously considering how to kill myself.

CHAPTER THREE
THREAT LEVEL

I stare at three laptop screens while a technician hooks up a computer to the gymnasium's overhead projection system. On one screen is the drone, another shows the engine damage, and a third displays the flight path.

"Well?" asks Lowell.

"It's only been four minutes," I reply. "I'm thinking."

"Is this how you usually work?"

"There's usually no usual. Except maybe for a few bodies."

McCallum points to the drone. "Then I guess that's your body."

I point to the airplane. "Technically that's the body. The drone is the weapon. Or in biology it'd be the pathogen. I don't know—analogies can be misleading." I gesture to the map. "What's important to me is the timeline. The drone, the plane, and the person or people who controlled it all have their own trajectories. We know where the drone ended up, and the plane. The question is, where are they now?"

"Or where did the drone come from?" asks McCallum.

"Radar has nothing," says Lowell. "Too low and too small."

"What about eyewitnesses?" I ask.

"Nada. We have a phone number and email address for witnesses. Our people are going through those reports now."

"About how many?"

"Right now, a few thousand tips. We'll get a few hundred typically every time the contact info is shown in a major market."

"And you're able to process all those that fast?"

Lowell gives me a dumb look. "What? No. That can take weeks. We have people transcribe them, and then agents go through them."

I turn to her, shocked. "Wait. Are you saying that someone could be calling right now and saying, 'I did it,' and you might not know for weeks?"

"No. Don't be ridiculous. If they got through to a person, we'd escalate it and have dozens of agents reading it right now."

"But if they don't get through, it could take weeks or not at all if it's not taken seriously," I reply.

"Do you have a better solution?"

"Yeah, you can get on the phone right now with whoever handles the email account and ask them to do a keyword search for 'buzzing.'"

"I could, but it won't be much help. We've already been looking for reports of people hearing drones flying overhead."

"And?" asks McCallum.

"People can't tell the difference between an electric Weed eater and a hexacopter. We've had reports from all over with conflicting time stamps." She waves a hand around the screen. "Take your pick."

"And eyewitnesses?" I ask.

"Conflicting, nothing concrete. We have people canvassing neighborhoods. We're also pulling surveillance footage from any street cameras we can."

"Lowell, come take a look," calls another DHS agent working on a laptop.

We follow and glance over her shoulder. On-screen is a piece of black metal on the ground.

"FBI just found this near the crash site. Our FAA guy says it's probably from the drone."

Etched into the metal are the letters *VTXI*.

"What is that, Latin?" asks Rossman.

"Probably an acronym," says Lowell. "We found anything on that yet?"

"It's a luxury model for a Cadillac with a lowercase *i*. But we haven't found any other manufacturing marks. No known terrorist groups use the term," says the agent.

"Okay, that appears to be deliberate. Anything else on the drone?" she asks.

"The parts appear to be laser cut. We haven't found the electronics yet. Chances are it's a standard radio set and won't tell us much. We haven't found any exotic materials. Forensics is going over it for prints and DNA, although the explosion probably cleaned most of that off. Our military experts think the portion we have survived because the drone got ripped in half on impact and was ejected in the explosion."

Lowell checks her watch, then looks at me. "Fourteen minutes have gone by, Cray. What've you got?"

"I think you're ignoring the most important evidence right now."

"Oh really? And what would that be?"

I walk back over to the map on the table. "You said you had multiple witnesses who reported hearing the drone fly over?"

"Yes. But they reported it in different places at the same time, and we know in some cases it was lawn equipment. It's Saturday," she explains. "Lots of lawn mowing going on."

"If you have a blood test with too many false positives, you don't throw out the blood samples. You refine the test. Here you have too many people saying they heard the drone fly overhead. That doesn't mean some of them didn't."

"I understand how statistics works, Dr. Cray. We've been playing drone sounds for witnesses, asking them if it's similar."

"From where?"

"What from where?" she replies.

"Where are you getting the drone sounds?"

Lowell calls over to a bald agent. "Addison, can you play the drone sound for Dr. Cray?"

Addison plugs his computer into the overhead projector and adjusts the sound input. "It's from a YouTube clip," he explains before filling the gymnasium with a high-pitched buzzing sound.

The distinct sound of a drone and the "whoosh" of the wind can be clearly made out. I glance over at McCallum. She hears the same problem I do and shakes her head.

"What?" asks Lowell.

"That's a quadcopter," says the retired air force officer. "The thing on the table was a hexacopter. Six motors, not four."

"And?" asks Addison.

"A hexacopter's going to sound a lot more like a lawn mower than a leaf blower," McCallum explains. "It might make no difference or all the difference." She turns to me. "I'm not sure if it would make a difference, Dr. Cray. People are unreliable either way."

She has a point. I shake my head as I stare at the map. "That still leaves too much uncertainty."

"I'm not going to hold you to your promise, Cray," says Lowell.

"I'm not done yet," I snap back. "Can I borrow a laptop?"

Addison unplugs his and hands it to me. I sit down at a table and pull up a 3-D aerial view of the neighborhood where the plane crash-landed. From my pilot's-eye view, I navigate to the point of impact.

The houses and trees look like fuzzy cartoon images as they scroll by. I point the view in the direction the plane was heading and from which the drone probably approached to cause a head-on collision with the engine.

"Angle up," says McCallum over my shoulder.

"What?"

"The plane would have more pitch as it took off," she explains.

I tilt the view so that I'm no longer looking at the ground.

"Hmm, the drone had to come in from pretty high up," she observes.

"What's the ceiling for one of those?"

"High enough. But it would've needed to build up some speed and get the aim just right. Tricky . . ."

She gets it at the same time I do. "Hey, Lowell, have there been any reports of pilots getting hit by lasers out of this airport?"

"I'm on it," says Addison.

I tilt the image down and scan the surrounding area. If I wanted to take out an airplane like this, I'd do two things: The first would be to put a laser pointer on the drone so I could see what I was about to hit. The second would be to hide my point of origin.

"Can I see something?" McCallum tilts the perspective downward again, then spins the world around to see what's directly behind the flight path. "Maybe find out if anyone saw someone suspicious there?"

"Possibly," I reply. "Can you go back to the point of impact?"

"Sure." She swivels the view back to where it was pointed. "Too bad we don't have a gunshot listener for drones."

She's referring to a system deployed in cities and war zones that uses microphones to trace the source of a gunshot. In an urban environment with lots of echoes, it can be next to impossible to triangulate the source of a noise without the help of a computer.

I zoom in to a neighborhood that was almost certainly in the drone's flight path. It's filled with lots of nice homes with big, sprawling yards.

I'm sure we could keep canvassing until we had enough data points to figure out an approximate point of origin, but that could take weeks and still give us an imprecise answer as to who is actually behind this.

If only we had McCallum's gunshot listener.

Oh wait.

Maybe we do. Kind of.

"I need to make a call."

CHAPTER FOUR
TRIANGULATE

I've done a lot of bad things. The first time I crossed the line was when I broke into the ambulance to examine Chelsea's corpse back in Montana. Then came the trespassing . . . lots of trespassing. I've put spy cameras on private property, broken and entered buildings. I've stolen evidence. I've even manufactured my own bacterial agents so I could track down people—an act that could be considered biological warfare. I killed a man in cold blood and let everyone think it was self-defense. He was a serial killer, so nobody looked too hard into it. I've butchered corpses on multiple occasions and led authorities on dead ends that could get me federal prison time.

I can live with those things, because inaction would weigh even more heavily on my conscience. I do those things because if I don't, people will die. The rationale of a vigilante.

I used to tell Jillian most of what I did. I stopped after Butcher Creek. I try not to think about that.

I definitely haven't told her about Mycroft. He's five miles away from here, and if anything's going to get me jail time in this day and age, it would be him.

Mycroft is thousands of lines of Python code running on several servers in a small office space I rent in an industrial park ten minutes from my home. At any given moment, Mycroft is breaking the laws in this and just about every other country, although he's not doing anything that the NSA, NRO, DIA, or other spy agencies don't already do to you.

I suspect there are hundreds of different variations of Mycroft in China and Russia. And I'm fairly sure I'm not the only civilian to have a Mycroft.

Mycroft started as a project to grab every publicly available image of a face and build up my own database for facial recognition. Then, one day, I read about a DNA database that had been left unprotected. How many others had such poor security? I wondered. It took only a couple of hours to find some of the more common exploits. I then identified several dozen targets to try it on.

I hesitated for a moment before running my scripts. I'd covered my tracks as best as I could. Everything would be run from remote servers that didn't belong to me, and all the data stored in Mycroft would be thoroughly encrypted.

My finger hovered longer over pressing the button to start Mycroft than it did when I took my first life.

I told myself that nobody's privacy would be violated if I never needed to use the information. If I did, then it would be to save a life.

That's how I started stealing DNA information. If you read the news, you know that such information is especially valuable these days. If the brother or even a cousin of a suspect has their DNA in a public database, that's enough to tell the cops which family tree they should be looking at. Some high-profile cases have been cracked this way, and chances are that thousands more will be.

Why should I be left out of this?

I did not, however, stop with stealing DNA files. Faces were creepy enough, hacking to get access to DNA was worse, but what I did next crossed every line.

I read another article, this one about how a company's security camera had a vulnerability that made it easy for anyone to access. Which meant that if you had one of those cameras in your living room watching for burglars while you were sleeping, someone could also be watching you and your mate getting in some one-on-one time on the couch while the kids were away.

At first I contemplated having Mycroft collect all the footage I could find. Who knew whether the next Toy Man or Grizzly Killer might be found using such data?

Then I had a thought . . . What if there was another way to get that data? I wasn't sure if I wanted to store millions of hours of security camera footage—especially if someone else was already doing it.

Security is hard. And the more complex your system, the harder it gets—even for spies.

I bought several different security cameras and tried an experiment: I started them all up using either the default password or the most commonly used passwords.

Of all eight cameras, care to guess how many of them experienced intrusion in the first ten hours?

All of them.

Most of the intrusions were probably only attempts to find vulnerabilities in order to install Bitcoin-mining software or other malware and couldn't tell a Wi-Fi camera from a Linux server. In two cases, though, the intrusions appeared to do nothing . . . until I realized they did something particularly devious—they rewrote the firmware.

The cameras behaved exactly as designed, except for one out of a hundred data packets was sent to a different destination from the camera-company server.

To make a long story short, someone had managed to hack the cameras. When I followed the trail, I discovered a server at the other end. Searching for the IP address of my own camera as a file name, I found a folder full of videos my camera had taken since it had been hacked. When I searched file names by zip code, I found a directory containing thousands of folders and an incredible amount of potential blackmail fuel.

Someone was building a comprehensive database of Wi-Fi camera footage. When I tried to calculate the storage bill for it, I realized it was being done either by a country or an extremely wealthy person.

The dilemma I faced was that, while this could be extremely useful to me, it was also a privacy-invasion nightmare. It would be bad enough if our own government was doing this, but it would be even worse if it was the Chinese. The amount of personally embarrassing blackmail material I saw simply scanning random home-security-camera IPs was mind-blowing. I'm never walking around the house naked again while Jillian isn't home.

As tempting as it was to study what I'd found, the scale of the operation was too big to ignore. I had to report it.

As a government contractor, I have the phone number for the department within the Department of Defense that I'm supposed to contact when I suspect there's been an intrusion in our lab's computer system. The operator put me in touch with the head of the security-network operations center. I explained the intrusion, and he gave me a different number to call.

"Dr. Cray?" said the person at the second phone number. "I understand you're experiencing a potential intrusion on a lab camera?"

This is not what I'd told the dispatcher. "Not quite." I explained the sequence of events without getting into why I had originally been curious.

"And you're saying that you can access the files without a password? But it's not a camera at your facility?" he asked.

"Uh, correct."

"Okay, we'll look into it."

I've seen some chilling things in my life, what happened next was one of the more disturbing ones.

Ten minutes later the files were gone. All of them.

This told me whose side the people collecting the files were on.

It also told me whom to contact when the situation called for it.

And right now, the situation is calling for it.

❧

"Hello?" says a familiar voice.

"I'm at the crash site in Austin," I reply.

"I understand."

"I need the point of origin for a hexacopter," I explain.

"We wish we had that, too. Small things can be hard to see," he answers vaguely.

"Yes. But they can sometimes be easy to hear."

There's a long pause before he replies, "Okay, we'll look into it."

Click.

"You got fifteen minutes for your miracle," Lowell shouts at me from across the gymnasium.

❧

Nine minutes later, her phone rings.

"Looks like you lose, Cray. We just got a call from the DoD. They say they picked up an acoustic anomaly that may be the drone's source of origin."

"What the hell is an acoustic anomaly?" asks McCallum.

I suppress a laugh. Whatever they want to call it is fine by me. And it's actually better that my secret friend didn't tell me the information directly. That would lead to too many questions. I can handle all the contempt Lowell wants to throw my way.

McCallum, Rossman, and I step to the sidelines as the different agencies swarm over their computers and bark information back and forth while the new lead is chased down.

Addison, who had loaned me his laptop earlier, turns up the volume on his radio so we can hear the field commander of the FBI team approaching the suspected launch point.

"We've spotted the clearing," he calls out over the radio. "Perfect spot to launch from. I've got two on the ground approaching."

"We have traffic-camera footage from an intersection near there two minutes after the collision. Blue SUV," announces an FBI agent.

"Tags?" asks Lowell.

"Affirmative. Sending the owner's address to the SWAT unit and ground units."

"We found some wiring and a hex wrench," says the commander at the clearing. "Fresh tire tracks."

"Same make as the vehicle on the traffic cam," says Addison.

A few minutes later, a SWAT commander calls in to say they're at the house that matches the truck's registration. "We're going in."

We hear someone shout, "Police!" and orders for everyone to get on the ground as the team rushes the house.

Minutes later the commander calls into his radio. "Clear. Suspects apprehended. One white male named Brad Yullen, age sixteen. One Hispanic male named Kevin Ortiz, age fifteen."

McCallum and I exchange glances. I think she's thinking the same thing I am.

"Kids?" says Rossman. "Just a couple of kids?"

"Would you rather it was ISIS?" asks Lowell.

"I'm not sure what world I want to live in," replies McCallum. "One where international terror groups are bringing down planes again, or one where a couple of teenagers can pull this off using stuff they bought on eBay."

"Nobody said they aren't terrorists," replies Lowell. "I'll have the deputies take you home. Thank you for your help, for what it was worth."

I simply nod and walk toward the exit.

McCallum catches up with me. "Who did you call?"

"It doesn't matter."

She looks back at the gymnasium. "Right. I guess you don't like the attention."

"Let's say I've had more than my share."

❦

I'm back in my study by the time Jillian comes home. "Did you see the news about the plane crash?" she asks as she walks into the room.

"A little," I reply.

CHAPTER FIVE
Not So Easy

It's kind of pathetic that it requires a passenger jet crash that almost took the lives of six hundred people to lift me out of my funk. Maybe *sick* is the right word. And *pathetic* is the wrong word. What I'm suffering from is severe depression. The MRI machine at the end of the hospital hall isn't a treatment for my depression; it's more of a glimpse at a watch that may or may not tell me how much time I have left. However, unlike the other patients waiting for their trip into the MRI, I'm not going to learn how much time I have left to live. But the machine could tell me how much time I have before I take a life.

Seven months ago, I was asked to look into a case involving a forensic technician who went berserk and killed several of his coworkers at a crime scene I'd discovered.

What I found was an evil bastard who'd been cultivating a virus that basically makes people homicidal—a concept that would have gotten you laughed out of the academy until scientists started making connections between pathogens and mental disorders ranging from hoarding to full-blown schizophrenia.

Between the time I spent unconscious and strapped to a wheelchair on the lunatic's back patio and the little parting gift from my former lab manager, which may or may not have contained the so-called Hyde virus, I've been doubting my own sanity and wondering if the tissue-thin layer of nerves that keeps me from going berserk is being worn away by the proteins the virus produces.

Of course, we can only tell if you have the pathogen after you get it. And right now, the only surefire way to know is by looking at the part of the brain that is affected.

We think we found all of the doctor's victims, but we can't be sure. We have no idea if the virus he made can go dormant or if it simply takes longer for some people to show symptoms.

I've kept my suspicions to myself, because there ain't exactly a cure for this, and the people working on it aren't quite as motivated as yours truly. That's why every week I have a brain scan done in a different hospital under a different name.

I do this on the sly, because I don't want the people who fund my nice government lab to decide that I'm about to become a murderous psychopath; they have enough doubts about me already. God knows what they'd think if they knew all the things I'd done in the name of science.

Today, I'm at Merced Medical Clinic in Baton Rouge to get this week's scan. Officially I'm in town to speak at a nursing college on behalf of the Juniper Parsons Scholarship Project.

The project was Jillian's idea. We'd had a discussion about gender representation in the computer sciences, and I'd opened my big fat mouth and said how you can't blame schools if not enough women apply. Jillian had responded that if I cared about the issue, I'd try to encourage more women to apply to those programs. Fast-forward to today, and every other week you'll find me visiting classrooms to speak about the joys of data science to mostly female audiences, with what I expect is a negligible effect.

The upside is that the scholarship itself gets hundreds of applicants, and Juniper's mom gets to help decide which ones get a nice little check underwritten by Dr. Cray to help with their college expenses. If nothing else, I'm glad it helps Mrs. Parsons feel that her daughter didn't die completely in vain.

Juniper was my student and the first murder I investigated. Also the first murder I was implicated in. She'd been following in my academic footsteps, which led her to cross paths with Joe Vik, the Grizzly Killer—the first murderer I investigated and the second murder I was implicated in. Prosecutors declined to charge me on account of it being self-defense. Which it sort of wasn't. But that's between me and Jillian. Every couple has their secrets. Ours are a bit darker. But the one I'm dealing with at the moment is too dark even for her.

"Mr. Gibson?" asks the nurse standing by the door.

It takes me a moment to remember that's the assumed name I'm using. "Here," I reply as I stand.

She leads me down a hallway to a small curtained-off area. "Please remove all metal objects and put on the gown."

I follow her instructions, keeping only the USB drive, which she doesn't notice.

"This is George. He'll be your imaging technician," she says, then departs.

George is my age, late thirties, with dark hair and bushy eyebrows. "Hello, Mr. Gibson. I couldn't find a chart for you. I understand your doctor in Australia requested that you get a checkup while you were here?"

"Yep. And please put the images on here," I say, handing him the USB drive.

He stares down at it as if I've just given him part of a UFO. "We don't usually give patients the images . . . directly."

"How often do they ask?"

"It's not our procedure."

"I already paid. Check with billing."

"Um, I believe you. Okay. Um, no metal objects? You know the procedure?"

Do I.

He straps my head into place, and I stare up at the inner ring and try to think happy thoughts and not about what would happen if a piece of metal was in the danger zone near the magnetic field. There are all sorts of gruesome stories about patients and medical people getting caught between something metal and the powerful magnetic pulses the machine generates.

"I have seen my death," I whisper to myself. This is what Wilhelm Röntgen's wife said after he showed her the skeleton of her hand, the very first X-ray photograph. The first X-ray *image* had come weeks before, when Röntgen accidentally moved his body between the X-ray source and a fluorescent screen and saw his own bones like a ghastly shadow.

The entire history of trying to see inside the human body is filled with horror stories, almost as if we've been punished for our curiosity.

The first experimenters to work with X-rays reported odd burns, bald spots, and lesions that refused to heal. It took decades before anyone suspected that this ray that was powerful enough to penetrate the human body might actually do some damage if it's exposed for too long. In the early days, it wasn't uncommon to have someone exposed to an X-ray source for more than an hour.

Thankfully we learned something from that. X-ray technicians now stand behind lead shielding, and the machines themselves use sensitive digital sensors requiring much less exposure. We also use devices like the MRI whenever possible and metal projectiles can be kept clear.

While theoretically my repeated use of an MRI shouldn't cause problems, every time I hear the loud knocking sound of the pulsing magnetic coil, I begin to worry about the software running the machine or whether the technician used a metal nut instead of a plastic one. It's the little things that make me worry.

The machine finally stops, and George unstraps me from the bed after it slides me out like Pez from a dispenser.

"It'll take a moment for me to transfer your files," he explains. "You can get dressed."

As I put my clothes back on, I wonder what I'd do if I saw that my dorsolateral prefrontal cortex was showing signs of damage. It's hard to tell from one MRI image; that's why I take them every week.

I use signal processing to try to discern changes over time and create a clearer image. So far, everything has been okay, but the Hyde virus can work fast. In the case of the Pale brothers, there wasn't much left of one sibling by the time we got him strapped into an MRI. Our poor FBI forensic tech may have had his brain erode in the few days before he went on his killing spree.

I might be kidding myself if I think I can outrun this thing once it's decided to make me go berserk.

What *would* I do?

I tighten my belt, reach into my pocket, and pull out the small steel washer I keep mixed in with my change. I found it in the parking lot of my lab the same day I received the potentially infectious *FU* note, presumably from my disgruntled lab manager.

As I sat on the curb thinking about the implications of being infected with the virus, I saw the small piece of metal glinting in the hot Austin sun. And that's when I thought of the first way to kill myself.

I'd pop that washer into my mouth before I went in for an MRI and let it punch a hole through my skull.

Except . . . it wouldn't. At best it would heat up and press uncomfortably against my mouth. Maybe it could lodge itself in my trachea. But, even then, it is only a washer. I'd still get air. When the medical personnel found the grown man gasping because he had a piece of metal in his mouth like a small child, questions would be asked.

Still, I keep the washer as a reminder:

If you're going to do it, Theo, don't fuck it up.

CHAPTER SIX
DARK SIDE

I stand in front of the auditorium at Lionel Nursing College and go through my rapid-fire talk about computational biology and the big, amazing world of machine learning and neural networks. When I get to the part about free online courses, a few actually write down the URLs, but most of them stare right at me, waiting to raise their hands for questions. Not because I've suddenly got them excited about TensorFlow or Jupyter notebooks, but because they want to ask about the other stuff. The dark stuff.

Once upon a time, I used to lecture to students in my own classroom, and the discussions were filled with talk about data collection, model sizes, tensors, and other things I use to put Jillian to sleep. Now whenever I'm in a classroom, they want to talk about the things that are the reason I can't teach anymore.

It wouldn't bother me as much if the questions were about the forensics, but usually they're not. They want to know about the men I've caught. They want to talk about Joe Vik and the others like they're discussing the villains in a Marvel movie. It's no more real to them.

I know we all have a dark side, the part of us that's fascinated by the things that should frighten us. For some of us it's curiosity—that compulsion that makes us want to look when we see an accident on the side of the road and spot a group of people standing over a body. It's the reason some of us wake up to read the news. We don't rush to make sure a tsunami *didn't* wipe out a South Pacific island. Reading that an earthquake *didn't* kill two thousand people in Turkey wouldn't trigger any dopamine receptors in our brains. When the news feels too normal, we stop paying attention. But bad news grabs us by the throat—which we willingly bare—especially when it's the kind of news that feels proximal but somehow doesn't quite touch us.

When three of my high school classmates skipped class one day and were killed in a car crash, you could tell the students that were really affected from the ones who weren't. The ones that were hardest hit were silent; the ones that weren't couldn't shut up about it. I remember watching people who'd trash-talked the guys the day before tearing up on local news cameras about how tragic the loss was and then laughing with friends at lunchtime and whispering morbid jokes. Part of that is the warped psychology of a teenager—the rest is human nature. They get to feel as though they came close to death without actually being touched by it.

Perhaps this explains why people love vampire stories or women write to serial killers in prison. We all like to come close to death but not actually touch it. Maybe there's some little survival lesson we can learn, or perhaps our brain makes us think that we're somehow winning by not dying.

I'm sure there's some evolutionary advantage to wanting to get close enough to death and evil to gain some awareness without getting too close. Maybe seeing how that person died on the side of the road will remind us to look both ways. Maybe learning a fishing village was wiped out makes us feel better about our expensive mortgage or not living in a fault zone.

Maybe our lizard brain can't tell the difference between our choices and our random circumstances well enough to know that bad stuff sometimes just happens and no matter what perverse pleasure you get in knowing it didn't happen to you . . . it can.

Juniper Parsons was as bright as they come. Joe Vik still found her. John Christian's victims were kids. They could have been anyone. Forrester's victims were as random as you could imagine. If he'd had his way, you'd have been one, too. But don't expect the CDC and the FBI to make that well known.

I take a deep breath and then ask, "Any questions?"

More hands go up than I can count. I point to a young woman in the middle at random. "Yes?"

"What was Joe Vik like in person?" she asks.

"I didn't really get to, um . . . talk to him that much. He was actively trying to kill me when we met," I reply.

"Oh," she replies. "In the movie you and him talk at the diner."

The damn movie. I don't bother to ask if this is the TV or theatrical version. "I've never seen it."

"Really?" she says, baffled that I wouldn't want to watch a movie about one of the most horrific periods of my life. She seems embarrassed by her question, but only for a brief moment. "It might be therapeutic."

I blink. The scent of the decomposing corpse of Joe's first victim comes back to my nostrils. I can feel the texture of the moist dirt through my gloves. I remember the elation of discovering the body and then the horror of what Joe Vik had done buckling my knees. I remember the last time I saw Amber and Devon as we pulled their friend's body from the ground. They were never seen again. I hope they ran away, but my gut tells me Joe Vik got them.

"Watching Joe Vik die was cathartic enough," I reply.

"Anybody have questions *not* about . . . um . . . Dr. Cray's criminal investigations?" interrupts the instructor.

I hold up my hand. "No, no. Those are fine. Nothing is off-limits." That doesn't mean I'll tell them anything . . . but I'd prefer that they understand what an evil place our world can be. I point to another young woman in the back row.

"Do you have any regrets about killing Joe Vik or John Christian?"

"I wish they could have been taken peacefully. In Joe Vik's case, he was trying to kill me and my girlfriend." Several hands go up. "And John Christian was about to shoot me. He also had two children hostages."

"And Forrester," someone comments.

"He shot himself," I reply. "And he's still alive," I add, almost grudgingly.

"You and your girlfriend are still together?" asks a student.

"To my delight and her frustration." I point to a petite young woman to the right who had been taking notes throughout the lecture. "Go ahead."

Usually discussions of Jillian bring up questions about marriage and kids. I prepare myself for my nonanswers. As awkward as they are, I prefer them to the fetishization of Joe Vik.

"How many active serial killers do you think there are right now?" she asks.

"Too many," I reply.

"Make a guess," she insists.

"Some estimates say over two thousand."

"Isn't Joe Vik the most prolific killer ever?" someone interjects.

"That we caught. There are over five thousand unsolved murders a year, and there're something like two hundred and fifty thousand total unsolved murders since 1980."

"And those are just the ones we know about," says the young woman who asked the original question.

"How can you have unknown murders?" asks someone else.

"Missing persons, undeclared, misdiagnosis," says the young woman, who then looks to me.

"Correct."

"What profession do you think has the highest number of serial killers?" she asks, baiting me for an answer she already knows.

"The FBI will probably tell you mechanic. But that's not the question you asked . . . or the answer you're expecting."

"What is it?" asks another student.

"Yours. Nurses probably kill more people than anyone else."

"Bullshit," someone says from the back.

"The hardest to detect and the most opportunity," I reply. "The numbers don't look good."

"I've never heard that," someone else complains.

The young woman who began this conversation starts rattling off names of suspected serial killers who were nurses. She finishes by pointing out, "And those are just the ones they caught."

"Well, that's been enlightening," says the instructor, clearly not happy with the direction of the discussion. "Let's hope this has been a deterrent to any of you considering becoming serial killers. I'm sure you wouldn't want Dr. Cray after you."

"Don't be so sure," someone says, making me blush and a little worried.

The young woman with the morbid line of questioning pushes past the others as they gather their books and hands me a slip of paper.

"I'm Emily," she says. "I think I know of one."

"One what?" I reply.

"An angel of death—a killer nurse," she says under her breath.

I stare down at the folded note, afraid to open it. "Tell the FBI."

"I'm telling you," she says.

"I don't do this anymore. It's not something I have time for."

Does she know how hard it is to do these things between planning your own death and waiting to become a killer yourself? Not to mention the Department of Homeland Security knocking on your door unannounced to ask you to stop world terrorism?

"If you can make the time, please call me," she says before departing between a group of students approaching me.

"She didn't waste any time," hisses one of the few men in the class.

I place the note in my pocket. "It was a professional question," I explain, still trying not to blush.

CHAPTER SEVEN
SWAMP FEVER

I'm sitting in a conference room with a view of the Pentagon while a group of people try to talk themselves into an agreed-upon hallucination. The hallucination is that seven months ago when I pulled a shipping package containing tainted vaccine samples from a cargo container on an airport runway, the package never would have made its way to its final destination—a medical facility that was supposed to use those samples to create one hundred thousand doses of flu vaccine for distribution to our military.

Thomas Grant, the facility manager in charge of making the vaccine, has insisted multiple times that "Protocols would have prevented the Hyde virus from making its way to military personnel." And that "Accepting the protovaccine in that manner would have been completely irregular."

Okay, that's comforting, but the pedant in me can't help but pay attention to his word choice. While everyone else *seems* satisfied and relieved that Edward Forrester's plot to turn one hundred thousand soldiers into Hyde-infected sociopaths was thwarted, I'd like to know for certain. I raise my hand, even though it's not really that kind of discussion. Grant's red eyebrows flare over the gold rims of his glasses, and I can see his skin turn crimson where his fleshy neck meets his sweat-stained white collar. "Um, Dr. Cray?"

"When you say that it would be completely irregular to accept the protovaccine in this manner, do you mean to say that it's never been done? That your facility has never used materials that have been shipped this way in the preparation of vaccines?"

While my question isn't exactly welcomed by the others in the room at first, I see a few faces turn toward Grant, curious now that I've thrown this shiny object out there.

A moment ago, we were all in a reality where there was no way that box could have wreaked mayhem, and now I've introduced a small degree of doubt.

Although nobody has told me this directly, I'm considered a pain in the ass when it comes to meetings. It's probably why I don't get invited to many of them anymore. I'm sure there was a discussion to keep me from this one.

"Dr. Cray," Grant says with frustrated formality, "I find that question a bit insulting. We've been creating vaccines for the military for a half decade without incident. We have very strict protocols in place."

I kind of feel for the guy. Multimillion-dollar contracts could be on the line. I don't doubt his lab is run any more poorly than my own, but being polite can cost lives.

"No offense intended, I don't enjoy it when the integrity of my facility is questioned. But, please tell us, have you ever used materials that have been shipped this way?"

Grant glances over at the meeting chairperson, Olivia Perez, to intervene, but her face scrunches up as she waits for his answer.

"I'm not aware of that ever happening. Like I said, we have protocols—"

I interrupt, "Protocols are ideals. They're things we aspire to." I throw in an analogy that Jillian gave me when I explained the situation. "They're not enchanted proclamations from the Ministry of Magic that can't be broken. We break them all the time. I'm sure there's some protocol here that says I shouldn't interrupt you, but here I am, interrupting you."

"Well, we're well aware of your penchant for breaking protocols, Dr. Cray," he says, scoring a few laughs at my expense. I have to admit he's not wrong.

After the room catches its breath with his little tension-breaking comment, I stick my finger in the punch bowl again. "So when you say you're not aware of it happening, that's another way of saying, 'I don't know'? And that would be because it's unknowable? You haven't bothered to ask? Or because you've intentionally avoided asking for fear of the answer?"

Grant turns to Perez. "Olivia, we've gone through our procedures. My facility never even made contact with the Hyde virus. I'm not here to have *him*, of all people, question my integrity!"

Back in Austin, those are step-outside words. I'd reply to the insult, but I don't need to. I've made the intended point and put the question into everyone's minds. I don't think Grant committed any great sin. He's here because we're concerned about a hypothetical that didn't happen and hopefully never will.

Grant is the center of attention because his facility would have been the last line of defense for a situation that nobody was even contemplating. Edward Forrester knew the weak links in the system because he'd worked inside it for decades.

"Thomas, if you can look into that, we'll need to know for the report," says Olivia. "And it would be better if you uncover any breaks in protocol before an audit does," she adds. "Let me be very clear to everyone. This committee is not about pointing fingers. It's about making sure something like this doesn't happen again. Right now, I feel confident that the new tracking system will help us ensure that the transportation of materials is secure and not vulnerable to compromise."

I raise my hand. Olivia's eyes flash with frustration. "Dr. Cray, we have your report and suggestions for procedures. Is there anything else you need to add?"

That was kind of a shutdown, but I persist. Hell, I'll even get a little melodramatic, because I gave away all my fucks back when Joe Vik came after me. "You know, when I was strapped to the wheelchair in Forrester's backyard, gunshot wound still bleeding, and I looked into the face of the monster that made the Hyde virus, I wondered why no one else noticed that something was off about the man. Why didn't anyone else find his behavior suspicious? Why did it have to get this far?"

"We may never know," says Joshua Pykeman, cutting me off.

I proceed anyway. "But I think I do. The last time we dealt with a similar crisis was when we had anthrax attacks, and our chief suspects were also the first people the government had asked for professional opinions. Our world was so small that anybody who knew anything was just as likely to be the one who did it. It's not out of the question that if Forrester had succeeded, he'd be sitting where I am right now trying to come up with protocols to help stop the next national disaster for whatever was left after the Hyde virus became a full-blown epidemic."

"We have no reason to think Hyde could have become airborne," says Laura Tanaka.

"No, it merely could have crippled our military," I reply. "My point is that we need to be asking more questions about each other. We need to be paying more attention."

"I choose not to live in a constant state of paranoia," says Dr. William Bryn.

"Then get the hell out of the business of protecting the public. Because if you aren't constantly looking around and trying to figure out who could be the next Edward Forrester, then we're screwed."

"Thankfully, we have you for that, Dr. Cray," Bryn says snidely. "I have no doubt you'll find some new crisis to bring to our attention." He watches my face flare and speaks before I can think of something to say. "How has your health been, by the way? I understand that you were at first concerned that you may have been infected with the Hyde virus in your own lab. No symptoms yet?"

At this exact moment I'm reasonably sure the Hyde virus hasn't taken hold of me, because I haven't lunged across the table and ripped this guy's throat out.

"I'm feeling fine, thanks for asking. If I need treatment, I'll wait until the plumbing is fixed at your clinic, if it's all the same."

Cheap shot on my part, but six patients treated at his facility died from *Sphingomonas koreensis* infections stemming from the bacteria making its home in the pipes. It's nothing exotic like the Hyde virus, but it doesn't have to be to kill you. Doctors washing their hands were actually lathering them in bacteria before surgery.

This is the kind of thing that scares me. Grant's facility is a good one; so was Bryn's until we found out it wasn't. God knows what mistakes I've made and don't know about. The ones I do know about would keep a pathologist up at night. I've performed autopsies in motel rooms . . .

"Can we tone things down a bit?" Olivia pleads, mainly looking at me. "If you were to sum up your suggestion into one brief statement, what would it be?"

This is her way of getting me to shut up. My ego wants to wave it off, but the saner part of me doesn't listen to it. "Pay attention. If something sounds suspicious, ask questions. Don't ignore it just because everyone else does. Our tools give us capabilities the rest of the public can't even imagine. If we're not vigilant, something bad could happen, and we might find those capabilities taken from us. I make mistakes. You make mistakes. Don't run from them. Seek them out. Correct them. Listen when someone is telling you something is suspicious. Don't ignore it."

My words strike a chord in my own head, and something that was lurking in the back of my mind comes to the fore.

During the break I take the slip of paper from my pocket and send a text to Emily back in Baton Rouge.

Let's talk.

CHAPTER EIGHT
SUSPICIOUS MINDS

"What's up, babe?" asks Jillian as she picks up the phone back in Austin. It's 4:30 p.m. there, which means she's probably at the bakery right now. I'm calling her from the airport while waiting for my flight to board.

"I'm stopping back in Baton Rouge to visit a nursing student I met yesterday," I reply.

"I hope she's good at stitches, because you'll need them if you want to have your balls reattached after I rip them off," she says without missing a beat.

Jillian is well aware that I can be completely blind to a woman showing interest in me. I unintentionally made her laugh so hard she spit out her drink at a party when I stared at a business card a woman had handed me and asked, "What's this for?" I'd spent the last twenty minutes explaining my field, assuming my conversation partner was really interested in how generative adversarial networks could be used to create synthetic, two-dimensional cell structures. Jillian had been watching the exchange unbeknownst to me from behind until I felt her drink on the back of my neck. She then walked away cackling. The woman asked, "What's her deal?" I could only shrug.

"Possible killer nurse," I explain.

"The one you're meeting?" she asks, sounding almost bored.

"No. Well, she's not a nurse yet. So she'd technically be a killer nursing student. She says she has suspicions about a nurse who may have caused some patient deaths, including the son of a family she knows. I don't have a lot of details."

"Any idea how much time it will take?"

"The plan is to go there and talk to her, poke around for a day, then head home."

"Poor choice of words, Theo."

"Oh, right. Poke—" I cut myself off before making it worse.

"I think you're further on the spectrum than when I met you. How does *that* happen?"

Although she's joking, it stuns me for a moment as I wonder if an early symptom of Hyde is lack of social awareness. I start to think about a number of Forrester's victims. Daniel Marcus was a forensic technician and probably a bit an introvert. The Pale brothers were definitely not the outgoing type. While a lot of spectrum diagnosis is highly subjective, there is a correlation between certain genes and extroversion. Also, some recent possible connections between people susceptible to Epstein-Barr virus and schizophrenia have proven quite intriguing—and frightening.

Damn it, I need to send a memo back to the working group in DC—especially to Dr. Tanaka. She thinks I'm a meddler and a borderline crackpot, which isn't inaccurate, to be honest, but she's thorough and will likely seriously consider what I have to say.

"Was it a good one?" Jillian asks, observing my little mental trip from my long pause.

"Yes. Could be very helpful." I don't tell her that her prompt has also given me one more thing to be paranoid about with my own behavior.

"Okay. Don't forget your call with Dr. Paulson. I spoke to her yesterday. I think she's having health issues, just so you know."

That hits me like a slap in the face. My former professor Amanda Paulson is as close to me as my own mother, which you can't judge by how infrequently I talk to her, and she's had a profound effect on me. Part of the little voice in my head is hers.

Along with Juniper Parsons's mother, Amanda is one of the people who helps evaluate the applicants for the scholarship program.

"I'll call her from Baton Rouge," I reply.

"Please do that. You know she thinks very fondly of you," Jillian reminds me.

"Yeah. I know."

"So, killer nurses?" Jillian says, changing the topic.

I get the feeling she's trying to keep me on the phone talking because I've been rather disengaged lately. She's still trying to figure out if something is up or if that's just my temperament.

I still haven't had the whole "Hey, I love you, but I'm afraid at any moment I could go berserk and kill you" conversation.

I really just want a clean bill of health so it never has to come up, but Hyde is such a devious little prick I don't know if that's even possible. Hyde's closest cousin, rabies, can lie dormant for twenty-five years or more.

Happy thoughts.

"Yeah, killer nurses. Possibly the most prolific profession for a serial killer," I explain.

"Makes sense," says Jillian. "Have you been looking into this?"

"Honestly? No. I'm a bit out of my element. I'm going to have to do some reading on the plane."

"It's a short flight," she replies.

"I'll read fast."

She groans. "Okay, wise guy. Just replay our last talk about getting yourself into these kinds of cases and putting yourself in harm's way. In any event, the bakery and the house are in my name, so that's settled."

"So are the vials at the sperm bank," I add, trying to land a half joke and an "oh by the way" and crashing instead.

"What?"

Oops. I forgot to tell her. "I had some frozen a couple months ago. I just got into this tissue-preservation kick." There was a clinic next to the facility where I was getting my first MRIs. For some reason it seemed like a prudent thing to do.

"Okay, so there's that, Theo."

Uh-oh. That's Jillian code for *There will be a longer conversation when I get home.*

"It's not a big deal."

"No, only a few billion little deals you decided to have frozen in carbonite on impulse. Was this a Groupon thing I don't know about?"

"Uh, no."

"You haven't arranged to have your head frozen, too, have you?"

"God, no."

"Glad to hear that."

"I couldn't put you through that. They'd have to saw it off in the first few hours and drop it into liquid nitrogen."

"Well, that'd certainly make an open casket interesting," she replies. "Although probably not a complete shock to some."

"I'll be careful. Don't worry. Anyway, killer nurses generally only kill their patients," I explain.

"Oh. That's a relief. Because, let's see, you've only made it how long without an emergency room visit since I've known you? Five months?"

"Fair point. But they only tend to kill the old, the young, and the terminally ill."

"Well, gee, then, you're fine."

"Oh, wait, I can think of at least three cases where nurses say they killed patients that annoyed them."

"You're screwed."

"I'll be careful," I say again.

"Will Hailey be helping you?" she asks out of nowhere.

Was that a hint of jealously I detected? Now is the time when my lack of human interface skills makes me panic. Should I call this out with a joke? Or is the right thing to ignore it? I wait too long and reply, "I haven't talked about it with her."

"But you've talked?"

Oh man. Think, Theo. We exchanged emails a couple of days ago. We're sending each other links to research papers just about every day. Two days ago, she had to explain the stupid space puppy meme that was going around.

I wait too long to reply again.

"We communicate all the time." *Jeez, great word choice, Theo,* communicate.

"Flight 211 to Baton Rouge is now boarding," a flight attendant garbles into the loudspeaker.

Perfect.

I have a sudden realization: I became obsessed with the idea that I might have dormant Hyde at the same time I met Hailey. As far as Jillian is concerned, my even more aloof degree of aloofness only has one new variable, and that's the presence of a young, very, *very* smart, and admittedly attractive woman in my social sphere.

While Jillian doesn't see other women as a threat, Hailey is different . . . and Hailey and I shared an experience somewhat like the one that bonded Jillian and me.

This looks bad.

"Uh, Jillian, this is going to come out awkward, but you know that I love you and no one can come between us? Right?"

"Right. That does sound awkward, Theo." She lets out a sigh. "I know you have secrets, and I accept that."

"Well . . ."

"You just told me you had your boys frozen on a whim. Who knows what other weird things you're up to? My point is that I get it and I know you'd never lie to me. You'll evade the question or seize up, but not lie."

"That sounds accurate," I reply.

"But you'd be okay if I went through your text-message history?"

"Sure," I blurt out.

"You idiot. I'm kidding. I trust you. I'm human, and my mind starts to wander when I'm back here in the bakery covered in flour and cinnamon frosting. And anyway, if I stop trusting you, I'll kill you. Fair?"

"Fair." Although I won't put cheating on Jillian on the list of ways to kill myself. "I love you."

"I know," she says, then cuts the call.

Smart-ass.

As I walk down the Jetway, I ponder the difficulty level of a conversation in which I explain that I haven't been cheating on her, only keeping secret the fear that I might spontaneously turn into her killer.

CHAPTER NINE
VIBES

Emily carefully pulls back the lids on three vanilla-flavored creamers and pours them into her coffee as she thinks about how to phrase her thoughts. We're sitting in a Denny's near the airport. She's wearing a jogging jacket and yoga pants, revealing an athletic build. Her posture is impeccable. There's an interesting inner discipline she has about her. People have never been my strong suit, but I still try to pay close attention. I'd bet she worked her way through high school and had brothers or sisters who were dependent on her. From her diction, I can tell her parents probably weren't overly educated. But her word choice tells me she's an excellent student.

Her inner world is a complete mystery to me. She could be sincere or pulling a complete con on me. Everything she says is carefully composed. However, I suspect it's because she's afraid of my disapproval.

After she stirs her coffee, her left thumb flips through the pages of a notebook she brought with her. She's avoided eye contact since I sat down.

"I didn't think you'd get back to me," she says after collecting her thoughts. "I'm sure you're working on a bunch of different cases right now."

For some reason, her comment catches me off guard. "No, actually. My main work is in a government lab that does Defense Department contracts. Boring biology."

"Oh really? I thought you were out there looking for the next Joe Vik. Seems like a waste. You're, like, really, really good at it."

If I told her some of the nonsense government projects I work on, she'd be surprised at how big and expensive a waste it can be.

"Thank you. I think I've been lucky and fortunate to be one of the first people to use techniques that haven't made their way into forensics yet."

"You're very humble," she replies.

I don't hear that too often. "Lucky, to be sure."

"I'm surprised you don't get more credit."

"Tell me about your case," I say, moving the discussion away from my most awkward topic, myself.

"Cooper. Yeah. Sweet kid. I used to babysit for him. After his accident, I used to visit him in the hospital. He's what made me want to become a nurse."

"Not a doctor?"

"They were nice enough. Some of the ones he saw were kind of dicks, if you'll pardon my language. They kind of had an attitude at that hospital."

"What happened to Cooper?"

"It happened three years ago. He rode his bicycle down a hill into an intersection and got hit real bad." She points to her head. "Fractured skull, broken ribs. He was in and out of the hospital for surgery. The last one was for a plate in his skull and some internal infections from a fracture that hadn't healed. That's when . . ." She pauses. "That's when he died. Heart failure, they said at the time."

"Heart failure? But you think . . . ?"

"Sergio Filman," she replies. "That's who I think killed him."

"A nurse?"

"Yes."

"And why do you think this?"

"Have you ever put something together long, long after it happened? Like, you have enough perspective to see what was really going on? You were too close at the time, but later on you got the whole picture?"

"More or less. Science is like that. I sometimes come up with answers to questions I hadn't realized I'd been thinking about. But that's a lot different from pointing my finger at someone years later and accusing them of murder."

"I'm not accusing. Not publicly. That's why I wanted to talk to you. I need your help. Maybe I'm not looking at things right. Maybe I'm totally wrong, and Filman is the greatest guy in the world. Or maybe Filman did kill Cooper and the others."

"The others?" I ask.

"Yes. I told you this was about a serial killer, right? I think Filman may have killed at least six other kids, maybe more."

"But the doctors said Cooper died from natural causes?"

"Yes, not that they could agree at first. Finally they settled on an explanation. It seemed a little odd at the time—now it seems like bullshit to me," she replies. "That place was a real mess of a hospital. I wouldn't take my dog there."

"Did you see Filman do something to Cooper? Was he attending to the kid?"

"Not directly. Listen, I don't want to sound unscientific, but there was a vibe about him. Do you know what I mean?"

"Absolutely."

Jeffrey Dahmer's neighbors complained about the smell. Lonnie David Franklin Jr.'s friends weren't completely surprised when he turned out to be the Grim Sleeper. Charles Cullen, a nurse who admitted to killing as many as forty patients, was followed by suspicion throughout his career.

Still, there's a fine line between suspicion and irrationality. A juror should never make decisions with their gut, but an investigator should never ignore it.

"Tell me about Filman."

"I guess he's around your age. Taller. Serious guy. He never said much when he'd come into the room. He didn't work that area often, but they said he was the one who'd hook up equipment."

"So he had access everywhere?"

"Probably. I never really saw him interact with other people. He kind of just did his thing."

"But you suspect him. Why?" I need to see if there's something more than a suspicion. I don't want to find myself on a witch hunt.

"Little things. But I guess the thing that creeped me out was when I went to go see Cooper. I was supposed to watch him while his mom was gone. I was about an hour late, and I walked in on Filman."

"Doing what?" I ask.

"Staring at Cooper. He was sleeping."

"What happened?"

"Filman turned around and shoved his hand into his pocket. He didn't say anything—he just left. It was weird."

"Like you caught him in the middle of something?" I ask.

"Yeah. But he wasn't close to the bed. He was just sort of hovering. It was creepy, but I forgot about it. Two days later, Cooper died right there."

"Was Filman around?"

"He wasn't there when I got to the hospital. Nobody mentioned him—Coop's family may have seen something."

"What about them?" I ask. "What did they say?"

"Coop's mom was a wreck. His dad didn't say much. We didn't really talk about it, although I remember Coop's dad, Mr. Hennison, getting pissed off when the doctors couldn't make up their minds at first about the cause. You'll have to ask them about that."

"And what does the family think about Filman?"

"Again, you'll have to ask them. Mr. Hennison doesn't like talking about it, but Darcy's the one who got me thinking about Filman. It was a year ago—I'd already decided I was going to do nursing, and I was talking to her about hospital stuff, and she made a comment about hoping I don't turn into that weirdo nurse who watched Cooper. She thought he was a child molester or something."

I nod for her to continue.

"That got me thinking. Both Darcy and I got a strange vibe off the guy but didn't say anything about it for years."

"And that's when you decided that Filman may have killed Cooper?"

"No. Darcy brought it up once, more as a casual question—if nurses had ever been known to hurt patients. I know, a naive question, but she's sweet like that. I asked her why she said that, and that's when she said something that made me feel like my heart stopped. Know the feeling?"

"Very much," I reply.

"She said that one of the other women in her prayer group had also mentioned Filman."

"Prayer group?"

"Oh, it was a group of women who met on Facebook and who'd all lost children. Three of them died in the same ward as Cooper. Only one remembered the nurse's name, but all three moms remembered being creeped out by him." She sits back and sighs. "Am I crazy? Or is that suspicious?"

Three different people lose a child in the same hospital ward, and all three randomly come to wonder if the same person may have been involved?

"Yeah, that's suspicious."

CHAPTER TEN
PRAYER CIRCLE

The next morning, Darcy and Isaac Hennison are sitting across from me in their living room. Krista and Robin, their two daughters, are sitting on chairs near the open kitchen, half listening as they play on their phones. Robin is nine and Krista sixteen. Cooper is half smiling in the family photo in the living room taken three years earlier. I'm not sure if it's painful for the kids to see that every day or if it's just part of the background.

I know looking at it is hard enough on me. Mr. Hennison almost seems to be avoiding it with his shoulder tilted away. God knows what he still feels.

The house is in a working-class neighborhood. There are bass boats in driveways and trampolines in front yards. Some lawns are kept better than others. Isaac Hennison's work truck was parked in the driveway when I arrived. Darcy's minivan still has a stick-figure family on the back window with all three kids next to a Mickey Mouse sticker.

"I asked Dr. Cray to come hear about what happened to Cooper," Emily explains after the two of them settle into their seats.

"About Filman?" Darcy asks.

There's tension in her voice as she almost spits at the name. Interesting. I need to de-escalate things before we get a lynching.

"Emily asked me to come talk to you. That's all. This is well beyond my area of expertise. I'm not sure I can be much help." Translation: I really have no idea what I can do here, this is so outside my knowledge base.

"How much do you know about soccer?" asks Darcy.

"The game?"

"No." She spells it out: "S-O-C-C-R, sudden onset cardiac collapse response."

"Less than nothing. I've never heard of it. What is it?"

"It's what they say killed Cooper," Emily offers from her spot on the couch next to me.

"It's what they *eventually* said killed Cooper," Darcy adds, correcting her.

"Before I make myself into any more of an idiot, mind if I google that?"

Doing so, I find only a handful of results. It's described as a kind of sudden cardiac arrest with unknown causes. There are only two medical papers on the condition, both written by the same person: F. Caputo. It sounds like a made-up phenomenon to me, but I don't say anything.

"Okay. So, this is what they say killed your son?"

"Eventually. It's the only explanation they gave us. I'd never heard of it before. Nobody had. The only other person I'd ever heard mention it was Cassie Quatrain."

"She's from the prayer group," Emily interjects.

"Her child died of that, too?"

"Same hospital," says Darcy. "Same ward. Same creepy nurse, Filman. I never thought I'd hear his name again until she said it. If it wasn't for that Facebook group, I probably never would have."

"Tell me about this group."

"I joined it about a year or so ago. Dealing with Cooper's loss is still hard. I thought maybe if I could talk to some other people, heck, maybe I could even help someone else. Do you have any children, Dr. Cray?"

"It's Theo. And no."

"Oh. What kind of doctor are you?" she asks.

Krista calls from across the room. "He's a biologist, Mom. Don't you watch television?"

"I didn't know you're on television," she replies.

"*He's* not on TV. Someone plays him on television," Krista corrects her again.

"Do they pay you for that?" asks Robin, looking up from her phone.

"I've never even seen the movie," I reply. "It was kind of, um . . . traumatic. I'd hate to see everything they got wrong."

"Well, I hope they make a movie about Filman when you catch him," says Darcy.

There's a knock at the door, and a man enters the house, then pulls up a chair next to the kitchen counter. Isaac and Darcy both give him a wave.

"I'm not sure Filman had anything to do with your child's death," I tell Darcy. "You have to accept the possibility that he had nothing to do with what happened to Cooper. Dozens of people interacted with your son, and chances are your son died from the complications the hospital described."

"You sound just like the hospital," says the man who just arrived.

"Theo, this is Tom Saunders," Emily says. "Tom, this is Dr. Theo Cray."

"Theo," I reply.

"Tom and his wife lost their daughter about six months after Cooper passed away."

"Same weirdo fucking male nurse, Filman," says Saunders. "The Quatrains got delayed, but they have the same story. Their kid goes in with some minor stuff, and a few weeks later, a coffin comes home. Meanwhile, that Filman's still lurking around."

There is not a lot of love for Filman in the room. "Why not the head of the ward or one of the other nurses? Why him?"

"Have you seen the creepy asshole?" Saunders glances over at the Hennisons' daughters. "Sorry, ladies."

"We're used to it," says Robin.

"Okay, but being creepy-looking isn't enough. And if I'm not mistaken, none of you even considered him at the time. Correct?"

"Not at the time," replies Saunders. "But when your child suddenly dies, you tend to be a little preoccupied."

"I understand."

"I'm not sure you do," he shoots back.

"Tom, shut up," snaps Darcy. "Let the man talk."

"Sorry, Dee." He waves a hand at me, as if permitting me to proceed.

While I'm grateful for Darcy interceding, I'm not too sure if she's going to be happy with what I have to say next. "Chances are he didn't do anything. And if I'm going to go any further with this, I need you to back off a little and entertain that maybe it is a misunderstanding. There have been more than a few cases where angry parents convinced themselves of things that didn't happen and people were wrongly convicted, or worse. Last year two men were killed outside a Mexican police station when an angry mob set them on fire because they thought they were kidnapping children. Nobody was actually missing a child. It just blew up over social media, and the townspeople got themselves worked up about the strangers."

"Are you always this condescending?" asks Saunders.

"Two out of the three men I went after are dead. The last one is still in the hospital. I don't tread as lightly as I would like to, Mr. Saunders. An abundance of caution on *all* our parts is a condition of me looking into this."

He throws up his hands. "As long as you take a close look at Filman, that's fine by me."

"Okay. Next question. What happened when you went to the hospital with your suspicions about Filman?"

There's a long pause. Finally, Emily breaks the silence. "They haven't. Not about Filman." She waits a moment, then asks, "Is that good?"

"Yes and no. It might make it easier for me to get information on him if he's not under suspicion. But otherwise bad."

"Bad?" asks Darcy.

"Of course. Assuming what you say is true, then the man is a serial killer. Your children aren't the only victims. And if he's still working at the hospital . . ."

I can tell from the reaction around the room that they hadn't considered this. *Weird.*

"He's right. I told you we should have gone to the police," says Isaac, finally speaking.

"And why didn't you?" I ask.

Nobody responds, so I look Darcy directly in the eyes. "Why?"

"Tom wanted us to find a wrongful-death attorney first."

"That wouldn't make a difference," I reply with a glance at Saunders.

"Well, we wanted to hear that from an attorney," he replies.

"And how is that search going?"

"That's the tricky part," says Darcy. "We've talked to one already. He says we can't sue."

"That's ridiculous. Of course you can sue. You may not win, but you have that right."

"No. We already took a settlement from the hospital. We gave up that right."

Emily interrupts. "The hospital waived their bill and gave them a cash settlement when they agreed not to sue the hospital for wrongful death."

"How much?" I ask.

"Fifty thousand," says Darcy.

"Which sounds like a lot more when you're also facing over a hundred thousand in medical bills," says Isaac.

"I get it, I get it. And when you made this settlement, was Filman's name ever mentioned?"

"No," replies Darcy. "We hadn't even thought about that by then."

Curious. The hospital settled with them so quickly, the actual reason why the children died wasn't even an afterthought. The settlement also seems quite low. The hospital administration might have exploited the fact that these were poorer families who didn't fully understand their rights.

Whether Filman had anything to do with the deaths of their children or not, something odd is going on here.

CHAPTER ELEVEN
HOUSE CALL

"Dr. Cray, I apologize for the miscommunication. Your visit is a bit of a surprise to me."

Regina Spicola, the director of the hospital group, greets me with a half-hearted handshake and a forced smile in the lobby of the administration wing of Ivy Medical Center. She's dressed in a gray pantsuit, with curly black hair spilling over her collar. In her late forties, she's got a slight southern twang that sounds like it's from Georgia or Alabama.

"My apologies, Ms. Spicola. Apparently, there was a miscommunication somewhere back in DC. I only found out about the error after I got on the plane."

"The email was rather brief. Explain to me what this is about?"

"My group is looking into ways to help improve the protocols for preventing the spread of pathogens." This is technically true but not why I'm here.

"Is there some problem I should know about?" she asks, even more guarded than before.

"Oh no. The NIH is looking to make new guidelines. I want to make sure that they're practical."

"I see," she says, still suspicious. "Let's go to my office. I've got about thirty minutes before my next meeting."

She leads me over to an elevator and presses the "Up" button. "Cray? Why does your name sound familiar?" she asks before we step inside.

I shrug and deflect. "I went by the Woodland Lake Clinic before coming here."

Woodland Lake was where Cooper and the other children died. I went there first, expecting to find an administrative building, only to find the hospital shut down and sealed behind a fence.

We step out of the elevator and head to a corner office at the end of the hall.

"We consolidated that facility about two years ago," she explains.

"Consolidated?"

"Merged, basically. We have six other hospitals in our group. The children's wing is now here. It's much nicer than Woodland Lake." Her words trail off as if she's said something she shouldn't have. "Here we go."

I take a seat in a chair opposite her desk. Stacks of folders cover every single square inch. She has a desktop computer and a laptop.

"Pardon the mess," she says.

"You should see my office."

"Back in DC?"

"I'm out of Austin now. That's where my lab is."

"Oh. Lab?"

"Biological research."

"Right. You're here about pathogens?"

"Correct."

She looks past my shoulder, and I turn. A man in his midfifties enters. He's shorter than me and wearing a suit that costs about as much as ten of mine.

Spicola introduces us. "Mr. Anderson, this is Dr. Cray from the NIH."

I may have been a little vague about my position.

He gives me an overcompensating handshake. "Dr. Cray? Like the guy in the movie?"

"I guess so," I reply. The advantage of having an actor play you is that nobody ever connects your face to your name.

"I can walk you over to our billing manager if you like, also show you the facility," he offers with an overly sincere smile.

Spicola quickly cuts him off. "Dr. Cray is actually here about NIH guidelines regarding pathogen eradication."

"Oh, my mistake. That's way above my grade level. Well, glad to meet you, Dr. Cray. Let me know if you need anything."

"Thank you," I reply. I'm not sure what the billing questions were about, but I can guess there's a constant paranoia in hospitals about that.

After he makes a quick exit from Spicola's office, she says, "I think we had our wires crossed. So, no billing questions?"

"Nope."

She makes a little nod, more to herself than to me. "All right, then. What can I help you with?"

"I have some questions about the deaths of Cooper Hennison, Veronica Saunders, and Michael Quatrain."

The look in her eyes tells me she wishes I had billing questions. "Who?"

"Those are patients. Children, actually. They all died at the Woodland Lake facility."

"I'm not sure if I'm aware of them. We treat over a quarter million patients a year," she replies.

"Yes, but these ones died."

She types into her keyboard for her desktop computer. "Hmm. No. Cooper Hennison died at Fairway Emergency Clinic. Same as Saunders and Quatrain."

This is news to me. "Don't you mean Woodland Lake?"

"No. It's right here."

I'm at a momentary loss for words. *Could the parents have been confused?*

"Either way, Woodland Lake was within the national average for similar facilities."

"The average for patient fatalities?" I ask.

"Yes. Average."

She says that word like an enchantment, which only makes me more suspicious.

"Okay, but why did you tell the parents that their children died at Woodland Lake?"

She seems frozen for a moment. "I'm not sure I understand that question."

I reach into my case and pull out the copies of the letters the families provided me. "These are condolence letters signed by you." I set them on her desk. "Do you write a lot of these? It's not normal for hospitals to do that. Nor to proactively offer some kind of compensation. Also, notice that it says Woodland Lake, right there."

"That's something our attorneys decide. In certain cases—"

"There was something wrong at Woodland Lake, wasn't there?"

She shakes her head. "I don't know what you mean."

"Why did you shut it down?"

"Consolidation. Any other questions?"

"Yes. Can you tell me the cause of death for the children I mentioned?"

"Excuse me?"

"You should have that information in front of you."

She glances at the screen. "Heart failure."

"Which ones?"

"All of them, Dr. Cray. You're not a physician, are you?"

"No."

"Then maybe I should have one of ours explain it in greater detail."

She meant it as a slight—I take it as an opportunity. "That would be very helpful. I'd like the contact information for the attending physicians, if possible."

"Dr. Cray, I'm not sure if I'm capable of answering any more of your questions at this time. Perhaps you can schedule another visit and I can have the appropriate people here to give you the details you're seeking."

"How about Sergio Filman?"

"Who?" she asks.

"He works for you, I believe. Would he be available?"

She taps into her computer. "Filman? The only one I see here is a nurse at our Concord Medical Center."

"Where is that?"

"Downtown. Why do you want to speak to him?"

"I just had a few questions. Thank you for your time. If you can forward the attending physician contact information to my email, that would be great."

She picks up her phone. "Miriam, could you please show Dr. Cray out?"

A moment later a woman is standing at the door. Spicola stands and give me a curt nod. "Dr. Cray," she says with no trace of cordiality.

I rise and return the gesture. "One more question."

"I'm very sorry, but I must take this call," she replies as she picks up her phone.

"No problem. I'm sure Miriam can guide me over to billing."

She slams the phone back down. "You'll have to schedule an appointment for that."

"I see." I spin and follow Miriam to the elevator.

I'm fairly sure that her next call was to her boss and the topic was me. The interesting thing is that of all the questions I asked, the one about Filman didn't even get a blink. There's a lot more going on here than I can understand.

While I'm sure they may have some questionable billing practices, her reaction to Woodland Lake was very, very curious.

CHAPTER TWELVE
ON-SITE

Concord Medical Center is pure chaos. It reminds me of movies set in New York during the 1970s. It's all cinder-block walls, torn linoleum, and people packed into buildings that should have been demolished after World War I. The crowd in the emergency room is like a coughing, bleeding, moaning version of what you'd find at the DMV, interrupted only by the occasional police officer marching a homeless or handcuffed person through the sliding doors.

With my lab coat and DoD badge clipped to my lapel pocket, nobody stops me as I stroll through the emergency room doors, down the hall, and into the hospital.

In the first two minutes, I feel the hair on the back of my neck rise at the sight of plastic gloves being stored next to medical waste, nurses failing to change gloves as they go from patient to patient, and clearly infectious people touching surfaces that nobody bothers to wipe down before the next person sits to be examined.

It's as if germ theory is really still a crazy theory. A plague mask would be more effective than some of the procedures I'm seeing here.

In defense of this hospital, even the cleanest-looking ones have their problems and often confuse well-mopped floors and the scent of antiseptic as proof of cleanliness. A swab test on stethoscopes revealed that they're one of the dirtiest instruments in a hospital—essentially the hospital equivalent of the bathroom on a long-distance commercial airliner.

If I taught physicians, I think my first test would be the one I use in my own lab: "Is it clean enough that you'd lick it?" Ask yourself that about your hands the next time you leave the bathroom.

I make my way to the second floor, where the hospital rooms are located. Some of them have three beds. Some have singles. Medical staff wander in and out of them along with visitors without supervision.

The nurses' station on this section is at the back of the wing and, at the moment, unstaffed. I spot patient files spread out around the desk behind the U-shaped counter and a computer terminal with a Post-it note that says: "Username: Admin. Password: LQ44sXXX."

I take out my phone and snap a photo. A nurse walks up to the station as I'm doing this, takes one look, and then walks away like I'm the paparazzi.

I pocket my phone and walk over to another nurse pushing a cart. "Excuse me, do you know where Filman is?"

"Who?" she asks.

"He's a nurse. Tall guy?"

"I think I've seen him. But this isn't his regular floor. Try the morgue."

"Downstairs?"

"What? No. Not the morgue-morgue. Fourth floor. Geriatric care." She shakes her head and continues on her way.

Jeez. It's not a good sign when the staff refers to the old-person section as a morgue. Medical people have dark senses of humor, but that's a little too dark.

I take the elevator with an orderly and a man in a wheelchair drooling on his hospital smock. The orderly is on his phone watching a music video while the man rubs at an open sore on his arm.

I can only pretend to be uninterested for so long. I make a show of putting my hands into my pockets, then turn to the orderly. "Could you get a nurse to put some Neosporin on that? I'd write it up, but I left my pad downstairs."

"What? Uh, yeah. I think there's some at the station."

I'm not sure if he meant antibiotics or nurses. Either way, his reaction seemed sincere enough. As he pushes his charge onto the third floor, I wonder how disorganized a hospital has to be to miss a golden opportunity like an open wound to overcharge.

When I get to the fourth floor, the smell hits my nose first: the unmistakable scent of people defecating on themselves poorly masked by disinfectant and whatever else they use to cover it up here. Pro tip: change their undergarments and bedding more often. It's not pleasant. I had to do it when I was getting my paramedic certification, but it's part of the job.

A woman sitting at the nurses' station doesn't even look up from her phone as I walk onto the floor. What did they do here before mobile? Sit around staring at *Reader's Digest* magazines?

If I were a patient here, I'd argue that I should only be billed for the time when staff wasn't looking at their phone. They'd probably end up owing me money.

I walk around the floor, poking my head into rooms and observing the overall state of things. Some patients are asleep. Others are watching television. I hear the unanswered call for a nurse from across the ward.

This place is a disaster. It's understaffed by an uninterested crew. I'm sure the pay sucks, but I'd also bet they earn more than their European counterparts, who tend to make half what American medical professionals do.

A nurse walks past me.

"Excuse me, is Sergio Filman around?" I ask.

"Filman? I saw him a few minutes ago. He should be back soon. What do you need, hon?"

"Oh, just a couple questions."

She notices my DoD badge and points to it. "Wrong one. You guys are always forgetting them."

For a moment I thought I'd been busted. "Ha. Oops. I just grabbed the first one in my briefcase."

"No worries. If you need to get into the cabinet, just grab me. Or ask Filman," she says before going down the hall to answer the nurse call that's been sounding since I stepped onto the floor.

I assume "the cabinet" is the slang here for the medical locker. It's nice to know that all I have to do is ask Nurse Fiona and I can get whatever I need. I'm sure I'll have to enter a patient code, of course. God forbid I swiped some benzodiazepine for my next party and there was nobody to bill it to.

Instead of waiting for Filman, I take the elevator to the first floor and make my way back to the loading area of the hospital. The back door—the first I've seen that requires a key card—is conveniently propped open with a chair.

If I want to ask questions, this is the real place to look. I step through and find two female nurses and an orderly puffing on cigarettes while a doctor tokes on a cigar as he paces around the parking lot.

This, I tell myself, is why you'll never get rid of smoking. I'm sure somewhere in their medical education someone must have mentioned that smoking is unhealthy, but here they are.

I walk over to the nurses. None of them looks Filman-like. From my pocket, I pull the pack of cigarettes that I purchased at the gas station thirty minutes ago.

"Any of you fine people have a lighter I can borrow?"

"Sure," says a sturdy woman with a gap-toothed smile. "You just have to tell us your name."

"Theo," I reply.

"Is that Dr. Theo?" she asks.

"Am I famous already?" I joke, assuming that she has no idea who the hell I am.

The nurse to her right, a taller woman with short brown hair, hands me a lighter. "I'm Connie. That's Jen-ah-qua."

"Almost," says the first woman, holding out her hand. "Jen-ay-qua. She makes it sound like I'm Aquaman's girlfriend. This is Bernie the Orderly." She points to the quiet man between them. "He doesn't talk much."

"Hello," I reply.

"So, who are you? Why are you here?" she asks.

"I actually work at the bank across the street. I just dress up like a doctor so I can get the discount at the cafeteria."

She lets out a laugh. "Well, if you were a real doctor, you'd know better than to eat there. That place has killed more people than the fourth floor."

Double jeez. The fourth floor again? I decide to go for an inside joke and see if it lands. "Imagine if they made Filman the chef?"

Jenaqua lets out an explosive laugh. "Oh, you did *not* just say that!"

"Fatal Filman's Café," says Connie, shaking her head. "That's messed up. Poor guy. If I had his bad luck, I'd consider another occupation."

Well, damn. I have to fake a laugh and a smile, because I'm horrified right now. My little fishing expedition to find rumors about him losing patients just landed a whale shark.

Okay, Theo, play it like you know it, but get more information. "It's not as bad as I've heard?"

"If you heard, then it's bad," says Jenaqua.

"It's overblown," replies Connie. "We always stick him with the hard-luck ones. And the fourth floor is basically God's waiting room."

"Was it that bad at Woodland Lake?" I ask.

"Woodland Lake?" asks Connie.

"That's over by Hobart," says Bernie.

"Oh."

Jenaqua shakes her head. "He came here, what, October? The streak up there started before then, I think. The hospital started taking people that should have been sent to hospice, if you ask me."

This is curious. Filman may well be the victim of bad odds, but I've witnessed several rationalizations for what should be a very, very suspicious pattern.

"Yeah," I reply. "I just hope nobody starts saying things like *killer nurse*."

"Who are you again?" asks Jenaqua.

"Don't tell anybody, but when I'm not running my secret military lab and troubleshooting for the government, I hunt serial killers as a hobby."

"Right. Right. I saw that movie," she replies. "I'm sorry, but you are not as good-looking as what's his face."

I check my watch and stub out my cigarette in the ashtray sitting on the edge of the wall. "Well, I have to go make sure it looks like I'm doing something responsible."

"Bye, Dr. Theo," says Jenaqua.

As I walk through the door, I hear a voice that must belong to Bernie the Orderly whispering to his friends, "That was the real guy."

I head straight to the elevator before any more questions can be asked, although I'd like to be a fly on the wall and hear how they take Bernie's revelations. If I had to guess, Jenaqua will try to convince him that he's wrong.

When I get to the fourth floor, the nurse I spoke to before is sitting at the station. "Did you catch Filman?" she asks.

"No. Was he here?"

"Yes, but then he left."

"Where?"

"I thought he went to find you when I mentioned someone wanted to speak to him. You can try back tomorrow if you like."

Interesting. I wonder if Filman decided to be elsewhere when he heard there was a stranger on the floor who wanted to talk to him?

Either way, I'm going to make sure that our paths cross again. I get into the elevator, joining the nurse who turned the other way when I was photographing the desk.

She's facing forward, but she steals a glance at me. "You don't work here."

"Nope," I reply.

"You're investigating this place."

I turn to her. "Correct."

"I thought so." Her hand goes into her pocket, and she pulls out a slip of paper. "Talk to her."

She gets out on the second floor and keeps walking without looking back.

CHAPTER THIRTEEN
SYSTEMS ANALYST

When I step inside the small community-college conference room space Marcie Quan reserved for our meeting, I find a table with more than a dozen folders and colored binders carefully laid out across it in perfect alignment and an equally organized young woman sitting behind them with a business jacket and blouse that make me feel as if I've walked into a job interview.

"Dr. Cray?" she says, greeting me with a polite smile.

"Yes. Ms. Quan?"

The woman whose name and number the nurse gave me in the elevator points to the chair across the small table. "Could I see some ID first?"

"Pardon me?"

"I just need to make sure you are who you say you are."

I'm more amused than caught off guard. She reminds me of the little kid in *Uncle Buck* interrogating a babysitter through the mail slot on the front door. I hand her my Texas driver's license. She snaps a photo of it, then aims the camera at me.

"Will you state for the record that you're not employed by or working for or on behalf of Southern Star Medical Group or any subsidiary?" she asks.

"Um, okay. Who are they?"

"They own the hospitals. Ivy, Concord, and the others," she explains.

"Okay. I don't work for them or their lawyers. Good enough?"

"It'll do," she replies.

"Are you in some kind of legal situation with them?" I ask.

"Not immediately. They've filed and dropped charges twice. They don't like what would happen in a discovery phase," she says.

"I see." I look down at the files on the table. "I assume it's about this?"

"Some of this. I was hired two years ago as an independent contractor to work on their software systems. Technically, I was hired by a small company owned by Ryan Anderson—he's the CEO of Southern Star Medical Group."

"I met him at Ivy Center," I reply. "He seemed concerned that I was asking about billing. So did Ms. Spicola."

Marcie nods. "That would be them. I was hired by Ryan to help develop billing software for the hospital. Which seemed odd to me at the time, because that's the kind of thing you buy from a company that specializes in that. You don't develop your own in-house. That should have been the warning sign."

"The warning sign?"

"Okay, it's no big revelation that hospitals have sketchy pricing. There's one price they'll charge the government, another for your insurance company, and even those fluctuate as hospitals try to figure out what's the maximum price to charge for something like a Tylenol pill before it triggers a rejection in the payer's system. It's like stock-market arbitrage. The insurance companies and the government have pricing limits, and the hospitals look for the closest margin they can get to them. If they can't charge forty dollars for an ibuprofen, they'll look for something else to charge more for, like X-rays.

"On the flip side, while as grossly inefficient as that system is, the alternative is state-controlled pricing across the board, which means chronic drug shortages like they have in Canada, where they run out of things like EpiPens. I don't think anybody has it figured out, but companies like Southern Star take it to an entirely different level."

"How so?"

"The system I was asked to work on had crooked billing methods you wouldn't believe. It would actually change a physician's diagnosis to something requiring more expensive treatments, and the patient surveys were designed in such a way that someone who was suffering a headache would appear to describe symptoms requiring MRI scans and expensive medications—which, by the way, were sold by the pharmacy at the hospital, which was actually owned by a separate entity controlled by Southern Star.

"My boss, Anderson's partner, was a former billing manager for an insurance company, and he had another guy there who'd actually worked for Medicaid, advising us off the books."

"That sounds . . ."

"Illegal?" she replies. "Most of it. A lot of it wasn't, strangely enough. You'd be surprised at what you can get away with. Our current medical plan laws were written by insiders who had no desire to disrupt the system."

"Okay. So, what happened?"

"First, I pointed out the things that were illegal to my boss and Anderson. Things like saying a patient spent one day longer at a hospital than they did or charging for a specialist visit that never occurred."

"And?"

"I was told to stay in my lane. Ivan Maguire, my immediate boss, told me that those were flaws that were going to be fixed and the most important thing was that the medical group had an excellent record.

"Which made me curious. That's when I discovered that they weren't only fudging their billing, they were outright lying about their treatment quality. Their cardiac unit had had one of the worst success rates in the country, and all of a sudden it was performing just above average. How was this possible? By reclassifying patients that had negative outcomes with terminal conditions."

"How's that?"

"They created an ad hoc postoperation panel that would reevaluate the diagnosis based on the outcome. It's literally one drunk doctor who sits in his home in New Orleans, rubber-stamping recommendations made by the computer.

"Anyway, I had enough, so I grabbed what documents I could and quit. I hadn't been home more than two hours before two sheriff's deputies showed up at my door with a warrant to seize any files I had. My parents were thrilled when those two marched through the house, grabbed my computer, and ransacked my room.

"The next day I'm sent a cease-and-desist order, and an attorney for Anderson says I'm going to be sued for ten million dollars for attempting to steal intellectual property. Which is ironic, because the property in question is the software they created for stealing."

I can see the frustration in her eyes, but also the fire. "So, what's the current situation?"

"They've made it clear to me that if I say anything, they'll go after my parents, too, because I was and still am living at home. I'm young, but my dad is eighty. He survived Vietnam, but I can't put him through this. So I'm just biding my time, building the case against them."

"To sue?"

She shakes her head. "In *this* state, with a judge they play tennis with? Nope. I'm just gonna WikiLeak it. Put it all out there. Let them sue me then."

"You're brave. Real brave," I reply.

"I'm not brave, Dr. Cray. What they're doing is wrong. It's evil. They're ripping us all off. Isn't that why you're here?"

"Uh, well. Kind of. I'm curious about a man named Sergio Filman. He's a nurse that works for the hospital group."

"What about him?"

"I think he's been killing patients," I reply.

"Really? Wow. That wouldn't surprise me. Lord knows how many people they've killed in that disaster of a hospital. They'd have been bankrupted by medical-malpractice lawsuits if it wasn't for the fact that every lawyer billboard you see near there is for someone who has a sweetheart deal with the hospital. The record they're proudest of is how few cases ever make it to court." She sighs. "So, what's up with Filman?"

"I met with the parents of some children who died suddenly at Woodland Lake Clinic. They suspect Filman did it. I was hoping you might be able to help me."

"Woodland Lake?" she replies. "They shut that place down. I didn't have access to the individual records there. A lot of stuff was lost because of a 'virus'"—she makes quotes with her fingers—"when a new state investigator was asking about billing. Those crazy computer viruses . . ."

She stops for a moment and studies me. I sit still, trying not to be too unnerved by the experience.

"You a computer guy?"

"I dabble."

"Their system is extremely buggy and easy to hack into."

"Like if I found a password on a nurses' station?" I reply.

"Yeah. Of course, it would be illegal for you to do that. Although, rumor has it that the same front end that gives patients access also gives access to hospital records . . . if you have the right password."

"That's . . ."

"Stupid? Welcome to the world of health-information technology. How many times have Patient Protection and Affordable Care Act servers been publicly hacked?"

"Fair point."

"Maybe you can find something in their system. Although I wouldn't expect a smoking-gun memo that says they think this guy is killing patients. Hell, they wouldn't know if Jeffrey Dahmer was eating patients in the emergency room. But you can be sure they'd find a way to bill for it."

CHAPTER FOURTEEN
THE HAPPY PLACE

Back in my hotel, I log on to the Southern Star patient portal using my "clean" laptop with an LTE account I paid for with Bitcoin. As an extra precaution, I use a VPN in Brazil to mask my point of origin.

While I doubt Southern Star is using the best intrusion-prevention standards, I can't be too sure. There's also the remote chance that this is all some kind of setup. Marcie Quan could be a hospital employee sent to trap me, as crazy as it sounds.

Everything about her checks out online, but that's not too hard to fake.

I would know.

The first thing I do is find my way to the hospital's in-house billing system, which isn't available through an interface in the patient system, but adding "billing" at the end of the URL takes me to an admin screen where I'm able to log in again using the code from the nurses' station.

In direct violation of federal law, I pull up two random patient billing records and find variable pricing between similar treatments.

When I enter Cooper Hennison's name into a general search query, I find multiple records. Under billing, there's a long list of medications and materials used during his stay. I notice a prescription for several expensive antibiotics that were made and filled a day after he died.

While I'm no expert on medical billing, I understand something about prescriptions. There are at least six scrips signed by physicians for Cooper *after* he was declared dead.

Looking at the room rate they charged the Hennisons, I see it's the price of a nice used car. I notice that another patient who had Medicaid paid a fraction of the rate. I also discover that Cooper was booked into two different facilities at the same time. While most of his stay was at Woodland Lake, they had him booked at the Fairway Emergency Clinic at the same time. Curiously enough, the same prescriptions were made and filled for him at both locations, but by different doctors.

Saunders's daughter, Veronica, has records as well. Her bill is a lot less than Cooper's. That might be because her father had an insurance company that was savvier to Southern Star's billing hijinks. Her last stay was also at the Fairway clinic. There's an ambulance bill as well, although it's called a "medical transportation fee."

It's weird that the families say their children died at Woodland Lake, but the hospital says otherwise. I give Emily a call.

"Hey, it's Theo. Quick question. Where did they see Cooper's body before it was taken to the funeral home?"

"The morgue in Woodland Lake," she replies. "I went there with Darcy that night."

"Was anybody with Cooper when he passed?"

"No. Darcy went home for a few hours after he went to sleep. She usually slept there."

This is interesting. "What about Saunders with Veronica?"

"No one was there, either. Oh, that's something I forgot to tell you: all the kids were alone when it happened. Which seems weird, because most of them had someone there most of the time."

"That is odd. But none of the kids were at Fairway Emergency Clinic?"

"What's that? I never heard of it."

"Interesting," I reply. "Thank you." I hang up and call Quan.

"Marcie speaking," she says in the same eager voice.

"What's Fairway Emergency Clinic?" I ask. "All the kids I'm looking into passed away there according to the records, but the parents say otherwise."

"Fairway?" She laughs. "I shouldn't laugh, but that's another scam. Let me guess, there's a transportation fee for that?"

"Yep."

"Fairway's the other side of the Woodland Lake facility. It's actually owned by a separate entity that leases the space, but it's operated by guess who?"

"Southern Star," I reply.

"Correct. The transportation fee is the gurney rental and the orderlies. They actually work for a third company . . . on paper. A lot of that is just employee numbers. Some staffers are listed multiple ways. John Allen Smith might be J. A. Smith or J Allen S. Anyway, the hospital charges patients when they're transferred to that part of the hospital, because technically it's leaving hospital grounds."

I do a search for Fairway in the portal. "I can't find anything for Fairway in the last two years."

"You won't," says Marcia. "It no longer exists."

"Did they close it with Woodland Lake?"

"Before then. They change the ownership of the clinic every year or so."

"That just seems inefficient . . ." Then it hits me. "Oh."

"Yeah. It's not about the money—well, not specifically. It also avoids red flags."

"Do a lot of these transfers happen after the fact? Postmortem?"

"On paper. I don't know how many patients ever made it down the corridor there. The hospital just transfers them to there . . ."

"To lower the hospital's mortality rate. Nobody dies at Disney World," I reply.

"What's that?" she asks.

"It's kind of an urban legend. People used to say that nobody died at Disney World because the company had an agreement that authorities wouldn't declare someone dead until they were transferred off park property. It's not true, of course. But it sounds cool. Is this how Southern Star was able to avoid raising too many red flags? They'd transfer just enough patients on paper to avoid looking like a death trap?"

"Exactly."

"Marcie, that's not just corrupt, it's evil." I can kind of understand trying to maximize patient billing for a financial gain, but manipulating records so people think your hospital is safe . . . that *is* killing people.

"Have you listened to anything I've been saying? Of course, Southern Star isn't the only one. Even state-owned hospitals have their own scams. Look at the mess at the VAs. I don't know what the solution is," she says, exasperated.

"You're the solution," I reply.

"What?"

"Saying things. Doing the right thing. Speaking up. Any system can be corrupted as long as people will pretend it's not their problem."

It took a murder accusation and a dead body to get me to do something, but Marcie saw this from the start. How do we get more of that?

"I could use your help on this," she says.

"I'm on board. Nailing Filman would be a big deal. It'd bring people here asking questions that they don't want to answer. The thing is, I can't find him in the portal other than the last three months. There's no rotations for Woodland Lake."

"Yeah. That'll be a problem. Their 'virus' ate a lot of records. I'm sure there are no records left of him being at Woodland Lake."

Damn it. I need to show Filman was there when the children were alone, and I need to know who else he had access to. Short of a confession, there might be no way to prove anything.

"Nothing?" I ask.

"Not that I came across. But I'm sure there are scattered records around. I doubt Anderson managed to wipe everything."

"What about Woodland Lake itself?" I reply. "Could there still be records there?"

"Maybe. They still own the facility. It wouldn't surprise me if they just took whatever was valuable and locked the doors."

"Why did they close it?"

"From what I heard it was the rent."

"But they own it?"

"Anderson does. But Woodland Lake is a nonprofit. I heard that in order for him to raise the rent on the facility and pay more to himself, he had to shut it down and rent it to another party at a higher rate. It's some weird rule to prevent people from using nonprofit hospitals for profit."

Universities do similar things. Some of the shadiest things I've seen have been done by institutions everyone perceives as being noble minded. In fact, I think the opposite is true. The more noble appearing the institution, the more prone it is to corruption, because everyone is looking the other way.

"Maybe you could get a subpoena for the records there?" says Marcie.

"I don't have that kind of pull," I reply. At some point I could contact someone friendly at the FBI, but I'd need a lot more than what I have now.

"Too bad."

I glance over at my suitcase and my little set of lockpicks resting on my socks. "Maybe there's another way."

CHAPTER FIFTEEN
WOODLAND LAKE

Woodland Lake is neither a lake nor a woodland. It's actually a dark-green pond infested with filamentous algae floating like alien globules waiting to slide ashore in a slimy mass and pull some unsuspecting person into the black depths to be slowly devoured. Or at least that's what it looks like. Actually, it's a fascinating little ecosystem. Years after the owners of Woodland Lake turned off the fountain that kept the water moving and the mosquitoes to a minimum, the pond has reverted to its natural state.

Frogs chirp, and the occasional splash tells me that something else lives in there, possibly a small alligator or catfish that made its way into the lake during flooding.

My curiosity is piqued by this giant petri dish, and I'm tempted to use one of my sample vials to bring some of the pond back home to find out what surprises lie inside. This close to a hospital, there could be all kinds of antibiotic-resistant bacteria living in the water.

But that's not why I'm here. Woodland Lake Clinic, the building, is the focus of my attention. Not the murky, poorly named lake.

I've been watching the facility for the last two hours. Approximately once an hour, a private security guard in an SUV pulls up to the locked outer gate, unlocks it with a key, and then drives inside and makes a complete lap around the building, using the spotlight mounted above his driver's side mirror to check all the doors and windows.

The man is thorough. I suspect he's probably retired or part-time law enforcement. Which also means it's likely that he's armed, unlike mall cops and the minimum-wage people hired to walk around apartment complexes.

After he leaves, I park my car at a strip mall where a McDonald's is still serving at the far end next to a twenty-four-hour convenience store. Making sure I'm not being watched, other than by whatever surveillance cameras the closed businesses might have, I make my way to the back of the parking lot and hop-trip through the small hedge that separates the back of the hospital complex from the mall.

Sticking close to trees and hedges, I sneak to the loading dock behind the hospital. The double metal doors next to the roll-up gate have a keypad next to them. Fortunately for me, I have a list of pass codes that were saved on the internal email system for the hospital.

The second one on the list elicits a buzz-click sound, and I'm inside the building. Getting inside just about anywhere is pretty easy once you understand its blind spots. In the case of a hospital, though, finding your way in is only the first step. Anything valuable is kept under a different set of locks and keys.

The inside loading area of Woodland Lake has desks stacked on top of each other, piles of broken machinery, and plastic bags filled with leaky things that glisten in the light of my flashlight. I smell water rot and rat droppings, but nothing too pungent. Of course, I've only just stepped into the structure.

The only light sources other than mine are the red glow of the emergency exit signs scattered around the facility.

I make my way through the next door, which is propped open with a trash can, and follow the hallway past several doors with windows revealing rooms that are either empty or have been mostly stripped clean except for empty moving boxes and trash on the floor.

I pass a bathroom, and the scent of stagnant water makes me quicken my pace. I keep going until I pass a reception area, careful to turn out my light so it's not visible through the glass windows that face the parking lot.

I take the stairs to the second level and find myself in the children's ward. A waiting area has magazines and a play pit with some broken toys waiting for children to return.

Through the next set of doors, I find another waiting area. This appears to be a place for adults to sit while their children convalesce in the ward at the end of the corridor.

In the ward proper, moonlight from a window overlooking the dark pond bounces off the damp floor tiles. A nook with some small couches and kids' furniture sits below the window, which seems set a little too high. This is the kind of place a parent would step into, take in the pond, and think how nice it is that their child will have this to gaze at while they recover, not realizing that a small patient in a wheelchair will only see a gray wall.

Well, not only a gray wall. On one side there's a mural of superheroes painted by someone whose only exposure to Marvel and DC characters must have been from melted Popsicles of them. A large green tangle of lines vaguely resembles the Hulk, if Bruce Banner had a tumor on the left side of his forehead and skipped his legs every workout. Thor is more recognizable but bears a frightening resemblance to an Aryan Nation tattoo.

The rooms are arranged in a U shape around the nurses' station. Each room has two beds. Several beds are in the ward itself, with only curtains to provide privacy.

I walk to the back and spot the location where Cooper had been in the photograph his parents showed me. It's in a semiprivate area with a couch below a window. The opposite wall is an accordion-fold screen that can provide total seclusion.

When I walk back to the nurses' station, I notice that large parts of the ward can't be seen because of the tall cabinets placed in front of the counter.

The computers in the station have all been removed. The metal cabinets have been mostly cleared out, and the office area behind the station contains only broken furniture.

Well, there goes finding a treasure trove of forgotten documents. Anderson and Co. made sure to remove everything of importance, or at least to move it to another part of the hospital.

I take one more pass through the children's section. Already thoroughly creeped, I try to imagine what it was like for a child in the middle of the night with the sounds of whirring machines and beeping monitors, and tiny islands of fluorescence in otherwise pitch-black darkness that must have looked like menacing eyes watching from the shadows.

The sound of something clanking almost makes me gasp. I stand perfectly still and listen for any other noise.

I'm a scientific man, but I can't ignore the fact that several children died here—not only died but were *murdered* here—and I'm pretty sure I'm not completely alone right now.

Large animal? Raccoon?

A security guard?

I stay motionless and continue to listen. There's an echo of a door shutting. Yes. Someone else is here.

It's possible part of this hospital is still used for some reason. But I didn't see a car in the parking lot.

Maybe other employees discovered the keypad trick and came here to screw around?

I wait another few minutes and hear no more sounds. Hopefully they're gone or at another part of the hospital.

I decide to keep my light off and explore the rest of the building, careful to use my ears as much as my eyes. The children's ward may be empty, but that doesn't mean there aren't other secrets here.

I take the stairs back down and head for the opposite end of the facility. As I walk by brochure racks and lonely signs about getting your flu shot, I spot a solid-looking door with no window. A piece of bare adhesive in the middle is where the sign describing its function used to hang.

I kneel and pick up the plaque, which has fallen due to the humidity. It reads "Server Room."

Curious.

The door is locked, but there's a keypad. I take out my list of numbers and keep entering them until the lock makes a clicking noise.

I step inside and smell glue traps and dead rats. After I close the door and turn on my light, the decaying rodents are visible an inch in front of my toe, caught in traps with their withered bodies contorted into painful positions.

The server room itself is more of a closet. I scan my light across a rack that holds telephone switches. Another has five servers. The lights are out, but the cables running into the back of them tell me that these were still in use while the hospital was operational.

A dust-covered binder sits on the topmost one. I open it and find a manual for the hospital records software system, including passwords.

If this were a movie, I'd plug in a hard drive and download the contents of the servers. I flip a switch to see if they're still plugged into power, but nothing happens. I doubt there's even a working internet connection.

If I want to know what's on them, I'll have to take them with me. Which is theft. But upstairs was murder, so it balances out in my conscience.

Each server's the size of a pizza box. I unscrew them one by one and place them into a cardboard box that previously contained light fixtures.

My plan is to wait for the security guard to do another pass and then make a run for my car with the box, looking about as suspicious as possible.

I carry the boxes back to the loading area and keep watch through the glass window, waiting for the car to pass.

While staring out, I hear the very clear voice of someone on the inside. On the first floor. Heading in my direction.

CHAPTER SIXTEEN
ARRESTED MOTION

Footsteps approach from the hall, and the sound of the voice grows louder. I can't quite make out the words, but the tempo is like one side of a phone conversation. I can't tell if it's a security guard or someone up to no good like myself.

Encountering either would probably not have a positive outcome. It's not like a meth head who breaks in is going to give me a high five when he discovers someone else holding a box of stolen goods.

Doing my best not to step on anything and make a sound, I slide closer to the doorway and look out. A beam of light washes past the window from the end of the hall. I also hear the sound of doors being opened.

Damn. It's probably the security guard, and he's almost definitely armed.

The light gets brighter, and I pull away from the window.

I scan the room for someplace to hide. There's a laundry bin at the other side of the storage room. I make three strides across the floor, willing myself to step lightly, and carefully step into the bin, still managing to make a squeaking sound as the wheels strain under me.

I curl into the fetal position, and suddenly I'm four years old, hiding under my blankets and hoping the monster in the hall closet doesn't see me.

Was Filman a monster to these children? Were they scared of him? Did Cooper look up into his eyes moments before he died?

The door opens. I want to kick myself for the stupidest of stupid plans. In daytime, I probably could have talked my way out of this with a fake ID and business card. But no. I had to do this in the middle of the night so I could catch a flight back to Austin.

Light flashes around the room and lands on the laundry bin I'm trying to hide in. It stays on the bin. It's still on this bin. The batteries should have run out by now. The sun is going to enter its last stages and expand into a red giant by now. Earth should be a burned husk absorbed by our dying sun by now. The damned light is still on the bin.

And then it's gone.

The door shuts.

The footsteps go away.

I wait.

And I wait.

Finally, I crawl out of the bin.

I go to the back door that faces the loading dock and see blue and red lights in the distance.

The distance part would be good, but they're coming from the strip mall where I parked my car. That is not good.

Someone must have seen me climb over the hedge and called the cops.

I don't think the person with the flashlight was talking on a police radio, but that doesn't mean he wasn't a cop. It also doesn't mean cops aren't coming.

I'd leave the car at the strip mall, but the rental's in my name. I could wait them out, but that might not help. They could have it towed.

I know for certain I can't waltz back to my car holding a box filled with stolen computers. But do I want to leave them?

No. I do not. But I don't need all their bulk, only the hard drives.

I take out the utility tool on my key chain and start to unscrew the servers' housings. I probably should have done that in the first place, but I really only wanted to grab everything and run. Plus, this feels too much like vandalism.

I need to rethink my sense of ethics. I'll decapitate stolen corpses in a state park to fake a crime scene, but I hesitate to use a Phillips screwdriver on abandoned property?

I get the first hard drive out and jog back to the window to have a look.

Lucky break: the cops are gone.

Or did they simply turn off their lights? Let me think . . . how would I lure someone back to their car?

I'd turn off the lights and wait.

I remove the other three hard drives and shove them into the pockets of my cargo pants, which are really convenient for little excursions like this but suspicious as hell if the cops see me. I haven't quite figured out the right kind of fashion for my line of work. Although black is convenient for the bloodstains.

Okay, the hard drives are in my pockets and the cops are probably in the parking lot over there. What's my plan?

I'll bet anything that the security guard is in front of the building, which kind of, sort of makes me trapped.

New plan . . .

What if I call the cops on myself?

Better yet . . .

I call the number for Eagle Watch security.

"Eagle Watch. How may we assist you?" says a man with a Louisiana drawl.

"Hello, I'm calling from Southern Star. One of our employees called in about a possible break-in at the Woodland Lake facility?"

"Yes, sir. We're on the scene right now. We have local police there, too."

"Oh, great. Great. Our employee's a little worried. He's afraid someone's inside there. Could you have someone meet him at the front entrance? His name is Ted."

"Sure. One second." The dispatcher calls into another phone or a radio. "Hal, could you meet someone from Southern Star at the entrance? He's the one that called it in. Hold on, I'll ask." He gets back on my line. "What was your employee doing there?"

"We had a problem with our emergency line and sent him there to figure out if Woodland Lake was causing the problem." Vague but specific enough, I guess.

"Understood. Tell Ted to meet Hal by the door."

"Thank you. He'll be very relieved. Poor guy is scared witless."

By the time I reach the lobby, Hal is standing outside waiting. I greet him with a sheepish wave and unlock the door from the inside to let me through.

"You Ted?" he asks.

"Yes. Hal?" I shake his hand. I point to the unlocked gate. "Sure, they give *you* the key."

"Anyone else in there?" he asks, flashing a light into the building.

"I think I had a false alarm and scared myself. This place is scary at night," I reply.

"Tell me about it. Need a ride back to your car?"

"You're a prince, Hal."

CHAPTER SEVENTEEN
GRAY MATTER

My brain doesn't look that special. Even displayed in 8K on the huge monitors looming over my workstation, which more closely resemble old-timey Burma-Shave billboards than the miniature screen of the ancient Macintosh I played with as a boy.

The cross sections of my latest MRI scans rotate at the touch of my mouse while imaging software I borrowed from a signal-processing project try to enhance and clarify the region in question.

Signal processing is a fascinating area of research. In a way, it kind of underlies all science—trying to find something significant in a pile of noise. Right now, I'm trying to take a number of fuzzy MRI images and see if I can see something that's not obvious.

I'd be much better off using a CT scan from a series of X-rays, like that taken shortly after my encounter with Forrester, but the radiation doses would be a little too much to endure on a weekly basis. So instead, I'm trying to use the MRI with data from known Hyde virus infection cases to see if I can spot it before it gets out of hand.

The specific trait I'm looking for in the MRI images is the thickness of the tissue in part of my dorsolateral prefrontal cortex. In particular,

I'm looking for either a sign of abnormal swelling, which would be the virus attacking it, or a sudden thinness—a sign that the virus demolished that area and I've lost my ability to control my anger.

Because every scan is going to have a margin of error and a borderline hypochondriac is not the best person to interpret his own images, I trained a neural network to look for abnormalities and flag them. I could second-guess myself over and over again regarding whether this is sufficient, but unless I'm going to turn myself over to the doctors at the CDC looking into Hyde, I'll have to convince myself that it's enough.

I plug one of the hard drives from Woodland Lake into a housing so I can divert myself from my descent into madness. What a strange world I live in, where the relaxing part of my day is hunting a child killer.

A little poking around the file system on the first drive reveals dozens of MySQL databases. When I take a look at the tables, I find medical-supply inventory logs and related billing. The next drive contains employee hours, and the third and fourth are backups.

It's kind of sloppy to keep the backup drives in the same place as the others, but nothing about Southern Star surprises me. Still, I'd bet they at least kept off-site backups for billing. God forbid they forget how much to charge a patient—although I'm sure they'd figure something out.

I copy all the data over to my system so I can make cross-database queries. What I'm hoping to do is build up a timeline for Sergio Filman and track his actions over time.

After a few hours, I'm able to get a pretty good view of his time at Woodland Lake, and it's pretty incriminating. He was on shift or leaving shift for each of the deaths of the three children in question.

Curiously, on the copy of their files at Woodland Lake, I notice an internal code, XP4003, and an internal memo that simply says: Determination SOCCR.

SOCCR again . . . exactly what the parents claimed. My internet and Medline searching hasn't been fruitful, so I decide to try some off-line questions.

I call Dr. Giles Emmerson. He's a researcher at the United States Army Medical Research Institute of Infectious Diseases, the place other researchers go when they're stumped. If there's an Ebola outbreak, he'll tell you the name of the bat that was probably the source.

"At this hour," he grumbles into the phone, "it'd better be the plague."

"It's Theo Cray."

"That's worse. Found something else to keep me up at night? Hyde wasn't enough?"

"I didn't try to find that," I reply.

"People spend their entire lives trying to discover something that's maybe at best a mutation on something we know. You come in and bring us a whole new category. A mathematician, of all people. Not even a real doctor."

"I'm a biologist, Giles."

"Yeah, whatever you tell yourself. Why are you bothering me? Is it to tell me that the team at the CDC is screwing things up?"

"Do I need to tell you? How are they doing at USAMRIID?"

"The army has no interest in weaponizing viral agents," he says, yawning the lie.

"Right. Actually, I'm not calling about Hyde. I want to know about something else."

"If you discovered something new, I'm going to have you sent to a primate research center as a test subject."

"That could happen sooner than you realize," I say, thinking of my own concern with Hyde.

"I don't get your sense of humor," he growls.

"I was told I didn't have one. Anyway, I didn't discover Hyde. That was Forrester. Who I believe you and your friends knew, by the way."

Emmerson suggests that I eat a part of my own anatomy.

"SOCCR," I say, then spell it out for him. "Ever heard of it?"

"SOCCR? Why does that ring a bell? Hold on a second. Let me think. Caputo?" he asks.

That was the name of the researcher I saw associated with the phenomenon. "Yeah. That one."

"It's bullshit. She was doing some data mining for deaths with undetermined causes and came up with what she thought may have been previously unknown conditions."

"What do you mean?"

"She was trying to apply a catchall term to what was very likely a misdiagnosis of known conditions. It's really a way of saying, 'I don't know,' while sounding extremely certain. Which can also be a way of covering your ass if you think you know, but the answer would reflect badly on the caregivers. Like if a patient comes in with respiratory problems and a possible infection and you accidentally give them penicillin, causing anaphylaxis. If a penicillin allergy isn't mentioned on their chart, but you suspect that may be the actual cause, a less-than-ethical person might be inclined to say that they died of cardiovascular-triggered anaphylaxis."

"How would that hold up?" I ask.

"Where? You think a medical examiner is going to pay that much attention if everything seems in order? As long as no foul play is suspected and the hospital appeared to make best efforts, nobody would care."

"Except the family," I reply.

"Good luck proving it. Some people claim medical errors kill more people every year in the United States than soldiers we lost in Vietnam. I'd take all those facts with an iceberg-size grain of salt, but they do happen. We're all human. If you lose a patient and one way of looking at the data makes you not culpable and the other does, which would you choose?"

"How many cases of SOCCR are there a year?" I ask.

"You tell me. It's not a real thing. Nobody keeps tabs."

I check the screen in front of me. "I'm looking at a hospital that claims eight cases in one year."

"Then you're looking at a bad hospital. That many cases? They should have reported it to NIH and the CDC."

"I'm pretty sure they didn't."

"What's the name of this facility?"

"Woodland Lake. It's a clinic in Baton Rouge."

"Never heard of it. How many beds?"

"Forty, I think."

"That's a high rate. Real, real high." His voice trails off as he thinks this over for a moment. "Can you check something?"

"What's that?"

"I don't want to know how or why from you, of all people. But can you get pharmaceutical records for the patients involved?"

"Let's say I can. Why?"

"Can you see if any of these patients were given digoxin?"

"The heart drug? Hold on." I do a search for the databases for digoxin and its analogs. None of the children were given it. "Nope."

"Hmm. It's very useful stuff . . ."

"But an overdose can cause heart failure," I say.

"Yeah. I was wondering if they had an accidental overdose or were given some from a supply in which the amounts were too high."

"Cullen," I reply.

"Who?"

"Charles Cullen. He killed forty patients with digoxin overdoses. But why would someone try that same method again?" I ask.

"Are you kidding? Because it worked for him. If what we're talking about is what I think we're talking about, serial killers get their best ideas from serial killers. Right?"

"Sad but true. Hold on." I do a query in the Rx database for digoxin requisitions. "This is interesting. My subject in question has requisitioned a ton of digoxin, using different brand names when they're available." I study a chart for a moment. "Normal doses are about seventy-five hundred to fifteen hundred micrograms. I'm seeing several seventy-five-thousand-unit requests."

"He's adding a zero to a written prescription," says Emmerson. "It's cheap enough that nobody would notice. It's not much of a party drug, either."

My mind races with the implication of this, and I stab my fingers at my keyboard.

"What's that sound?"

"I'm typing. Shut up," I snap.

I grab the data from my queries and put them into a graph. "I'm sending you something. Take a look."

A minute later Emmerson lets out a sigh. "This data is real?"

"As far as I know. I can only pin an eight-month period on my guy, but the graph itself covers a several-year period until the records stop."

Emmerson is looking at three scatter plots. The first one shows deaths at the Southern Star hospitals. The second one shows when digoxin was prescribed for other patients in an abnormally high amount. The third is the two plots combined.

"Within twenty-four hours of your nurse's requisition, someone dies from a condition that could be caused by a digoxin overdose," says Emmerson. "But never the person who was actually prescribed the digoxin?"

"The only ones I can prove conclusively are at Woodland Lake. But there's a pattern at other hospitals my suspect worked at."

"It's a bit erratic," Emmerson comments.

I know what he's referring to. There's a period before Woodland Lake when Filman appeared to go on a frenzy, sometimes two patients in a week. And then a lull of about one digoxin-related death a month for half a year, followed by another frenzy, and then back to two uses a month.

"He may have been worried about getting caught and then slowed down for a while," I reply.

"You know these sickos better than me. So, what are you going to do?"

"I have to stop him. He's still working and presumably killing."

"Godspeed, Theo. Godspeed. After you're done and we can meet in person, I'll tell you what I unofficially know about Hyde."

A week ago, I would have been on the first plane to Maryland to find out what he's hinting at. But right now, the most urgent ticking clock isn't the one in my head. The thought of Filman taking one more life sickens me.

On the drive back to meet with Jillian, I contemplate some kind of quick stopgap. But before I do anything drastic, I need to talk to her. She's my moral baseline in these matters.

CHAPTER EIGHTEEN
Big League

I've seen Jillian's face react to all kinds of horror. There was the first time we met, when I stumbled into her diner back in Montana, bruised and bleeding. She thought I was some jerk who got his ass kicked trying to pick up a hooker. The truth was a lot harder to explain.

Weeks later, we were alone in the forest with Joe Vik, and I watched her as he was about to kill her. She was calm and cool, telling me to save myself. Jillian had been a soldier. She'd lost a husband. She understood death more thoroughly than I could comprehend.

When I explain to her about the children in Baton Rouge, it elicits the same reaction she had when I explained what John Christian had been doing to children.

As I lay out my reasoning, Jillian nods and keeps glancing at a framed photo of the Little League baseball team we sponsor through the bakery. In truth, it was Jillian who arranged to pay for equipment and made sure the kids didn't have a game without cupcakes. I've gone to maybe two games with her. She knows all their names. She knows their parents. The kids are abstract notions to me. They're real to her.

As I tell her about Cooper, Veronica, Michael, and all the other likely victims, tears well in her eyes. "And he's out there right now."

"Probably killing old people," I reply.

"People, Theo. People. Like right now? You know where he is?"

"He's on the night shift at Concord Medical Center. I don't have recent records. But he . . ." I trail off in thought.

"Could be killing someone right now?"

"I called the hospital on the way over."

"What did you tell them?" she asks.

"That I thought Sergio Filman may be a serial killer."

"And they said?"

"They could put me in touch with a grief counselor."

"I don't understand."

"They thought I was just a bitter family member."

"But then you told them who you are? They have to listen, right?" she asks.

"Do they ever listen?"

She shakes her head. "So, what are you going to do?"

"It's a seven-hour drive. After I talked to you, I was going to drive straight there so I could be at the district attorney's office first thing in the morning."

She nods her head. "Good. Good." She pauses as she thinks this over. "Are there others like him?"

"Killer nurses? Probably dozens around the country."

Her voice goes soft. "Those poor children. What about the other killers out there, Theo? What can be done about that?"

"I don't know. And I only know about this one because someone said something to me."

"But you said people at the hospital suspected."

"Yes, but they move him around from facility to facility. Nobody gets too suspicious, I guess."

"And the night Cooper died, this Filman was there?" Cooper is already a very real person to Jillian. That's how much she feels for these children. "Where were his parents?"

"Work. Watching the other kids. They assumed he was safe at the hospital."

"But he wasn't. Nobody was there to protect him." Jillian shakes her head. "They should have some kind of camera or something."

"Most hospitals do," I explain.

"But the hospitals *control* that," she says. "There's no way for the parents to know. You can put a camera in a teddy bear and watch it with an iPhone these days. Somebody should make a smarter version of that."

"Maybe. Maybe. When I get back, we can talk about it."

"Hailey makes kids' games, right?" Jillian asks out of nowhere.

"Yes."

"Okay, maybe I can talk to her."

Something is different about Jillian. I can't quite place it. She's handling this differently than I expected. Not better. Not worse. Just different.

"That might be a good idea," I reply.

"Have you told her about this?"

"No."

"You should. Call her on the way?"

"Okay." I can't figure out what's going on. "Is there something else?"

She stares at me for a moment. I know that stare extremely well. We have an agreement to say what's bothering us, even if it is trivial.

"I saw your credit card receipts. I saw the one for the clinic," she explains.

"The fertility clinic?"

She rolls her eyes. "That's a separate conversation. No. I'm talking about the one for brain imaging. What's that about?"

I know I can't lie to her—she'll see right through me. I was hoping I could avoid the issue until . . . I don't really know.

"It's Hyde," she says. "You're worried that you might be infected?"

"It's still a possibility."

"And the people at the CDC?" she asks.

"The CDC is great. The particular group working on this? Not so great. I've had some issues with them."

"Is this an ego thing?" she asks.

"Mine or theirs?"

"Theo. You're the first one to tell people we have to be aware of the limits of our expertise. I assume this applies to you as well?"

"Of course," I reply.

"And have you shared your concerns with the experts there?"

"It's complicated."

"Complicated? Is *complicated* the word you'd use to describe what happened to Daniel Marcus's coworkers when he went crazy and killed them?"

"Jillian . . . I'd never—"

She cuts me off. "Hurt me? Oh, honey, I'm not worried about that. I know your weak points. It's everyone else I'm afraid for."

"Afraid . . ." I repeat the word, hurt. "There's no reason . . ." I let my voice trail off.

"I'm afraid because *you're* afraid, Theo. I see it on your face all the time. It wasn't until I realized you were sneaking off to get your brain scanned that I realized what it was about. How am I supposed to feel?"

"I don't know."

"Is there somebody you can talk to about it?" she asks.

"If I go to the CDC group, they'll use it against me. And they're no closer to a cure for this, much less diagnosing it, than I am," I reply.

"Someone else?"

"Maybe. I don't know," I say, exasperated.

"Are you okay now?"

"Probably. Chances are I don't have it. But if I do, it could act fast. I'd probably see signs, like a fever."

"Okay, then that's something. Go to Baton Rouge. Take care of this asshole, and then we'll figure this out. Okay?"

"Okay," I reply, not feeling okay at all. She's looking at me like we're discussing a terminal disease. Which is technically true . . .

We have a long, awkward hug in the parking lot. As I watch her recede in the rearview mirror, she completely loses her composure. I've seen her cry, but never like this.

CHAPTER NINETEEN
LEGAL OPTIONS

Ella Bailey and Mark Versant, two prosecutors from the Baton Rouge district attorney's office, are watching me explain my suspicions with some interest, yet I feel more like I'm putting on a show than giving testimony in what's a serious criminal matter.

Bailey has short black hair in ringlets while Versant has a close-cropped military-style cut. They appear to be around the same age, a few years younger than me, and probably biding their time in the prosecutor's office until they're ready to go to a law firm doing higher-paying work or pursue a bench appointment.

I was able to get the meeting by dropping my own name. My reputation may not be the best in all circles—some people consider me an opportunistic glory hound—but I'm also a bit of a curiosity.

When the DA's office learned that *the* Dr. Theo Cray wanted to talk about a serial killer in Baton Rouge, an early-afternoon appointment was hastily scheduled.

I decided to go to the district attorney directly because it's a complicated case and wouldn't get as much immediate attention from local police.

Bailey waits for me to finish, then says, "So, let me describe what you just said, Dr. Cray. You believe a man, a nurse, Sergio Filman, is killing patients at Concord Medical Center?"

"I believe that's likely to be true. What I have evidence for is at least four patient deaths while he was at Woodland Lake." I push my scatter plots toward them. "Each one of the red dots represents a death about which family members were suspicious. The light-blue dot shows when someone removed an absurd amount of digoxin from the hospital's medical cabinet. You can see that always precedes a death under unusual circumstances."

"And how did you acquire this data?" asks Versant.

"I'd prefer not to disclose that," I reply.

"Patient records are protected," he says. "Possessing them is a violation of HIPAA."

"Possessing them without permission of the patients or their guardians is a violation. And since we're speaking about deceased patients, I'm not sure if that still counts. Where are you going with this?"

"I'm just making sure we're handling this appropriately. I'm also curious to how you got this information."

"Understood," I reply. "But let's focus on the more urgent manner of a man killing patients at one of the largest hospital chains in this state."

"Allegedly, Dr. Cray. All you've shown us is a graph. It's not exactly evidence," says Bailey.

"Yes. I know this. But it's a starting point."

"Why aren't the families here?" asks Versant.

"This seemed urgent."

"But you have their testimony?"

"I'm sure they'll be happy to come in here and provide it to you. They came to me." *Sort of.*

"Can I have their names?" Versant slides a pad and a pen over to me.

This feels fishy, but I can't figure out why. Of course, I'd have to tell them the names of the families involved. I write down the information for the Hennisons, Saunderses, and Quatrains.

"I'll be right back," says Versant as he gets up.

"What's that about?" I ask.

"It's what we do. So, Dr. Cray . . . ," says Bailey.

"Theo. Just call me Theo."

"All right, Theo. Is this how it usually works for you? Some family calls you up and asks you for your help?"

"I get asked all the time, but I don't really have the time. Nor is it my expertise. I generally refer people to their local law enforcement. Of course, by the time people talk to me, they've already tried that. But to be honest, I really haven't done this all that much."

"Two serial killers and that Forrester guy? What was that about? Poisoning the vaccine supply?"

His case hasn't even gone to trial yet. "Basically. The FBI pulled me in on that one." *And then they pushed me out of it.*

"So how does it usually work? You build up some evidence and come to us?"

"There is no usual. If something that doesn't make sense is brought to my attention, I look for a pattern. If I find something that the police didn't know, I go to them," I explain.

"And then what happens?"

"Generally, they tell me that I'm out of my element. What I have isn't enough and that I should basically stay in my lane."

"And then you prove them all wrong." She smiles as she says this, but it looks rather forced.

"I guess so."

"Ever been wrong?" she asks.

"All the time."

"I mean about someone you were convinced was the bad guy. Have you ever been wrong?"

"Not yet. Have you?"

"We have an eighty-one percent conviction rate," she says proudly. "Ten percent above the national average."

To keep things cordial, I don't ask her what that rate would be if they tried cases in which they knew the suspect was guilty but weren't sure how a jury was going to lean. "That's something to be proud of," I say instead.

Versant steps back into the conference room and returns to his seat. "So, I checked up on a couple things. I couldn't find a single record here of any of those families filing a complaint with us or anyone else."

"That doesn't surprise me," I reply. "They weren't even sure until quite recently."

"Yeah," says Versant. "Here's the problem: it's not much for us to go on. The last death was two years ago. There's not even a case for us to reopen, because nobody ever filed one."

"The last death involving the children was two years ago. The last murder committed by Sergio Filman could be last night, for all we know," I reply.

Versant nods his head. "Understood. Understood." He turns to Bailey. "Take it up to Oliver?"

She nods. "Yeah. I'd hate for us to overlook something." She turns to me. "Dr. Cray—or Theo. We're going to talk this over with our boss, Oliver Capstone. He runs the show around here and will have a better idea how to proceed."

"Okay. Understood. Let's go talk to him," I reply.

She stares at me for a moment. "Oh, not right now. We have a review meeting day after tomorrow. We'll bring this up to him then."

"You're fucking with me," I reply.

"Dr. Cray," she says, scolding me. "We don't have the luxury of choosing what we want to work on when we work on it. I have a desk filled with cases. Homicides, rapists, you name it."

I roll my eyes. "How many times have I heard that? Look, I'm not asking you to stop all other work. At the very least, call the Baton Rouge Police Department. Bring Filman in for questioning before he kills anyone else."

Versant lets out a chuckle. "I wish we'd known it was that easy."

I glare at him. "Catch many serial killers?"

"Your reputation isn't in question here," he says. "Just work with us."

"Fine. How about this? I come back here at 10:00 a.m. and we discuss this with Capstone. If not, then at 10:05, I walk across the street to the big newspaper building, tell them who I am, and explain that you didn't want to stop the most prolific serial killer in Louisiana history. And if they don't want to listen, I'll call the *Enquirer*. Sure, none of your friends take it seriously, but I bet a good number of people around here do."

Versant raises his hands. "Ease up there! I'll go into Capstone's office today. Okay? Happy? And then if you're not happy tomorrow, tell the world. Good enough?"

"We're all on the same side here," says Bailey.

I force myself to calm down. "Right. Sorry. I just . . ."

"Don't want anyone else getting hurt," says Versant.

Yet again, I chide myself for losing my cool. Jillian's right. My ego is my biggest enemy—well, that and literally whatever enemy I'm currently hunting down.

"Thank you." I point to the spreadsheets and disks I provided. "Should I leave this?"

"I don't think we can touch it," says Versant. "Just make sure we have your contact information."

CHAPTER TWENTY
Lunch Meat

Sergio Filman is sitting twenty feet away from me, eating his food and staring at his phone. If I had any doubts about him being a psychopath, they vanished as I observed him eat his hospital-cafeteria turkey and gravy without even wincing. I settled on the meat loaf and have spent the last half hour trying to figure out how it's physically possible for the pint of grease on my plate to have oozed out of something that's the size of a bar of soap and about as appetizing.

Filman looks like a normal guy, if there is such a thing. He's taller than me, in his midthirties, and has dark hair and eyes that seem like he's always thinking.

"What's going on?" asks Marcie Quan as she takes the seat opposite from me at my table by the wall.

I nod to Filman, behind her. "Him. I came here to watch him."

Marcie doesn't flinch. "I'll have to look when I get up."

"Look now," I reply. "I want him to know he's being watched. Less chance he'll kill tonight."

"You're like the most passive-aggressive serial-killer hunter I've ever heard of," she replies, then turns for a look. "Oh."

"What?"

"I didn't know what I was expecting. He looks like a normal dude." She turns back to me. *"Him?"* she whispers.

I nod. "That's how it usually works. The hard-to-catch ones are the most normal."

"Do they fake it?" she asks.

I shrug. "Some are just normal people but got a wire crossed somewhere. They have friends, wives, children, church groups. That's what makes them scary."

Sergio hasn't acknowledged our attention, but I think he's aware of it. The moment I left the DA's office, I called the hospital to see if he'd be working that night.

I got here two hours before his shift and spent that time talking to Mrs. Wilmington, whose husband is undergoing treatment for pneumonia on Sergio's ward.

Lotty, as she prefers to be called, was very happy when I offered to spend some time with her husband after she went home. Rufus Wilmington, heavily medicated and not very talkative, preferred to watch the sports channel than banter with me. Which was fine. I spent the time wandering into the other rooms, talking to any coherent patients, and making my presence known.

When Sergio showed up for his shift, I was chatting away with Barbara Kenner and getting chided for not having any children yet. Sergio walked into the room and was surprised to see me there. Not that I thought I caught him in the act; he simply seemed surprised that someone was talking to this lonely woman.

He checked her drips, then made his way to another room. I followed him in there. Sergio looked up from the empty bed where he was changing the linens. "Can I help you?"

"Me?" I held out my hand. "I'm Dr. Theo Cray."

"Cray?" he replied. The name was registering somewhere in the back of his mind. "Oh," he said, then went to the next room.

I lurked around the nurses' station, talking to Fiona, who was surprised to see me without a lab coat but forgot about it once we started talking about her favorite show on Netflix.

She introduced me to Filman when he walked by, eliciting a small grunt. She rolled her eyes. "He's in one of his moods."

Moods. Interesting.

When Sergio headed to dinner, I followed him down here. I'd asked Marcie to meet me so I could recap what happened at the DA's office.

"I'm not surprised," she says after I explain how I left things. "For a smart guy, you're kind of naive about how things work down here."

"What do you mean?"

"Hospitals are big business," she explains, to no surprise from me. "Which means they have a lot of money to spend locally. This is true everywhere. They create fake jobs to give to the wives and husbands of politicians. Look at the size of their PR department. It's ten times what a comparable company would have. Why? They're easy jobs to give out to people who have no medical background. Governors' wives, future presidents, people who sit on review boards are all in positions to financially affect the hospital."

"To bribe them? At that scale?" I reply.

"Are you really that naive? It's not a bribe. It just puts them on the same team." She realizes her voice has become loud. "I can't believe I'm in the belly of the beast. So where did you leave it with the DAs?"

"They were going to talk to their boss, Oliver Capstone. You know about him?"

Marcie groans, "Yep. His former law partners happen to represent Southern Star."

"Oh man. I didn't see anything bad about him online," I reply. "By local standards, he's a saint."

"I'm not saying he's a crook," Marcie replies. "You have to remember it's still the good ol' boy network around here. Which means if you come after someone's friend, you better have your ducks lined up. Why do you think I've been lying low? For crying out loud, Evelyn Cox, the governor's wife, runs a PR company whose sole client is Southern Star."

"I'm not after them," I reply, staring in Filman's direction. "He's why I'm here."

"And they made it possible for him," she replies. "If they have any reason to look the other way, they're going to do that. What you're talking about is far worse in the public's eyes. People couldn't care less about billing if it's not their problem. Southern Star cares, but it's an easy matter to control bad public relations. Serial killers? I guarantee you that Evelyn Cox will not be excited to tell people that her clients let a serial killer operate practically in the open for a half decade. A child killer, no less. You can only buy so much goodwill. Even around here. I hope you know what you stepped into."

Filman gets up and puts his tray in a bin by the exit. "I have to go," I say to Marcie and follow him into the corridor.

He steps into an elevator, and I hold the door open before it closes. "Sorry," I say as I step inside.

Filman is facing forward but watching me out of the corner of his eye. He has to be wondering about me. From his body language, he seems tense . . . angry.

"What floor?" he asks after a long silence.

"Same as you."

He stabs the button with his finger. I can tell that, in any other situation, he'd confront me. But right now, here where he kills people, Filman can't figure out if he's trapped or not.

The elevator doors open, and I realize we're in the basement. I wasn't expecting that. There's a long, awkward pause as he watches me from the side while I try to figure out what to do.

Finally, I step into the corridor. It's not as brightly lit as the upper floors, and large laundry baskets line the wall to the right. I start walking down the left, putting Filman behind me.

Bad move.

The corridor ends in a junction. As I slow and prepare to choose a direction, my body tightens like a coil, ready to spin around at a moment's notice.

Things happen in slow motion. I take a step; he takes a step. Our walking is almost in sync, but his longer strides mean that he's covering ground more quickly.

I feel a gust of wind on the back of my neck and wheel around as Filman enters a door that says **MEN'S LOCKER ROOM**.

I wait for him outside. Five minutes later he comes back out, wearing the same scrubs. I assume he used the bathroom, unless he simply waited inside there, trying to decide what to do.

Sergio Filman's eyes lock with mine for a moment, then he heads back to the elevator. He wants to say something. It's killing him. But he's afraid that I already know. He's afraid the whole world is onto him. He just doesn't know what to do. So he keeps going about his routine, trying to pretend I'm a figment of his imagination and, if he ignores me long enough, I'll go away.

I follow him into the elevator and notice something is different. Under his baggy dark-blue V-neck shirt, there's a square bulge near his stomach.

Filman has a gun.

I try to pretend like I don't notice. Now I'm the one unsure what to do. In my head, I was going to shadow him all evening, almost taunting the man. Now I'm afraid he's ready to explode at any moment.

The elevator doors close, and it's just the two of us. Filman doesn't even wait to ask me what floor. He punches "4," and we ascend.

It takes twelve seconds to travel from the basement to the fourth floor. That's twelve seconds I spend wondering if he's going to try to kill me.

It may not seem like long, but I bet between the two of us, there was at least a lifetime of contemplating what happens next.

I could take the gun from him. Then what? I've just committed battery against a man who so far hasn't done anything wrong in the eyes of the law.

I could disarm him and the gun could conveniently go off . . . How would that play out? There's already enough suspicion around me and the violent ends people meet in my presence.

Or I could just ignore it. I'm not sure Filman even knows what he's going to do with the weapon.

The doors open. I walk out and head toward Mr. Wilmington's room. I watch sports all night with him until Filman goes home, at which point I take a quick look around the ward to make sure everyone who should still be alive is still alive and then go back to my hotel.

The only person Filman was thinking about killing tonight was me.

CHAPTER TWENTY-ONE
Null Response

Bailey and Versant have been joined by a third person when I enter the conference room the next day at ten. He's older, bald, more heavyset, and has the look of someone who spends a lot of time hunched over a desk.

"This is Al Breaux," says Bailey. "Capstone wanted him to join us."

"Dr. Cray," says Breaux, shaking my hand. He has a briefcase on the table and a stack of folders next to it.

"We spoke to Capstone," says Versant. "Laid everything out for him. He definitely took an interest in this."

"Well, that's good," I reply.

"Yes, well, he had the same problem I had. There's not much to go on. All we have is your concerns. And they are appreciated."

"I'm not asking you to arrest Filman right now. I understand due process. At the very least, someone should question him."

"That could spook him," says Bailey. "We might not be able to gather any evidence if that happens."

"His evidence is empty syringes of digoxin and corpses. Are you waiting for more of them?"

Breaux speaks up. "You're an intelligent man. I don't say that to play to your ego, Dr. Cray. But you're here because you know more than we do. What is that?"

"I already told them that the families asked me to come here," I reply.

"Yes. And that's very noble of you. What led you to Joe Vik?" he asks.

"Bodies," I reply.

"Forensic evidence."

"Actually, no. You know what led me to Joe Vik?" I pull out my scatter chart. "One of these. I looked at a graph of missing persons and realized there was a pattern there. It was like the hunting ground of a great white shark. Only this was on land. Data. Data is how I found Joe Vik."

"Precisely." Breaux holds up my scatter plot. "Data. There is no data here. There are no citations. It's just dots. We can't call people in for questioning just because of a whim. Maybe you're right. We don't know. And last I checked, you're neither a medical doctor nor a licensed forensic specialist, are you?"

"No," I sigh.

"How much experience do you have with medical errors or even standard hospital procedures?"

"Not much," I reply.

"But you have a gut instinct. Or is this more than that? You claim that Mr. Filman was illegally withdrawing pharmaceuticals. Correct? Where is your evidence for that?"

I slide a CD out of my bag and push it toward him. "Database records."

"From where? How did you acquire them?" he asks.

"I'd prefer not to say," I reply.

"Am I to assume that you acquired them illegally? I can't understand how you'd otherwise be in the possession of hospital records."

Ever smell a trap and realize that you walked into it so long ago that you can't even spot the exit? "You can assume anything you choose."

Breaux pushes the CD back toward me with his pen, making a show of not touching it. "The only way those records exist is if you tell us where they came from."

"Why don't you get a subpoena and search the hospital records yourselves?" I ask.

"And what judge will issue that subpoena?" asks Breaux. "If you were willing to go on the record and verify the authenticity of anything, explaining the chain of custody, I might be able to get someone to entertain the notion. Of course, the hospital would be well within its rights to fight that order on the account of patient privacy."

"So that's it?" I ask, looking around the table.

"With all due respect, Dr. Cray," says Bailey, "we deal with cops all the time, good ones. People like you. They tell us they know for certain somebody is guilty. And we believe them. But that's not enough. *This* isn't enough. If a family member said they saw Filman in the act, we could go on that. Otherwise it's less than circumstantial."

"That's not how he kills," I reply. "I'm sorry. I don't deal with the kind of men you're used to convicting. My killers are smarter. Sometimes smarter than any of the people in the room. Myself included. They don't make it easy. And there are more of them out there than you realize."

"Tell us how you got your information," says Versant. "Then we have something to start with. It's that easy."

Time to test if this is really a trap. "Okay."

"You'll tell us?" asks Breaux.

"Yes," I reply.

"And you'll go on the record so we can make a solid case?"

"Absolutely."

Breaux glances at the others, then takes a tape recorder from his briefcase and sets it on the table.

I hold up my finger. "One second. First, I need you to grant me immunity."

"Immunity?" blurts Versant.

"Yes. I want whistle-blower status. I want a guarantee that you won't prosecute me for anything related to the documents you're asking about."

"This is a murder investigation," says Breaux. "Whistle-blower status doesn't really cover it."

"Perhaps. But I still want immunity. I also want federal prosecutors to sign off on it. And I'll want my attorney to look at it. I think a concise letter of intent would be fine. You can have that done in an hour or so."

"It's much more complicated than that," replies Breaux. "It's not like in the movies."

"It's as complicated as you want to make it."

Breaux shakes his head. "That's not going to happen. I can give you our assurance that we will be grateful for your cooperation and that we aren't looking to prosecute you."

"What does that even mean? You do realize that I'm well aware that I'm talking to a roomful of lawyers? Your assurances aren't very meaningful."

"Do you want this guy or not?" asks Versant.

"Do you?"

It takes a real long time for Bailey to interject, "Of course we do. We all do."

Breaux puts his folders back into his briefcase. "I believe we're done here. Let me know if Dr. Cray decides to take this seriously."

"Dr. Cray feels the same way," I reply.

I leave the room before Breaux has a chance to rise. I've become real good at dramatic exits. It's not something to be proud of. If I were better with people, I wouldn't need to storm out of so many meetings.

Bailey catches up with me in the parking lot as I try to remember where I parked my rental. "Hold up, Theo. Hold up."

I stop and let her speak.

"What now?"

"What do you mean? I told you what I'd do. Now I'm going to do it."

"We tried to work with you," she says.

"No, you didn't. Your boss sent that asshole in there to get me to implicate myself. What you really want is to be able to tell the reporter who calls you up for a statement that I didn't want to cooperate with you. I get it.

"I don't know if you all are too cynical to see it, genuinely don't care, or think I've just gone completely off my rocker. Whatever it is, I'm screaming I smell smoke. You won't acknowledge there's even a fire."

Bailey shakes her head and lowers her voice. "The problem is the place where you're yelling fire."

"I get it. Southern Star has deep pockets. Nobody's pockets are deep enough to buy everyone."

"Can I give you a piece of advice? Don't go to the papers. Let the problem work itself out. You made noise. People heard. If what you say is true, I guarantee they'll want to deal with the problem."

"They?" I reply. "And how would they deal with it? You know how other hospitals deal with people like Filman? They let them go and don't tell the next hospital why he was fired. Charles Cullen kept getting sent from one hospital to the next. They suspected, but they just kept sending him to new killing grounds."

"I understand that. I don't know what else can be done. But I can tell you that if you go to the press with this, they'll come after you hard. And whatever dirt you have that you don't think anyone knows about, they'll find."

"Courtrooms don't scare me," I reply. "As far as I'm concerned, I'm already living on borrowed time."

"Have it your way, Dr. Cray." She leaves me and heads back into the building.

I stand motionless, holding my keys, and remember they're *my* keys, not a rental's, and walk to my truck parked at the far end of the lot.

Why do they always ignore me? What the hell do they think some corporate lapdog lawyer can do to me that Joe Vik or Forrester didn't try? Didn't they even watch the damned TV movie?

CHAPTER TWENTY-TWO
PLAUSIBLE DENIAL

Regina Spicola isn't happy to see me, but she's also not surprised, from what I can tell. I called her office from the parking lot and said we had to talk. She simply asked when I could come in.

Two hours later and we're face-to-face in a conference room at the main offices, along with David Glassly, who is in charge of legal affairs. I expected other people to be in the meeting, and an attorney makes the most sense. The man sitting next to him is a much older man, Dr. Altman. No title given for him other than "Dr."

I'm here because they're not the enemy. They're not helping me, but they're not the ones intentionally killing people. Perhaps they're guilty of enabling it through neglect, but that's a grayer area than the one I'm here to talk about.

I want them to stop Filman. I want to make sure that he never kills again, and I want to see to it that he's punished. I also want to know the full extent of what he's done.

"I'm suspicious of one of your employees, Sergio Filman. I believe he may have knowledge about the murders of several of your patients," I say as neutrally as possible. I don't come right out and say he did it, but what I said is effectively the same thing.

"And how did you come to this conclusion?" asks Glassly.

"Initially I was contacted by a friend of the family of one of the victims. I then spoke to other parents whose children died under the same circumstances. When I looked into it, I noticed a suspicious pattern of behavior centering around Filman."

"Are you accusing Filman of murder?" asks Glassly.

"I think it would be a good idea to investigate him."

"So you're simply suspicious because of what the families told you? Or is there more evidence?"

"I've seen other evidence," I reply.

"Can you elaborate?"

"I think if you look into his pattern of behavior—pharmaceutical requisitions and hours on the floor—you'll see a correlation," I explain.

"What kind of correlation, Dr. Cray?" asks Dr. Altman.

"Your in-house medical examiner uses an obscure unproven condition as a cause of death at a statistically improbable rate. Patients under Filman's care die of unclear causes at a higher rate. Which is saying something, because your hospital has an already-high rate."

"Our survival rates are among the best in the country," Spicola interjects.

"Does that include all the patients you posthumously transfer to your rotating clinic? Yes, I know about that racket."

Nobody responds to this allegation. Glassly flat-out pretends I didn't even speak and looks off into space like he's zoning out. He's probably had plenty of practice.

"Can you back up to these alleged murders?" asks Altman. "What makes you think they were killed? I mean, actual cause of death?"

"They all died from heart failure, even children that had no prior symptoms. This happened shortly after someone using Filman's employee code withdrew massive amounts of digoxin," I reply.

"And how do you know this?" asks Glassly.

I'm having déjà vu from earlier today. "I just know. You can look it up."

"Dr. Cray, we're all concerned here," says Altman. "We take you very seriously. As you know, diagnosing conditions can be more art than science. Although you're not a physician, I know you're a very intelligent man, and I wouldn't discount anything you have to say. However, I think this may be more complicated than you appreciate. Critical care is a very big field. I'm learning new things every day. And hospital records, well, it's no secret that getting our member clinics in order has been a challenge. We're not as well funded as other hospitals. Many of our patients are on Medicaid or have the bare-minimum health plans you can buy. We have lots of single mothers, elderly, and people we know may never pay their bills. But we treat them. Anyone who walks through our doors, we do our best. I retired officially from the regular rotations, but when it's back-to-school time or flu season, I'm in these halls seeing people."

I believe his sincerity. I genuinely think he's the kind of doctor that wants to help people. But he's also incredibly naive. I'm not surprised he's unaware of what's going on around him. He's busy trying to perform triage in a state of constant crisis.

"Dr. Cray, Regina called me the moment you left the other day and asked me to personally look into Sergio Filman's history. You know what I saw? A man that was given the worst shifts and never complained. A man that was given the most difficult patients and treated them with dignity and respect. I couldn't find a single complaint from any of the families whose loved ones you say he killed. And when I looked into those cases, my heart broke all over again. I remember when the Hennisons' boy died. Same with the Saunderses. I remember them all. I remember holding the hand of a young woman last week as she passed away while we tried to save her.

"With all due respect, Dr. Cray, where you see murder, I see the hand of God. A god we don't understand. A god we get angry with. And in Sergio Filman, I see another man working for God."

"God's killing hand?" I ask.

Altman stares at me, then gives me a reproaching headshake. "I don't get your sense of humor."

"Doctor, I think you're a decent man who sees the good in people. But good people can have an evil inside as well. And if you think there's nothing suspicious about the official cause of death of those patients, then I don't know if you're in the right line of work."

"That's unnecessary," snaps Glassly. "And uncalled for."

"It's fine, David. It's fine," says Altman. "Our young friend here is a very intelligent man and used to being right. Maybe he is. What do I know? We'll continue to look into this. I'll speak with some other colleagues. I'll get their counsel." He stands up and offers me his hand. "You'll have to excuse me. We're a little short staffed."

After he leaves, Glassly turns to me. "That man is as good as they come. I think he's done as much as we can ask, but he's offered to look into this more. Are you satisfied, Dr. Cray?"

"Satisfied? You act like I found a Band-Aid in my salad and I'm asking the manager for an apology. I'll be satisfied when I know Filman isn't a threat. I'll be satisfied when your patients aren't being murdered."

"Fine. In the meantime, will you cooperate with us?" he asks.

"What does that mean?"

"Give us some time. Back off now. You've done your part. This matter has been brought to our attention."

"And what will you do now?"

Glassly stares at me like my head just did a three-hundred-and-sixty-degree rotation on my neck. "Dr. Altman is going to have some colleagues look at the case files. Isn't that what you want?"

"And Filman?"

"What about him?"

"Are you going to allow him around patients while you look into this?"

"We'll make that determination," he says.

"But you haven't. Is he on shift tonight? Do you even know?"

"Mr. Filman has rights, Dr. Cray. You may have convicted the man, but the rest of the world hasn't. I promise you we'll look into it. Just give us some time."

"I just hope you don't get another computer virus that erases inconvenient records," I reply.

Of all the things I've said in this room, this is the one that makes Glassly flinch. I catch Spicola throwing a glance in his direction.

They may be scam artists, but I don't think they're killers. Still, how can I expect them to investigate a crime while they're trying so very hard to throw away all the evidence?

CHAPTER TWENTY-THREE
Meet the Press

I'm in yet another conference room. This time it's on the seventh floor of the *Baton Rouge Trumpet*. Across the table from me sit Evan Caster and Kyle Waddell, a journalist team that has had a pretty good run breaking stories on their blog and then doing deep follow-up in the paper. Their editor, Stephen Raynor, is sitting in on the conversation because I called him directly.

While they look different, they all seem to have the same personality type—only at different stages of life. Evan is younger, Kyle a few years senior, and Raynor is the one whichever of the two who survives layoffs over the next decade gets to eventually become.

I called Raynor after my meeting with Southern Star. I surmised that any news editor that could hold on to his job in this age of consolidation probably knew who I was or would get it pretty quickly. When I said I had information about a serial killer active in Baton Rouge, he wanted to know how quickly I could come in.

"A killer nurse?" says Kyle.

"Yep."

"What's the kill count?" asks Evan.

I pull out a graph and some notes. "Best guess, sixty-three low end. One hundred eighty-eight on the high end."

"That's . . ."

"A record in the United States. If this guy confesses."

"Jeez," says Kyle. "All those families."

His sympathy for the families wins points from me.

"This would be number four for you?" asks Raynor.

"Four?" I ask, pretending not to know what he means.

"Your fourth high-profile serial-killer catch," he explains.

"Depends upon how they charge Forrester," I reply.

"That's like catching Ted Bundy, Jeffrey Dahmer, John Wayne Gacy, and the Unabomber," says Evan. "I heard a rumor about you."

Uh-oh. "I'm sure you have."

"One is that you actually work for some NSA-funded lab and that you have access to information that they can't use criminally, so instead they go through you. Secret phone taps. DNA databases. That kind of thing."

Sounds like my secret warehouse. "I wish that was the case. If it was, my life would be easier. I could just go over to the FBI and never have to show my face in public."

"About that," says Kyle. "A couple of eyewitnesses in Austin said you were brought to the crash site. Any truth to that?"

I shrug. "Let's talk about Filman."

"He's your guy?" says Raynor.

"I think he's very, very suspicious. Hospital records back that up. The data screams that he's a killer."

"How so?"

"Statistically speaking? Which is hard, by the way, because Southern Star already has an unusually high death rate because of the kind of patients they treat."

Evan speaks up. "They say it's because of the meth epidemic and fentanyl. Not that they have a higher number of overdose cases, just that the quality of health of their patients means they're harder to treat. I'm not sure I buy it."

"Maybe," I reply. "But even if you accept their already-high death rate, whenever Filman's on duty, it gets ridiculous. It basically doubles at whatever center he's at."

"And you have work records for him?" asks Raynor.

"Only at Woodland Lake. But I know that during his total term of employment, going back five years, the death rate has been consistently high."

"What do you have for us?" asks Kyle.

I place two thumb drives on the desk. "Hospital records. I won't tell you how I got them. I have two copies: one in which all patient names have been removed and the other an original copy of the files. It even includes the database with the encryption key in case you need to validate it."

"And how did you acquire these?" asks Raynor.

"No comment."

"Were her initials *M* and *Q*?" asks Evan.

"No comment. And I'm fairly positive she doesn't have the critical records. Assuming I know this person . . . You've spoken to her?" I ask.

Raynor shakes his head. "No. That's the funny part. The day of her departure, we got a cease-and-desist from a judge telling us not to publish any patient records she may have stolen."

"Hmm," I say. "Sounds like Southern Star kind of jumped the gun there."

"Right," says Raynor. "We'd never heard of her. We still haven't talked to her. We thought about filing a lawsuit against Southern Star to clear the way if she ever showed up, but decided otherwise."

"So where do we stand?" I ask. "Are you going to run this?"

Kyle and Evan turn to Raynor. He nods. "We'll run something. We just have to figure out what. If it's an exposé, then we'd need some time to corroborate what you're saying. I believe you're a thorough man and this Filman is probably as guilty as sin and needs to be taken out of there, but . . ."

I understand their position. Like the hospital and the DA, the newspaper is in a vulnerable position. If they simply run with what I have and something doesn't add up, it could cost them dearly, both financially and reputationally.

"We've got to get this guy off the street," says Evan. "He could be planning to kill someone right now. How long since the last one?"

"I don't know. Statistically? Maybe two a month. But I can't tell you which ones without looking at the records."

Evan turns to his boss. "What if we run something online first? Like 'Serial-Killer Hunter Theo Cray Investigating Baton Rouge Hospital'?"

"One, you write horrible headlines. Let Kyle do that. Second, then what? What will the article say? Are we writing blind items now? Third, will that even stop the guy?"

Evan leans back in his chair and stares at the ceiling. "We could work this tonight and tomorrow. Get statements from the hospital and the families." He looks at me. "Did you say the DA was taking this case?"

"That's not what they told me."

"Hmm. We can't really say that Filman is a person of interest, then, can we? And the families haven't filed a lawsuit naming him. What do you think, Stephen?"

Raynor's forehead looks like he's doing a really hard math problem and just realized he doesn't recognize any of the numbers. "I can't see us naming the guy on that little evidence. God forbid we do and some vigilante decides to go after him."

"I think Theo has that covered," says Evan.

"You know what I mean. A family member or someone. Naming him is a real problem unless we have him dead to rights."

"What if you interviewed him?" I naively ask. "Maybe he'll say something?"

"I doubt he'll talk," says Raynor.

"Maybe, maybe not," replies Kyle. "It might be worth a shot."

"I need more. I don't want us to start the story. Have you blogged about this or tweeted anything?"

It takes me a moment to realize that Raynor is talking to me. "Yeah, I have a whole Instagram story on it."

Evan almost leaps out of his chair. "You do?"

Kyle shakes his head. "He's messing with you, Evan. Dr. Theo's not the social-media type, are you?"

I shake my head. "Sorry."

What I don't say is how many times I've used social media to investigate, instigate, and even mislead. It's better they think I'm naive on the topic. But still, there's something to the notion. Heck, I even faked my suicide on YouTube to throw off Joe Vik. I think I still have the channel.

"What if I made a YouTube video saying that I was looking for information? Maybe even name checked Sergio Filman as someone who could help the case?" I ask.

"Would you?" asks Evan before turning to Raynor.

"That could work," Raynor says. "If you make him a person of interest, then we're pretty clear to repeat the name."

"They're going to go after you," says Kyle. "Filman, the hospital. Their friends."

"Fine. But will you run it?" I ask.

"I'm already writing the lede in my head."

CHAPTER TWENTY-FOUR
ALL AT ONCE

I leave my hotel before morning traffic picks up and head out of Baton Rouge. Before departing, I made a video at the library down the street from the *Trumpet* and laid out what I hope was a pretty straightforward case. I showed some graphs of the elevated number of deaths—pointing out spikes. I explained how this could be done and implored any family to contact an email account I set up for this purpose. The last part of the video is what I'm the most uneasy about: I named Sergio Filman. While I didn't outright call him a killer, I said that I'd like to talk to him and said that he was at the hospital when the murders were committed—which is basically the same as calling him guilty.

Driving back home, my mind goes over the data. What do I really know? What if someone used his employee number to access the heart medication? What if someone had already tampered with the data I saw?

This is what makes me uneasy. All I have is circumstantial evidence. Of course, that's all I'm going to get unless there's an investigation.

I try to make myself feel better by convincing myself of the fact that all this attention on the hospital will at the very least help improve things.

But I'm not even sure of that.

What if it doesn't? What if Southern Star closes overnight and shuts down all of their facilities? This will put pressure on the other hospitals and throw thousands of lives into disarray. Files will be lost. Conditions misdiagnosed. People will die.

But what alternative did I have?

Southern Star wasn't going to seriously pursue Filman. The DA's office might look into things, but unless Filman outright confesses, there's not much else they can do, because Southern Star doesn't want anyone looking at their records too closely. The Woodland Lake files I have are already "lost."

The cold, hard truth is, doing nothing means Filman will be quietly let go and will pick up somewhere else, like Cullen did. And if that hospital becomes suspicious, he'll move on and on, leaving a trail of bodies.

I had no other choice.

I spend the drive lost in thought. After texting Jillian, I turned my phone off. My mind doesn't get enough of these long, unplugged stretches. I get to turn inward for a while.

Times like these are when I fantasize about what I'd be doing if I weren't married to the government lab and getting distracted by bad people.

I miss teaching. I was hoping when I got the lab that I could get some undergrads in there and have fun exploring the unknown with minds not already calcified by concerns about grants, tenure, and mortgages.

I keep thinking about a start-up. Hailey has made it clear that she'll go all in on anything I want to do. We both agree that it's still the early days of AI and machine learning, especially when it comes to medicine. We could save a million lives with a slight tweak to an antibiotic. Thousands of drugs could be improved by doing some clever data mining. Or we could just make better tools. Hailey laughed when I showed her MAAT and some of the other early-iteration software I've created for computational modeling. She said my programs are designed around the particularities of my brain.

That could be fun. I think the only thing holding me back is that it would feel like cheating on Jillian. Not physically, but intellectually. Starting something like that would mean a lot of time on the phone. It'd mean time away from Jillian. No matter how earnest my intentions, it'd be a kind of betrayal.

It doesn't matter whether it would be the same if Hailey were a man. It's not about body parts. It's about two minds interacting.

If not that, then what? How else could I be applying myself? I can only pretend to care about the research I'm doing for the military for so long. I've made promises in order to get favors and then found myself afraid of what happens when those promises come due.

An hour away from Austin, I turn on my phone and find a blizzard of notifications. Three calls from Jillian alone.

"What's up?" I ask.

"Your video's all over the news. Everywhere. At least in my feeds. Your newspaper friends picked up the story, and it went nationwide. *Drudge Report* had it as the top story."

"Good lord. That wasn't the plan."

"And this Filman guy's name is everywhere. People picked up the hint," she explains.

"Hopefully they start asking questions."

"They are. There's a video of him leaving work and people yelling questions at him. The guy looked confused."

"I'll bet," I reply.

"He's the one, right?" asks Jillian.

For some reason, having her voice my doubts makes them a thousand times more worrisome. She trusts me, but she knows I'm human.

"I'm pretty sure. Pretty sure. Something weird is going on there, so if for some crazy reason it's *not* him, then he'd still have to know about it. A doctor? An orderly? But Filman's the consistent thread, Jillian.

The killings started when he got hired. The deaths followed him to Woodland Lake. I have his name on drug requisitions that nobody can explain." I sound like a man trying to convince himself.

"Good, Theo. Good."

"Will you be at the bakery?"

"No. I'm home. I let Emma and Ally run it tonight."

I spend the next half hour listening to voice messages. Most of them are from reporters who got my official phone number. I keep skipping through them until I get one from my office.

"Theo, it's Sheila. Figueroa wants you to call him ASAP."

That's not good. General Figueroa is my point man with the Department of Defense. He's the reason I'm working at all after Joe Vik and not cleaning bottles in a factory somewhere.

"Cray," says Figueroa the moment he picks up. *"What the hell?"*

"Could you be more specific?" I reply.

"You want to be a YouTube star now? The lab isn't enough? Maybe you want to be some jack-off on TV talking down to people about science like some kind of high priest? Is that it?"

"Um, no, sir."

"Of all the times to pull this crap . . . I'm still cleaning up your mess with the Hyde thing."

"Mess? I thought I did everyone a favor."

"Don't be cute. The mess is from *how* you did us that favor. You're not as good at covering your tracks as you think you are."

Damn. This is the first time he's even hinted at the fact that I did some highly questionable things to catch Forrester. Horrible things.

"This wasn't intentional," I explain.

"You accidentally made that video? What are you, ten?"

"I mean, I'm worried he'll kill again."

"Then you call the FBI. God knows they have you on speed dial. Let them handle this. You even have friends there. Friends you may not even realize you have."

I'm not sure what he means by that. "I understand. But they take time. This guy is an active killer. It's not a cold case."

"Then you should have called me. I'm on your side. But this . . ." He pauses. "Theo. This couldn't have come at a worse time."

"I'm sorry. I'll try to fix things." I don't even know what that means right now, but I say it anyway.

Figueroa makes a sound somewhere in between a sigh and a growl and hangs up.

I spend the remainder of my drive trying to figure out what he was intimating. Everything is a crisis between us, but this sounded like something else. As if he'd been trying to keep me out of trouble.

Any hope of this blowing over dies the moment I turn the corner and see two television news trucks parked on my street. I'd never wish ill on anyone, but I've never prayed harder that one of my neighbors got busted for running a meth lab or a prostitution ring out of their garage.

When I see the makeup-wearing faces of the newscasters turn their heads as I drive up, I realize that, sadly, that's not the case. They're here for me.

I have no idea what I'm going to say to them. Driving off or running away will only make it worse. I have to defuse the situation.

The moment I get out of my SUV, a lanky young man with a microphone rushes over and asks, "How are you going to respond to Sergio Filman's hundred-million-dollar lawsuit against you?"

Oh jeez.

CHAPTER TWENTY-FIVE
SLOW MOTION

I feel like I threw a chain saw into the air and just realized that it's going to come back down. I'm holding a subpoena sent by an attorney in Baton Rouge. I haven't opened it yet. It's sitting on the kitchen table in front of me. I've had others, and I knew this was coming, but for some reason I hesitate to open it.

After a long pause, I use one of Jillian's fancy knives to slit the envelope open, then set the blade aside in case the news is really bad.

A civil subpoena is a rather bland document. It's basically an invitation in the guise of a form that tells you some judge has ordered you to do something. In this case I'm being told that I have to give a deposition in a lawsuit. Filman's lawsuit.

Filman v. Cray.

While I can't say that I'm surprised, the timing has completely caught me off guard. Baton Rouge was only two days ago. Filman acted fast.

I call my attorney, the one my other attorney, Mary Karlin, recommended. Nobody should know this many lawyers. Not even lawyers.

"Cray," says Sam Goldman a second after I dial. "What's up?"

"I got a subpoena."

"The DA? That's good, right?" he asks, hoping they want my testimony.

"Nope. Filman." I flip through the pages. "Libel, tortious interference, stalking."

"Stalking?"

"I may have shadowed him at the hospital."

"You ran into him. Totally different and not stalking. Okay. We expected the rest. Send it on over, and we'll figure out a strategy for the deposition."

"It's next week," I reply.

"What?" He makes a sound almost like a cough. "No. You're reading it wrong."

I take a picture with my phone and send it to him. "Have a look."

A minute later he replies, "Jesus. I've never seen this. Hold on . . . Now it makes sense."

"What?"

"Filman's law firm, Lowry and Summer. That's the same firm Southern Star uses. I'm sure the judge is a good friend. This is your ticket to be railroaded," he explains.

"What do we do?"

"I'm going to contact the judge and point out how ridiculous this is. He's going to tell me that the good Mr. Filman's reputation can't wait. He'll then deny a stay and tell us you have to be in that deposition on Thursday or he'll have you in handcuffs."

"Delightful."

"It's not that bad. It's actually a good sign."

The legal system never ceases to confuse me. "How is it a good sign that they got a friendly judge?"

"It means that they want to settle out of court. We'll go in and make your deposition. They'll make a point of how incriminating your comments were toward Filman, and then they'll make some kind of offer to settle it quickly.

"The fact that it's Southern Star's law firm tells me that the hospital is behind this and wants closure. It's not a cash grab on Filman's behalf. I'd bet anything that they approached him with the idea for the lawsuit and that he's not paying a dime."

"What do they want?" I ask.

"Maybe an apology. Maybe they just want to say that the two of you reached an arrangement, which would look good enough," he replies. "Would you be willing to apologize to Filman?"

"Can we depose him first?"

When I first brought up the threat of a lawsuit from Filman with Mary Karlin, she mentioned the fact that in a civil lawsuit, I could ask Filman just about anything. Because he was suing me for slander, I was allowed to ask questions that might support my claim against him. She expected the lawsuit would never materialize because Filman wouldn't want to put himself in that position. Furthermore, she'd suggested that if the DA did nothing, the families should consider suing Filman for wrongful death. While they'd already accepted a settlement from the hospital, it didn't preclude them from suing an employee for criminal negligence.

"Yeah," says Goldman. "I'll make it clear that we plan to. We'll see what they say. But I have a feeling they're really just looking to save face for the hospital. I should have seen this coming, to be honest. The hospital wants to get you to retract without it looking like they're directly suing you if they can. I'll get back to you."

After we hang up, I consider the situation. So far Southern Star has avoided direct contact with me, although their PR flacks have been working overtime.

They made it clear that there is no criminal investigation into them, that they've always cooperated in these matters, and that they're taking my claims seriously enough to look into them, but I ran to the press within hours when I wasn't satisfied that Filman would be removed immediately.

Southern Star's public relations department has also been going on about the hospital's safety record and repeating the bogus mortality rates.

Curiously, I've noticed, they've made it a point to emphasize that Filman is licensed by the state and that he passed all state requirements. Which tells me they might be creating a scapegoat, in case something unexpected comes up, by blaming the government.

I hope Southern Star sues me, to be honest. Because that means I would get to depose them as well. While I may not be able to get them to reveal anything about Filman, there are tons of uncomfortable questions they don't want to answer about their billing practices. Especially with all the media attention that would fall on them now.

I think Goldman is right. This Filman lawsuit is the most they're willing to throw at me. I'm not sure they have anything else. I'm certain that CEO Anderson doesn't want to be asked about the intricacies of his shell clinics and how their billing software works.

Hmm . . . maybe my seeds aren't looking as bad as I feared. Filman's facing the scrutiny I wanted, and Southern Star's going to try to sit this one out on the sidelines, to the degree they can.

I pluck the knife off the table and slide it back into the stand. "Not today."

I can contemplate ways to kill myself after the deposition.

CHAPTER TWENTY-SIX
STATEMENT OF FACT

The Lowry and Summer law firm has the nicest conference room I've seen in my recent tour. The capitol building looms in the park to the north and the Mississippi River meanders to the west. While the room's designed to impress the clients who pay the bills, it's also intended to intimidate people like me when we come to give a deposition. On the wall opposite the capitol hangs a television big enough to be a garage door. At the moment it's frozen on the YouTube video of me incriminating Sergio Filman.

I spent the morning answering exactly the kind of questions that Goldman prepared me for. These were basic queries about my work, my past history investigating serial-killer cases as an amateur, and other routine background information. My main interrogator is an attractive woman named Carla Rosset, who tries using a mixture of flattery and fake friendliness to lull me into thinking this is just a minor matter. Filman's lead attorney, Lowry, gave me a firm handshake when I walked in and told me what a pleasure it was to meet me. The other three lawyers at his elbow also greeted me with smiles and handshakes.

This is the velvet glove over the gauntlet, as Goldman explained beforehand. Their goal is to get a quick settlement by being so gosh darn nice about the matter. They're hoping the introverted academic can be convinced to make quick restitution and exonerate Filman and the hospital, their real clients in the matter.

"Can you tell us how you acquired these files?" Rosset asks after I explain Filman's suspicious behavior.

"My client will not disclose that information, as it pertains to a confidential source," Goldman explains.

This is the moment Goldman told me to watch for. If we have any doubt that Southern Star is behind the lawsuit, their response will make that clear.

"Sam, come on. This is the crux of the matter. Your client is making a claim based on evidence he doesn't want to divulge? Or cannot?" says Lowry, as if the two were bantering over how to score a squash match.

"If we disclose the source, then the data itself has to be divulged, and that would of course make it a matter of public record," he replies.

Lowry is smart and sees where this is headed. If the files I took from Woodland Lake are entered as evidence, they become available to anyone who wants to have a look at them—which is something that Southern Star does not want. Because at that point we can call in a witness from them to verify the documents under oath and expose their billing practices.

While Lowry could ask the judge to seal the files due to patient privacy, it would be too risky, because in cross-examination Goldman can have the Southern Star witness read back any part he wants with the names redacted. At least in theory.

In reality, this kind of maneuver could hold everything up in court for a long time and deny Southern Star a quick end to the PR problem I caused.

"We can table that for later," says Lowry.

Goldman gives me the slightest of nods to let me know that our little "gotcha" tactic worked.

If they're going to claim that I knowingly defamed Filman's reputation, I have to be allowed to prove why I came to my conclusions. Those files are the main reason. And while they may not persuade a jury, suppressing them is Southern Star's intention. If Lowry and his pals were really working for Filman, they'd let the files become evidence and then explain how they don't show what I claim.

Because this is a civil lawsuit, I don't have to prove Filman did it. I just have to explain why a reasonable person like me would have come to that conclusion.

Everything is going as predicted by Goldman. Filman's attorneys are nailing down the specifics, getting me to admit what I did: talking to the hospital, making the video, and going to the press. This isn't something I can deny.

"Dr. Cray," says Rosset. "Could you direct your attention to the video screen. Will you state who is on that YouTube video?"

"That would appear to be me," I reply.

"Appear?" says Lowry. "Sam, can you get him to be more specific?"

"Dr. Cray is an expert in computer technologies and, as we all saw in the case of *United States versus Haywood* and Deepfake technology, it's hard to know if it's you or not," he replies.

Lowry rolls his eyes. "Play the video and then ask Dr. Cray if it's him."

The video runs for two minutes, until Lowry asks them to stop it while I'm holding up a graph showing suspicious deaths over time. "Dr. Cray, is that you so far?"

"I believe so," I reply.

"Care to check the transcript and see if there's anything you dispute?"

One of the other lawyers slides a document over to me with my words and screen grabs. I read through the text for a minute. "This appears to be accurate."

"How about a yes or no answer, Dr. Cray? You're a mathematician—you're familiar with precision."

I say nothing. I'd already talked this over with Goldman. I won't make definitive statements when I don't have certainty. I told him I'd be willing to risk contempt if I'm really not sure. He told me not to be such a pain in the ass.

"If you'd allow us more time to compare the transcript . . . ," says Goldman.

"We'll accept your answer as an affirmative," replies Lowry. He points to the screen. "So, that appears to be you?"

"Yes," I reply. My finger is pointing to a series of red dots after a peak on the graph.

"And that's the graph you made?"

"Yes."

"Can you explain the graph?"

"It shows the period in which Sergio Filman worked at Southern Star and the suspicious deaths that coincided with that period," I reply.

Lowry nods to the assistant handling the video feed. The screen refreshes to show a close-up of my finger and the graph. "And this period? How many deaths do you attribute to my client?"

"I haven't attributed anything to him. However, there were approximately two to three suspicious deaths per month based on other patterns," I explain. Before and after this time period came the two peaks when Filman appeared to be in some kind of frenzy. The "after" period came when he was working at Woodland Lake, and I have the pharmaceutical records and time stamps to nail him to the wall.

"And this lasted for how long? This period?" asks Lowry about the other period.

The graph has the months running along the horizontal axis. "Six months," I reply.

"So how many people total do you claim my client killed during that period?"

"Don't answer that," says Goldman. "My client has made it very clear that he only thinks Filman is a person of interest."

"Sorry. You're correct. So, Dr. Cray, how many suspicious deaths do you think my client would be a person of interest for during this period?"

Goldman's eyes shoot sideways toward me from the screen. A light-bulb just went off in his head. "Can we take a break?"

"Are you serious?" asks Lowry. "Can't your client just tell us the number?"

I'm not sure where this is going. Goldman gives me a reluctant nod, looking defeated.

"Approximately fifteen suspicious deaths," I reply.

"Fifteen suspicious deaths between January 2016 and June 2016 that you say is way above the norm for that hospital and evidence of a serial killer," says Lowry.

"Yes," I reply.

The elevated deaths are consistent right through the time Filman worked at Woodland Lake. The pattern is unmistakable. Sometimes he killed more, sometimes less. But there's clearly an elevated number of deaths that can be attributed to digoxin overdoses during that time.

"Kendall, could you go to the next slide?"

The screen changes, and all at once everything changes. Lowry doesn't have to speak for me to understand the point of everything he was leading up to. This isn't about the deposition. This is about destroying me.

"Dr. Cray, can you identify the man in the photo?" asks Lowry.

It's Sergio Filman. In a uniform—an *Army National Guard* uniform—standing next to two Iraqi soldiers with medical-corps insignias. The photo has a date stamp of March 2016.

Sergio Filman was halfway around the world when I accused him of murder.

CHAPTER TWENTY-SEVEN
MERCY KILLING

Goldman sets down two beers and takes the seat opposite from me in the booth at a bar called the Briar Patch. Edison bulbs light up the wood-paneled interior where peanut shells still litter the floor from lunch hour.

The beers-in-a-bar bit feels like a routine Goldman has performed many times in the past when something didn't go his client's way. Emphasis on "client," because no matter how much your lawyer pretends you're all on the same team, at the end of the day you're the one paying the price and their bill.

Filman's team ended the deposition shortly after dropping their little bombshell. That was the whole point of the show. They could have told us this at any point, but revealing it in the deposition put me on notice that there's a major hole in my narrative, and that if I keep trying to insinuate that Filman's a killer, I could be in even more legal jeopardy.

Filman probably won't prevail in his lawsuit in the long term if I stop implicating him now. In theory, all I have to do is prove that I had a reason to think he was guilty. They can make all the threats they want; I had good reason. Even though it *now* appears that I was wrong.

"So what happened?" asks Goldman.

Well, there's the million-dollar question, or hundred million in this case. "I don't know. I assumed the hospital records were accurate. Although now I feel stupid saying that. Of course they weren't accurate. They changed them all the time to boost their billing and cover up medical errors."

"I'm going to ask you a question: Is it possible that the cause of death that looked like a digoxin overdose could have been something else? Maybe some kind of cross malpractice." He struggles for an explanation. "Bad blood, some kind of infection? They shut down the Woodland Lake facility under some mysterious circumstances. Could it have been some kind of mold thing?"

"I don't know. But it looks like Filman requisitioned a ton of digoxin."

"Maybe he was selling it?" he asks.

"It's not that expensive." I go back through the data. When Filman was overseas, the death rates were as elevated as when he was there. "It could be a much more dangerous hospital than even I thought. But . . . the real Woodland Lake records."

"Could have been faked."

"Faked?" I ask, as if this is some new word I'd never heard of before. "You mean besides the overbilling? To frame him? By whom? For what purpose?"

"What if someone had a grudge against Filman? What if this was a setup? I don't want to get all conspiratorial, but maybe this Marcie Quan? She really has it in for the hospital. Could she have planted the evidence?"

"I'd say the circumstances by which I found that data would make that unlikely," I reply.

"But not impossible."

"But not impossible," I echo.

"Either way, we have to talk about the matter at hand. Filman's offer," he says.

"You mean Southern Star's offer."

"Same thing right now, I guess." Goldman checks the buzzing phone in his pocket. "It's them. Hello?"

I watch the less active side of a one-sided conversation as Goldman makes a series of "Uh-huhs" and nods his head.

"All right. I'll convey that to my client." He slides the phone back into his pocket. "Well, that was their offer."

"How bad?"

"It depends upon how you look at it. They really want to get this wrapped up. They're asking for one hundred thousand dollars. Which is a pretty steep discount from where this started. And they want a full apology to Filman and the hospital. Guess which one they care more about?"

"A full apology to the hospital? I didn't lay out any specifics against them. There's not much for me to retract."

"They're going to ask you to say you were looking at falsified records and you apologize for defaming the reputation of the hospital group. And that in light of new evidence, you fully exonerate Sergio Filman."

"I don't know . . . ," I reply.

"I understand. Just consider this: it's the hospital that's going after you. They're the one seeking the apology. That's really what they care about, and they'll do just about anything to get it. I'm serious when I say that I could probably get them to pay the hundred thousand Filman's asking for. Hell, if you want to push it, I might get them to pay you something, if I'm reading things right."

"Blood money," I growl.

"Peace of mind. Their next step won't just be a lawsuit of their own. This place plays a dirty game. They'll be coming at you behind the scenes in other ways. Ways we can't anticipate."

"What kind of ways?"

"Whatever Anderson and his partners can come up with. I don't want to scare you, but they have a playbook. It could be some prostitute that says you roughed her up while you were here. They might get someone friendly in the police to investigate you for something. All sorts of accusations could be made to undermine your credibility. This *will* get ugly," he explains.

"So, what's your position?"

"Whatever you want it to be. I'm a lawyer. I'm just telling you over beers that outside the courtroom, I have no way of telling you what's coming at us. The simplest route is to make a deal."

"I need to think about it," I reply. "I just don't know . . . I could see making a cautious statement about not having a rush to judgment and a need to look at all the facts."

"That won't cut it, Professor. They want an answer by midnight. They want to have it in the press by the time the morning news comes on. I can ask, but they're not going to be happy with a plea for caution. They want you singing Filman's and their virtues."

I shake my head.

"Talk it over with your girlfriend. You have a few hours. Don't be rash. They're not going to give us a second chance."

I already know Jillian's response.

"I'll tell you tonight. There's just one thing I have to do first."

CHAPTER TWENTY-EIGHT
FREE FALL

Sergio Filman's Kia Sorento is parked in front of a house in a poor neighborhood just outside the Baton Rouge city limits. The grass in the yard is overgrown, and the rusted remnants of a lawn mower can be spotted next to a broken concrete birdbath. It may have been a nice home once, but Truman was probably still the president back then.

This isn't his home. He lives seven miles away in a slightly less dilapidated neighborhood whose neglect started during the Ford administration.

I believe this is the home of the woman he sometimes appears with in his Instagram feed, Amelia Paredes. I'm not sure if they're dating, friends, or hookup buddies; either way, it's something I should have known about him before I ran to the press with his name. Or the fact that he had been in the National Guard up until recently.

When I saw him, my gut told me something was off, but I should be the first one to point out that your gut shouldn't be judge and jury.

John Christian—the man I put a bullet into, stopping his reign of horror molesting and murdering children—chose his victims because he thought their red hair or green eyes were signs of black magic. Just as he had done back in Africa, he killed these children based upon his gut instinct.

Am I no better? Yes, I have charts and graphs, but they're based on files from an abandoned computer. They could have been doctored. They could have been planted.

Emily and the grieving parents based their suspicions about Filman on his looks. Mine on a series of dots. Whatever the real picture, I jumped the gun.

Filman steps out onto the doorstep, and Paredes gives him a hug. A little girl, probably Paredes's daughter from another relationship, wraps her arms around Filman's waist. The nurse's reaction is anything but cold.

He untangles himself from her arms and heads for his vehicle. His eyes glance to the left and to the right, possibly expecting a news ambush, and then he gets into his car and drives away.

I wait for him to get all the way to the end of the street before I follow.

After leaving Goldman, I drove straight to Filman's to watch the man. Tonight's his night off, and I want to see his routine.

He didn't leave his house to visit Paredes until evening. Ten minutes after he arrived, a Domino's driver pulled up and delivered pizza to the door. Three hours later, Filman departed. Pizza night with his girlfriend and her kid. Nothing could be more mundane.

Twenty minutes later, Filman pulls into his driveway and parks his car. He's a street over from a Walmart and a strip mall. The houses in the neighborhood have sedans and Cadillacs parked out front, suggesting a lot of retirees live here.

Filman enters the one-story house, and a moment later the blue flicker of his television emanates from his living room.

I'd give anything to know what's going on in that head of his. Confusion? Anger? Remorse? Fear?

My phone buzzes, and I pick up.

"Cray?"

"Yes."

"It's Evan Caster from the *Trumpet*. Have a second?"

"Off the record, yes. On the record, I'm unavailable," I reply.

"Off. Just tell me when we're on. Fair enough?"

"Yep."

"We're about to run an article on Sergio Filman. A little background on the man. His side of things," he says.

"The National Guard rotation?" I ask.

"That's part of it. So I guess you know."

"I do now." *Understatement.*

"How does this change things?"

"Still off the record?"

"Yes."

"I don't know. I never said he did it. I just said he might have information," I say.

"While he was in Iraq?"

I get testy. "Is this an interview?" I snap, then regain my composure. "Sorry. It's a fair question. I don't know. I just don't know."

"I totally understand. So, the real reason I'm calling is that someone over at the hospital PR department told me that you might be making a statement to exonerate Filman."

"I'm not law enforcement. I don't convict or exonerate anyone. I just offer an opinion," I tell him.

"Sorry. Poor choice of words. But from what I understand, you've been negotiating with Filman's attorneys about a statement of apology," he explains.

"And Southern Star's PR people told you this? Isn't that kind of odd?"

"We all know who's behind Filman's lawsuit. But that's not what's relevant right now. Is it true?" he asks.

"I don't know."

"Can I run that?"

"No. When I'm going to say something, I'll say something," I reply.

"Fair enough. I know this is pretty hard on you. So I'm going to tell you something, and the reason I'm telling you is because if something develops or changes, I want you to come to me. If you get some break or find another killer somewhere else, I want you to think of me as someone who did you a favor. Okay?"

"Sure."

"They're coming at you hard. Rumor has it the hospital has put pressure on the DA's office to find out how you got those files. They're looking at ways to prosecute you that wouldn't put the data itself on the public record, like if you stole a computer."

Or a couple of hard drives . . . Damn it. I would have destroyed them if they weren't potential evidence against Southern Star.

"We'll cross that bridge if we get to it," I reply.

"There's one other thing. I've had two different people who I know are actually working for Southern Star try to feed me tips about your questionable mental health."

"I think that's a matter of public record."

"Something about a brain tumor? Perhaps you're on some kind of medication that's making you act irrationally? Possibly connected to a previous case?"

This is not good. "I have no idea what they're talking about."

"I'm sure. But they're claiming that you've been trying to keep it a secret and have been going to radiation therapy clinics under an assumed name."

I can tell by the tone of his voice that he thinks there's something more to this than idle chatter. He's trying to probe me for a response.

"Evan, I promise you I am absolutely not undergoing any kind of radiation therapy."

"And the trips to the clinics?"

I don't know what he actually has on me. "There's nothing to comment on."

"Okay. So, let me ask you one more time so Kyle doesn't jump all over me: Do you have a statement?"

I think this over. He was forthcoming enough with me. I could use an ally, even if it's a journalist who will turn on me in an instant.

"My attorney, Sam Goldman, will contact you later with my statement. You'll be the first. Good enough?"

"That would be great."

I hang up and call Goldman.

"Cray, what's up?"

"I've thought about what they want," I reply.

"And?"

"I'll give Filman an apology."

"That's great!" he says a little too enthusiastically.

"Not so fast. It's not the one they're asking for."

"All right. Do you want to send it over to me?"

"I can run it by you right now. I apologize to Sergio Filman for publicly mentioning his name without doing due diligence," I say.

"I don't think that's going to make them happy," says Goldman.

"It's not meant to. I'm only being honest. They can take it or leave it."

CHAPTER TWENTY-NINE
EVERYTHING

The sun is rising over the bay at Smith Point to the east. Drinking coffee and leaning against my truck, I watch the golden rays on muddy green water create a color I'm sure no artist who wanted to sell their work in a gallery would try to emulate. It's not an ugly shade per se; in fact, it reminds me of the skin of a river frog, *Lithobates heckscheri*, which isn't completely coincidental. Well-camouflaged animals don't simply emulate the environment around them; they also re-create the way light refracts around smooth and rough surfaces.

As the sun begins to ascend for its daily reign, the eastern-facing sides of buildings on a distant island begin to shimmer above the haze of the gulf. It's kind of appropriate, in a way, if I'm looking for a tortured analogy for my life.

Yesterday was like the San Ciriaco hurricane, a most unfortunate natural disaster among natural disasters. When the brutal winds of the longest-lived Atlantic hurricane had finished devastating the Caribbean and East Coast of the United States, more than three thousand people were dead.

"What could be worse than this?" many people probably asked themselves. One year later, Mother Nature had an answer: the 1900

Galveston hurricane, which killed as many as twelve thousand people. The first messengers to reach Texas City on the western side of the bay were accused of exaggerating when they told authorities how many lives were lost. As rescuers navigating through the debris-strewn waters of the gulf saw the bodies, they began to realize that the early death-toll estimates were a massive understatement.

More than a century later, I can see the shimmering, eastern-facing sides of Galveston in the morning light.

Yesterday was San Ciriaco. Today is Galveston.

My lab is gone.

Figueroa himself called me with the bad news. The Department of Defense suspended my security clearance, and my current research programs were put under the custodial supervision of DARPA.

It was a temporary precaution, he told me. For a man who hates to lie, I could tell that he was only able to say it with great difficulty.

The suspension wasn't directly because of my accusation against Filman. It was the last straw in a series of problems I'd created for my patrons at the Department of Defense.

The Hyde virus has turned into a political mess, and there's certainly a bit of shoot-the-messenger going on. There are two schools of thought. On one side, Theo Cray is a brilliant genius who single-handedly saved us from a national disaster that we were too dumb to see coming. On the other, Theo Cray is an attention-seeking glory hound who has blown this way out of proportion to exaggerate his own self-worth.

My running off at the mouth about catching another serial killer while I was supposed to be back in my lab and giving Hyde investigators help, not hindrance, settled the issue.

To be honest, I'm not sure they're completely wrong.

My lab. Sure, I spent as much time out of it as I did inside, but it was more than the time I spent there. It was my identity.

After the Joe Vik incident and the way I ruined my relationship with my university by not showing up to teach and through the initial negative attention I brought them, losing my professorship was humiliating.

Getting a government lab with even more funding helped salve my wounded ego. To my peers reading about me in the tabloid headlines, the new situation must've sounded downright enviable.

The cruel truth is, what I missed the most was what I didn't have and what they didn't want. *Teaching.*

Now I have neither.

About the only thing I have now is Jillian, and, if I'm being honest, I've treated her more like a roommate than a lover since I encountered Forrester.

After Figueroa broke the news about the lab, he dropped another little bombshell on me. The group at the CDC researching Hyde wanted to know my availability for more exams.

They weren't asking if I could come in. I was being told to come in sooner than later.

My second-guessing their conclusions hasn't won me any favors there. All it would take is one researcher to say that my brain shows possible signs of inflammation from an MRI and they could order me quarantined for observation.

Given the indefinite life span of Hyde, that could last the rest of my life.

I'd only ever thought about that in the most abstract sense, but now I'm facing the possibility of becoming a literal laboratory animal.

When we initially recognized the pathology of the Hyde virus, the first proposed treatment for people who had been exposed was massive antivirals followed by six months of hospitalization and then continuous monitoring.

I took all the antivirals, but there was no way I was going to let them keep me locked up for that long. Maybe it was arrogance, but I figured I was better off on my own.

Maybe it *was* arrogance . . .

That can explain so much in my life.

I reached my conclusion about Sergio Filman based on past experience. Not evidence. I became so damn sure of myself that I couldn't be bothered by mere empirical evidence. My mind said it was true. What could be better than Theo Cray's mind?

My conclusion wasn't the problem—it was the way I arrived at it. *Ego.*

I take my phone out and stare at it for a moment. Funny. The sight of it brings me actual pain. This was the messenger that told me a few minutes ago the one thing of value in my life had been taken away.

The one thing of value.

You're an asshole, Theo Cray.

How about the person who saved your life and endures your mood swings and weird tics?

I dial her number.

"Hey, babe," Jillian answers.

"They're . . . they're taking the lab," I stammer like a child who's had his bike stolen.

"Oh, Theo."

"I'm sorry. I'm sorry I've been so distant."

"It's okay. It's all right," she says.

I pull myself together. "I'll be fine. Are you okay?"

"Yes . . ." She hesitates.

"What is it?"

"Oh, Theo. I wanted to wait to tell you. Until all this was over."

Oh lord. "What?"

"I . . ."

"The suspense, Jillian. What have we said about that?"

"Sorry. It's your professor, Amanda Paulson. Her daughter, Jewel, called."

"Oh god."

"No, no, it's not that! It's just . . . well. She's not been doing as well. Apparently, she's undergoing cancer treatment. Jewel said she called to let me know that Amanda wouldn't be able to go over this year's Juniper applications."

Paulson was supposed to be immortal. This can't be the way the universe works.

"I know she's special to you, Theo. And maybe now is not the time, but you . . . she may not have it later," says Jillian.

"I'll go see her. Is she still at the ranch?"

"I think so."

"All right. I might be a few days. Is that okay?"

"Of course."

We hang up, and all I can feel is shame.

My Galveston?

Far better people than I are out there dealing with much worse. There may be a revolver in my head playing Russian roulette, but at least not all the chambers are loaded.

CHAPTER THIRTY
GOLDEN HOUR

Amanda Paulson is waiting at the gate of her ranch, holding it open while the largest English mastiff I've ever seen—easily mistakable for a small horse—sniffs around the dry yellow grass at the base of a post.

Amanda's thinner than when I last saw her, not healthy thin but the kind of thinness that comes from fighting a losing battle with disease. She'd always been on the hale side, strong and capable of lugging her own pack up a mountain well into her fifties, when I first had her as a professor.

Her smile and intense blue eyes are unmistakable, though, when I roll down my window.

"You here to make sure the rumors are true?" she asks.

"Nah, I still have a problem with the way you graded my paper on the Fermi-Pasta-Ulam problem," I reply.

"Consider what you're still calling it and then come talk to me, you dummy."

Dummy is a term of affection from Amanda, one she saved for her special students, the ones she expected more from.

Her class, the Quantitative Organism, was one of the first programs to explore computational biology. In particular, she combined computer modeling with field research. We spent a lot of time in forests, digging in the dirt and investigating ponds, while the classroom work consisted of reading about the early days of using computers to model living systems from Ulam and von Neumann to Alvy Ray Smith. It's an interesting field that attracts unusual minds. Ulam and von Neumann were instrumental in the Manhattan Project, while Alvy Ray Smith went on to cofound a little company called Pixar.

I get out of my truck and give Amanda a hug. She squeezes back. It still has the intensity of something you'd experience in a wrestling ring, but it's not the same mama bear hug we used to joke about.

I let go and almost buckle when my legs are nearly knocked out from underneath me as her dog decides to occupy the same space as me.

"Orion! Back off," she tells her beast.

"Nice boy," I say, patting the creature on its basketball-size head.

"Girl, Teddy. Orion is a girl. Anatomy was never your strong suit."

"Oh, I thought . . ."

"Because of the name? What did we say about labels? They're like maps. Not the same as the thing."

I've been out of my vehicle less than a minute, and I'm already back in her classroom. It feels good.

"Let's go inside. I have something I want to show you," she says, leading me through the front door.

The inside is pretty much as I remember—a wide-open ranch house packed with books, scientific apparatuses, stacks of papers, boxes of student essays, and little jars filled with curious things she's found on her field trips.

An Amanda expedition could be a backpack trip in northern Mexico or ten feet from the front of the biology building, where she'd have us dig a hole and inventory all the flora and fauna we could find in one cubic foot of dirt. Part of that exercise was to show us the real story, the one we didn't see.

The next week we'd take some of the worms we'd found and sacrifice them to the gods of science, splitting them open and examining their innards, from which we'd try to grow cultures of the bacteria found inside. From those cultures we'd try to find evidence of bacteriophages—viruses that infect bacteria.

"How do you model all of this?" she'd ask.

A few of the braver students would suggest computing clusters and fractals or whatever other buzzword was popular. The real answer, she'd explain, was that you couldn't. The parts were so complex you could never hope to re-create the entire system. There were too many unknowns. Our goal was to reduce the complexity and find simple rules that allowed us to build models that could make predictions. Dig, poke, and dissect to gain some insight, but don't pretend that you're seeing everything.

She would then demonstrate how a simple spreadsheet could better estimate the number of organisms than some of the more sophisticated computer models at the time.

"Come take a look at this," she says, shoving me into a wooden chair facing a large computer screen. Behind the display, a wide window faces a vast, green prairie.

This is Amanda. No *Hello, how have you been?* It's *Put your butt down here and see something I find interesting.*

She clicks away on her keyboard, using only her index fingers.

"I see that typing course worked out," I tell her.

She extends her middle finger and then uses it to type. "Here, smart-ass. You've seen this?"

On-screen, a green, glowing blob shoots a long tentacle out and snatches a red blotch, then retracts it back into its body.

"*Vibrio cholerae?*" I ask.

"Clever boy."

Vibrio is one of the bacteria that causes cholera. Recently, we've caught on camera one of its evolutionary tricks—its ability to quickly adapt new immunity to antibiotics. While we'd known for almost a century that seemingly asexual bacteria could evolve and even pick up traits from other bacteria around them, we didn't have a broad understanding of how. For decades we simply assumed that the bacteria would absorb the DNA when other bacteria died. But the rate of adaptation suggests that there's something more sophisticated at work.

When researchers first filmed *Vibrio* under the microscope, the bacteria appeared to be minding their own business, but when colored dyes were introduced, helping separate them from the surrounding medium, we saw a totally different picture. Those chill bacteria were actually using an appendage called a pilus like a harpoon. They'd snake out like a tentacle and stab into a pore of another bacteria and literally snatch DNA from inside its body and then pull it back into its own membrane.

Despite being a single-cell organism, it had evolved a sophisticated appendage to perform DNA transfer from a completely different organism—with a precision greater than what we can achieve today. The pilus itself, which we'd observed in the past, is simply a structure of proteins made on demand and then broken down when no longer needed.

I can see why Amanda is fascinated by the little creature. It's all of her lessons in only a few seconds of video.

"Pretty amazing?" she asks.

"Very." I notice a twinkle in her eye.

"Now the real question is this . . . is that bacteria just grabbing DNA at random? Is it looking for something when it stabs the other cell? Do the proteins have some kind of way of sensing what's needed? Or does the bacteria wait until it's retrieved the DNA strands to figure out if it's useful?"

"Does it need to test the DNA?" I ask. "If it works, it works. If it doesn't, it doesn't. There will be a billion other bacteria to take its place in a minute."

"It could. Or here's another theory: the bacterium only grabs the DNA when it's desperate. If a phage or something else is attacking it, then it makes sense to try anything, doesn't it?" She waves to her kitchen, where I notice a table filled with pill bottles and containers. "Look at me. At this point I'll put anything they tell me in my body." She tilts her head, reading my expression.

"Don't make that face, Teddy. I'm only making a point. I think the answer might be all of the above. The curious part to me is how the bacterium knows which part of the DNA to grab. I think it's more than chance. It also tells me that if we want to avoid going extinct, we have to realize we're already at war with an enemy that's mastered genetic engineering and is conducting trillions of experiments every second, figuring out new ways to kill us. As if our own bodies aren't enough of a threat."

She stops and breathes for a moment, as if slightly winded. "Okay, I'll shut up now. Time for small talk. How's the wife?"

"No wife." She already knows this.

"The kids?"

"No kids."

"The dog?"

"He ran away," I reply, completing an old joke.

"Great. Let me show you something else," she says before walking over to a box of papers. "I was going through this the other day. One second." She eases herself onto the tile floor next to the box. "I need to catch my breath."

She makes an exhaling sound. "It wouldn't be so bad if I wasn't losing my mind, too." She points to a large whiteboard at the other side of the living room. Once she used it to give lectures in her house. Now it's filled with an itinerary of chores and which drugs to take.

I think the sight of this affects me more than anything else. I remember lying on a pillow on the floor with a small group of other students drinking beer while Amanda explained some odd quirk about a species of river eel or whether Neanderthals made bread.

Her mind could wander anywhere, and she always had a little observation that made you think about things differently. The Neanderthal-bread question led to a discussion of the first gyro wraps and then a moonlight expedition into her greenhouse to see if we could approximate a Pleistocene baking recipe.

Amanda's greenhouse . . . just thinking about it brings a smile to my face. It's a botanist's version of Jurassic Park. If she heard some researchers had found an extinct variety of seed, she'd write to ask for samples if they became available.

She once brewed us Egyptian beer from some ancient emmer grain and yeast cultures she'd been sent by a biologist working near the Nile.

"How's the greenhouse?" I ask.

Amanda is digging through the box next to her. "Gone. It got to be too much trouble. Don't worry, I buried the seeds in bottles in the backyard."

"Upside down to keep the moisture out?"

"Just like Mr. Beal," she says. "Although there are much better ways. Here we go." She pulls a stack of papers out of the box.

"What's that?"

"It's you, Teddy. First week of class I asked everyone to write an essay. This was yours. Do you remember it?" She clutches it to her chest.

"What was it about?"

"Who you wanted to be."

"Um, headmaster of a prep school for nymphomaniac cheerleaders?"

"Hardly. Anyway, I kept it because I thought to myself, *This boy has potential.* World-changing, paradigm-shifting potential. And of course you turned out to be my biggest disappointment."

"Hey! I bet I have the highest number of citations of any of your students."

She shakes her head. "Is that how we measure success?"

"Um, I caught some serial killers. Maybe stopped a global epidemic . . ."

"I saw the movie. It was horrible. No, Teddy. I was hoping for more. I wanted to see what this young man was going to become." She reads from the paper: "I want to use science and computing technology to change the world like Salk, Fleming, or Pasteur."

"I was a bit full of myself," I reply.

"Wanting to do something great isn't being full of yourself." She laughs. "Maybe I was arrogant to think that one of my students would go on to do something at that level."

"The odds weren't exactly in your favor," I say.

"Well, I tried to stack the deck. So, what happened to that kid?" she asks.

"He encountered the world."

"Is that it?"

"Change is hard."

She sets the paper back in the box. "Especially when you're not trying to change it."

"I've stopped bad people. I've made a difference. Hell, Forrester? If that had succeeded . . . ?"

"Maybe so. I don't know much about that. But I do know that you had even greater potential."

"I'm not sure what you mean," I reply.

"Go get the box from the guestroom closet marked 'Project Shrinky Dink.'"

I walk down the hallway and find the guest room pretty much as I remember it. I slept on that bed more than a few times after having more than a few beers.

There's camping gear stacked in the corner, including a brand-new backpack. I find the box in the closet and bring it back to the living room.

"Planning a trip?" I ask.

"I was. Myanmar," she replies.

"Aren't there quieter places to vacation?"

"Yeah, but those don't have epidemics the government is trying to keep quiet as long as it keeps killing their enemies," she replies. "Anyway. I was planning, then my health got worse. We plan, God laughs. What I want to talk about is what's in that box. Take a look."

CHAPTER THIRTY-ONE
IMPACT

As the sun sets, school is once again in session as my former professor and permanent life coach tasks me with discerning the meaning of Project Shrinky Dink. The box is filled with lab notes, highlighted articles, and descriptions of apparatuses. At the very bottom, I find some grant applications and read through them, getting the basic gist of what it was all about. Amanda's name is all over them, along with a researcher named Joseph Chu, whose work I'm sure I've read elsewhere.

"Antibody research," I reply, remembering that was what she'd been working on before she got into computational biology. "Synthetic antibodies in particular. It's a hot field. Why did you stop?"

"The better question was why did I start."

"Okay . . . It looked like you had a novel approach here."

Antibodies, or immunoglobulin, are protein structures that the body produces to bind to certain pathogens like viruses, bacteria, and even cancerous cells. They're like the laser pointer a spotter uses to tell a sniper—in this case our immune system—where to attack.

Our body produces antibodies when it recognizes that it's being attacked. It tries to both create them on demand from cellular memory—programmed from evolutionary history and/or vaccination—and generate them on the fly. Really sophisticated bacteria and viruses are more problematic, because they change their shape so quickly that our body can't figure out an epitope to bind to.

Powerful antivirals, like the ones I took after being exposed to the Hyde virus, aren't very discriminating and can run the risk of attacking healthy cells if not administered carefully. A virus and a perfectly beneficial blood cell can be killed by an overzealous antibody. Anaphylaxis occurs when our body goes haywire responding to a threat to our immune system either externally or internally.

"You were trying to skip the cellular approach entirely?"

Current methods of making antibodies involve taking naturally created ones and attempting to produce them en masse outside the body, using either cell cultures or chemistry to re-create immunoglobulin itself.

"I'd been fascinated by molecular-imprinted polymers. We'd been working on them since the 1930s, with limited success."

Molecular imprinting is a process that makes a "mold" of a molecule or particle by using some material to bind to it, then removing the original object. These castings can then be used to detect the presence of similar molecules or structures.

Amanda's process appears to create impressions of viruses and bacteria and then use the impression as a kind of trap—similar to how immunoglobulin functions but created artificially.

"What if when you wanted to develop an antibody, you could just program it on demand?" she asks.

"It sounds great. But how?"

"Joseph and I were inspired by the way polymerase chain reactions worked. What we wanted was to build up our antibody one paratope at a time and then use a protein to bind to them."

"Randomly?" I ask.

"We had a crude process that worked a lot like modern protein microarrays. Emphasis on crude. Our skills as chemical engineers and grasp of proteomics were exceeded by our ambitions. It was a glorious failure," she says.

Most of their research was in the early 1980s, but the photos and diagrams of their processes wouldn't be matched until the 2000s.

"You were ahead of your time," I reply.

"Every wrong idea is ahead of its time, Teddy. It's not really a compliment. The key is to have a brilliant idea that's of its time. That's how the world changes." She gestures to the box. "I'm still proud of our failure. And that's my point. Had we succeeded . . ."

"You could have completely changed medicine. It would have been as big as antibiotics."

"Bigger," she says, pretending to nonchalantly admire her nails. "Joseph and I used to talk about this being the key to immortality. If we could dial up an antibody to kill a flu virus without having to wait for Mother Nature, we could attack cancer cells, too. Alas, we didn't. And that's when I decided to focus on plan B."

"Plan B? What's that?"

"That was the source of my even greater failure. You."

"Jeez, lady."

"Not just you. All of my miserable students. I tried to inspire you. I told you stories of people that shook the world. I told you to dream bigger, not to worry about your peers, not to seek out safety nets, but to be bold, to try to change the universe."

"Like I said, the odds were stacked against you."

"That's not the point. I didn't expect any of you to succeed. I expected you to *try*. Instead, my best students are trying to get cashew apples to produce two seeds instead of one, working on marijuana hydroponics, or, in your case, counting tadpoles in the goddamn forest so you can build a better computer model to make better computer models.

"Not one of you has a Project Shrinky Dink. Last I heard, your biggest project was trying to build a way to profile potential terrorists

Andrew Mayne

through DNA. Are you fucking kidding me, Teddy? This is what you're doing?"

"It's complicated. I took that on so nobody else would. I'm against it," I reply.

"Is that how it works? Are you against the funding? Or is that okay?" She stops and makes a wheezing sound. "Jesus, now look at me."

"I'm sorry. I'm sorry. After Montana . . . after Joe Vik . . . ," I try to explain. "Everything was different. No university would hire me."

"I'm talking about before then, Teddy."

"I was doing good research."

"You were doing safe research." She sticks out a leg and kicks the Shrinky Dink box. "Know what I'm really proud of? I had to go back to teaching because nobody would give me any serious grant money after *that* fell apart. I'd already knocked on every door; I'd twisted every arm. I gave it everything. That's what I'm proud of. What are you proud of?" She holds up a hand. "Yes, your science-cop shtick has saved hundreds of lives. Maybe thousands." She takes a deep breath. "But, Teddy, you were meant to save millions."

"No fucking pressure."

"You know what I mean. You didn't try. You did edge-case research. You never confronted something head-on until it touched you personally. Then you found something to focus on. A nice little win to give you some sense of self-worth."

"Well, if it's any consolation, I don't have the government lab anymore. My little vigilante hobby finally bit me in the ass," I say, sounding sorry for myself.

"What happened? Jillian didn't say anything."

"It all fell apart yesterday. I stepped on my own . . . Anyway, I ran off half-cocked, made some claims I didn't yet have the evidence for, and it all blew up."

"What do you mean?" Her attention suddenly jumps from eviscerating me to a new shiny object.

"I may have confused a hospital that had a ridiculously high death rate for a hospital with a moderately high death rate and implicated someone for murder. No big deal. I probably ruined a life," I explain.

"Then maybe you can get back to real research," she replies.

"Doing what? The government lab was my last stop. Nobody will fund me. My reputation has now been ruined in the academic, public, and private worlds. My Shrinky Dink box will be a bunch of *National Enquirer* clippings."

"So because of this you can't get back into research?" she asks.

"Basically."

"How bad did you screw up?"

"I'll let you read my notes," I say, then try to get off the topic. "You still have the telescope?"

"Yeah. Want to try to find Planet Nine?"

The odds of two amateur astronomers using an eight-inch telescope spotting a theoretical object at the farthest reaches of the solar system are . . . well, astronomical. But that's what I love about Amanda. A sky-gazing trip to the backyard to take our minds off the stress of the world is instantly transmuted into a crusade to answer one of the most pressing space mysteries of our time.

CHAPTER THIRTY-TWO
Planet Nine

Amanda's ranch sits far enough from the lights of the nearest city that the smoke-like band of the Milky Way is clearly visible overhead, and the stars are so bright that you feel like you're actually in space—which technically we are. The atmosphere and surrounding land seem to fall away.

As she adjusts the telescope, I watch Orion sniff around the grass and brush, constantly vigilant for predators, food, or, the best of both worlds, a predator that could also be food.

"Take a look, Teddy." Amanda steps back and invites me to gaze through the eyepiece.

I see the familiar dark bands along with two bright pinpoints of light, Europa and Io. "Planet Nine looks remarkably like Jupiter," I reply.

"Smart-ass. Out of the way." She pushes me aside and recalibrates the telescope. "I thought about becoming an astronomer," she says.

"But you hated the idea of never being able to touch the worlds you saw."

"Oh, I told you guys that?"

"Once or twice," I say. "But you're totally cool with touching the Lassa virus or *Vibrio cholerae*?"

"Still a smart-ass." She steps back from the telescope, and her breath makes an icy cloud in the night air. "What was I doing?"

"Planet Nine," I remind her. She was always a bit scatterbrained, but I can see how it's worsened.

"Right. Right. If it's at aphelion, that would probably put it right in the middle of the Milky Way band . . . and that only leaves it somewhere . . ." She adjusts the telescope. "Have a look."

The magic of Amanda Paulson is that, in this brief moment, I believe she could have found it—which is absurd, but it's her gift. She gets you to believe in the impossible. Even in yourself.

I look through the eyepiece again and spy several faint stars. "I'll call CalTech and tell them they can relax. Case closed."

"Okay, maybe not. But there are almost certainly planets around those stars. Who knows what else is out there? There could be a super-Earth there with a massive ocean and a giant kraken swimming underneath, contemplating their own existence."

I step back and see that she's staring up at the Milky Way with her head tilted back, smiling with joy.

"At times like this, I don't feel so bad. You know, out near Blackland Prairie they found some more arrowheads and bifaces. McDonnell tells me they're at least twenty-one thousand years old. Which puts almost eight thousand years between them and Clovis," she says, referring to what was the oldest recognized archaeological site in the Americas. "Think about that, Teddy. Someone probably stood right where we are standing right now. Literally right here. It's the highest point in the area. Someone stood here twenty-one thousand years ago and looked up at the sky like we are right now. And they probably asked, 'What is my place in all this?' They had to feel so tiny and yet strangely important all at the same time. What *is* my place in all this? What's yours?"

"Twenty-one thousand years ago?" I ask. It's an interesting time in human history. We still walked the world with some of our ancestral cousins.

"I know what you're thinking. You and your Neanderthal obsession," she replies. "You wrote a paper for me predicting we'd find their genes in our DNA, didn't you? Of course, that turned out to be true. I mean, other people thought the same thing, but they went out and did the actual research," she adds, deflating my moment of pride. "Wait a second . . . that was for my class?"

"Yes." Did she just forget what she was saying?

"I remember now. You did a computational part, didn't you? You predicted that people with European ancestry would have around two percent Neanderthal DNA. That's almost spot-on, Teddy."

I don't bother asking her how she remembered the number. Amanda Paulson had as close to a photographic memory as anyone I've ever met. "Lucky guess," I reply.

"No. It wasn't. You based the number on estimated Neanderthal population and something about gene flows between Nganasans and Sami peoples, right?"

"Something like that. I just tried to make it sound smart."

"You wrote again about Neanderthals, didn't you? You even did a computer model. Something about their range." She thinks for a moment, probably imagining the graphs in her head. "Your model showed them reaching North America during the Eemian period?"

"Yeah. I might want to change that prediction to Denisovans. Now that they're like a real thing and we've found little evidence of Neanderthals east of the Altai Mountains in Siberia," I reply.

"The paper's back in the house. You can go correct it if you like. I won't tell anyone."

She looks down from the stars and stares at me. "You had such big ideas back then, Teddy. Maybe it's time to start having them again."

"Yeah. Jillian's hinted at the same thing. It's just that right now . . . Well, right now, I don't know if it's time for big ideas."

"The lab and the other thing?" she asks.

"The other, other thing. The Hyde virus. We don't understand it. We don't know how long it lies dormant."

"You don't know if you have it?"

"Yeah. Our antibody test isn't the most reliable. And the people doing the research aren't the most confidence building for me. So here I am worried that any moment it's going to start attacking my brain and I'm going to turn into a raging psychopath," I explain.

This is the first time I've really externalized my feelings to anyone outside my confession to Jillian that didn't end so well. It feels different talking to Amanda . . . maybe because she's dealing with her own crisis?

"You're being stupid, dummy," she replies.

"Okay . . ."

"How many of the people who became infected with Hyde and turned into rage monsters knew they had Hyde?"

"None."

"Are there symptoms beforehand? Photophobia? Fever?"

"Fever. Possibly photophobia . . ."

"So you're saying you'll have at least two to three days' notice before the virus starts to cause serious damage?" she replies.

"Potentially irreparable damage that will turn me into a rage monster."

"So you're afraid of becoming Hannibal Lecter. Got it."

"I won't have his self-control. More like a PCP freak on a bad trip with a glimmer of self-awareness," I explain.

"You said 'potentially'? What do you mean?"

"It depends upon the severity. In some cases there was an inflammation that eventually receded, and they're fine now. In others it permanently damaged the brain."

"What was the mitigating factor?" she asks.

"From what I can tell, how quickly they got antivirals and reduced the inflammation," I reply.

"Knowing you like I do, you probably have a batch of those in your truck."

"Well . . ."

"Damn it, Teddy. What are you really afraid of? I get this is a concern. But it sounds very manageable for you. Scary, but manageable. I'd trade places with you in a heartbeat."

"There's Jillian . . ."

"Next time you have a fever, she can strap you to the bed like a werewolf. So, what's really bothering you?"

Damn this woman. It's not pleasant to have her scalpel-like mind focus on me. She's right. She's absolutely right. Hyde scares me. But it's probably manageable. This is really about something else. Something that was inside me before I encountered Forrester and his Hyde virus.

I glance around the prairie to make sure that we're really alone. It feels like the safest place to confess. "I killed a man. I killed a man in cold blood."

CHAPTER THIRTY-THREE
EXECUTIONER

"John Christian was a monster," Amanda says after I tell her the whole story. "It doesn't sound like cold blood to me. There were children there."

"I understand all that. I know he was a monster. It's not whether or not I was justified that keeps me up. It's the ease with which I did it. Did I pull the trigger because I came to some moral calculation? Did I pull the trigger because I was still feeling some kind of impotent rage at what Joe Vik had nearly done to me and Jillian?" The next one is hardest for me to admit. "Did I pull the trigger because I'd dehumanized him in my mind because of his race?"

"I think he dehumanized himself the moment he started killing children, Teddy. Maybe there's more to it. We're all twisted messes inside. What matters is how we manifest our actions on the surface. John Christian was a very bad man. You were in a situation that may not have been as cut-and-dried as someone like you prefers, but you had to make a decision."

"I know. I know. It's just . . . I'd do it again. I would have killed Forrester if I could have. I guess that's what's scary. I don't need a virus to be a killer. If I think it's called for, I know I'll do it again."

"You see yourself as something separate from society."

"I guess."

"Better?" she asks.

"What? No. Just not emotionally bound to the same rules."

"What brought you to Christian's house that day?"

"I don't know. William, the father of one of the children. There was a young man named Artice. They'd asked for help. Begged someone to do something. But nothing happened. They were ignored."

"But you listened," she replies.

"Eventually."

"Did you get pleasure from killing Christian?" she asks.

"Like did I get a hard-on? No. God, no. But it felt . . ."

"Right?" she says, completing my thought. "I envy you. Grab the telescope." She lets out a whistle, and Orion comes stomping back to us.

We start back toward the house with Orion threading her way around our legs like a much smaller dog. I have to do my best to not fall over and break the telescope. "Next time let's tie your beast to a wagon and have it pull us back."

We keep walking, surrounded by the sound of crickets and the distant call of a coyote that Orion ignores.

"It was in the Orinoco Delta," Amanda says after a few minutes.

"What was?" I ask.

"What I was just telling you about," she replies.

"I'm sorry, I must have been distracted. Could you tell me again?" I say, trying not to sound too worried about her lost train of thought.

"Did I space?" she asks, stopping in her tracks. Orion stops, too, almost mimicking her mother's stance.

"A little. You were talking about the Orinoco Delta. Venezuela," I add to trigger her memory.

"This was while I was working on my doctorate. I went down there with a team from the Methodist hospital. They were on a medical mission, and I was going to help out and also do a biological survey. We were vaccinating Warao children for measles whenever we came across a village. This was ages ago, and the government was doing a spotty job of it. We had one of their doctors with us, Ernesto.

"We came to one village, a bit more isolated than the rest, which is saying a lot. Half of the tribe had left when the fishing began to decline. Mostly it was the men who left, leaving lots of mothers and children. What was the name of that village? Something like 'the bend in the river.' Anyway. The elder refused to let us vaccinate the children. The mothers were willing. They understood, most of them. They knew what measles was. We argued—well, I argued. Our ethnologist went on and on about respecting tribal traditions. I pointed out that the women felt otherwise, but she insisted that the elder was the holder of the tradition and his word was law. Eventually I gave up, and we decided to leave the next day.

"That night I lay in my hammock and thought all I had to do was go get the key for the chest from Ernesto's tent while he was sleeping. I could vaccinate the children, going from hut to hut. Sure, there would be crying, but the elder was usually so drunk at that hour, he'd never know. Either way, by the time he and the others had realized what I'd done, it would be too late. The children would be vaccinated."

"Did you?" I ask.

"No, Teddy. I planned it all out. But I didn't. I was too afraid of the consequences." She sits down on the steps leading up to her back porch to catch her breath. "See if you can guess what happened next. A year later there was an outbreak. Half the children I played with, some of them I even held, died. No more Curva del Río. Except for that bastard of an elder. I'm sure that fucker is still there drinking himself to sleep every night."

I set the telescope down on the deck and have a seat next to her. Orion collapses at our feet like a fallen sequoia.

"I'm sorry," I mumble.

"You don't understand, Teddy. This is what true regret feels like. What you're feeling, that's your moral compass making sure that you're still in alignment, acting as a check and balance. That's not regret. It's a burden. Not a regret. But what I felt. What I still feel? Now *that's* regret. If you don't at least try to change the world, you'll know what it feels like. I don't want that for you." She sighs heavily. "It's past my bedtime. Tomorrow at breakfast you can tell me how you're going to make a difference after you get yourself out of your current mess."

"My mess," I reply. "My humiliating public shame and arrogance."

"At least it doesn't have seventeen faces you can still see when you close your eyes."

No, the faces I see when I go to sleep are the decomposing ones of all the victims I've pulled from the earth. Maybe Amanda's impossible challenge will give me something else to think about instead.

CHAPTER THIRTY-FOUR
N2

The light from the hallway catches Amanda's disheveled hair falling over her face as she shakes me awake. "Teddy! Teddy! Into! Into!"

Is this a nightmare?

I try to move, but my brain still hasn't booted up.

"Into!" she shouts at me.

Oh lord. She's having an episode. Some sort of fight-or-flight response kicks in, and I come out of my coma.

"What's wrong?" I ask, sitting up. "Do we need to go to the hospital?"

"Yes!" she yells.

I reach for my phone. "Let me call."

She swats my hand. "Not now! I have to show you!" Amanda's gaunt hand grabs my T-shirt and pulls me out of bed with unearthly strength.

Orion is standing in the hallway, watching the display with dog amusement as we shuffle past.

"Should I call Jewel?" I ask.

"Who?" she asks.

"Your daughter, Jewel?" I try to keep up with her as she moves down the hallway.

"Oh no. She wouldn't understand."

When we reach the living room, she puts a hand on my chest and stops me. "You're bright, Teddy. But you're right, you are arrogant. You can spot others' mistakes but not your own."

I can smell more beer on her breath than when we said good night. I glance at the sunken floor and see several beer bottles next to a stack of folders.

Oh lord.

"Amanda, maybe you should sit down?"

"Why?"

"Um, I think you're having a moment," I reply.

"No, Ryan, you're having a moment."

"Teddy."

"Whatever. You forgot about *into*! How many times have we talked about this?" she demands.

I don't know if I should humor her or call an ambulance. Other than being drunk and crazy, she seems physically fine . . . besides the cancer thing.

"I'm not sure."

"Dummy, look." She points to somewhere behind my shoulder.

I turn around and see her whiteboard has been completely erased and something else drawn on it: a hundred dots spread from one side to another with her chicken-scratch writing in random spots. They look like stars.

"Um, you found Planet Nine?"

Her face freezes. "What the hell are you talking about? Look, dummy."

I stare at the board again, and it hits me. The papers on the floor by the beer bottles are my notes on the Southern Star deaths. The dots on the board are my graph, reproduced in precise detail.

"I see," I reply, really not sure what her point is.

"I couldn't sleep, so I read your notes. Then I went to bed because I was tired."

"Drunk is what they call it."

Her hand lashes out and slaps me across the face. "Listen when I'm talking."

My face is still smarting. The only time I saw her this angry was when one of her students almost stepped on a rattlesnake pit while not listening to her.

"Sorry. Ah . . ."

"Look at your graph. Your assumption was all wrong. Wrong, Teddy!"

"My assumption? What assumption?"

"What got you into your mess?" she asks.

"The idea that there was a serial killer at the Southern Star," I reply.

"There's your mistake, Teddy! You didn't check your assumption!" Her skinny finger jabs at the whiteboard.

"Yeah, I think I realized that when they told me my suspect wasn't even there at the time."

She shakes her head. "Dummy. Your assumption is wrong."

"I'm really not understanding." Orion could explain this better. "Are you saying that I got the wrong guy?"

"I don't know. But your assumption is wrong."

"My assumption? My assumption that there was a serial killer there?"

"There! That statement! What does it assume?" she asks.

"Either there's a serial killer or there's not a serial killer," I reply.

She shakes her head so vigorously her silver hair whips around. "What are you assuming there, Teddy? Your problem is implicit in the way you phrased your assumption."

"Either there's no killer or there's . . ." *Oh shit.*

Amanda's eyes flash with manic intensity. "Yes, Teddy. Into . . . or more. Probably into."

Only she's not saying "into." She's saying "N2"—as in a second value. The first one being N1.

I look back at the scatter plot with new eyes. It's so clear now.

I sit on the steps, and Orion puts her head in my lap.

Holy crap.

My assumption *was* wrong. I assumed Southern Star only had *one* serial killer. Because . . . well, it seemed so unlikely that there could be two. But Southern Star's hospital group was so poorly run it would have been a magnet for bad nurses, the worst ones virtually being pulled there.

N2 is a second nurse. A second serial killer who was operating at Concord while Filman was there . . . and when he was gone. Unfortunately, I don't have all their records, and the ones I do have have missing names—otherwise I might be able to narrow the possible suspects to a few dozen.

Amanda goes over to the board and makes a hand gesture following a wave of dots. "N1, see it?"

I nod.

She traces a second wave, not as pronounced as Filman's but obvious when you realize it's there. "N2, Teddy. N2."

A simple statistical analysis would have revealed the two different waves if I'd bothered to even look. But I didn't. Because I'm a dummy.

N2 wasn't there nearly as long as N1. In fact, it appears that N2 vanished shortly after Filman returned from Iraq. If I had to guess, N2 realized someone else was doing the same thing and decided to leave. N2 may have noticed the peak at first, when their killings and N1's— Sergio's—caused a huge spike, then dismissed it when it declined, only to realize that the return of Sergio also meant that patient deaths were rising again.

"How do I catch him?" I ask.

"Her," says Amanda. "I mean, probably but not definitely. This one is a bitch. No offense, Orion."

The dog lifts her head up from my lap and glances at her mom for a moment, then falls back down and leaks syrup-like saliva on my shorts.

"You going to catch this one?" asks Amanda.

"What happened to changing the world?" I reply.

"Get this . . . c-word. Clean up your mess and *then* save the world."

I fixate on the dots and try to figure out how I can even go about catching N2. I'm sure she's long gone by now, off to another hospital, taking her wave of death with her.

Maybe that's how I have to treat it. The pattern is like a signal. I'll have to trace it. All the deaths in all the hospitals would be too much noise.

I'll start with hospitals that have stats similar to Southern Star's. I'll look for employee records. It could be an orderly or even a doctor. The only thing I know right now is that dark wave.

I'll find it again. I have to.

CHAPTER THIRTY-FIVE
PROWLER

Our living room is taken over by spreadsheets, scatter plots, and a long graph I made by taping printouts together that stretches from the front door all the way to the kitchen table. I'm sitting on the floor next to my laptop, triple-checking the program I wrote to look for patterns. It's a streamlined version of Predox, which was an elaborate version of MAAT, the program I used to hunt Joe Vik.

"It's like watching a seven-year-old," Jillian observes from the couch as she sips a glass of wine.

"Sorry about the mess." I run my fingers through my unkempt hair and feel the stubble on my face. I'm the real mess right now. "I just want to be really, really sure," I say. "Can I run through my thinking?"

"Sure. Then can I show you what I've been working on?" she replies.

"Yeah, sure."

"And then can we talk about the elephant in the room?"

I'm so out of it I look up, not for an actual elephant, but possibly some kind of elephant artwork or something else I didn't notice. "Ah, metaphor. Yeah, what's that?"

"I don't know, your lab?"

"We got money for a while. We'll be okay."

"Oh, thanks, big provider. Thank you for putting my tiny little lady mind at ease," she says in a high-pitched voice.

Jillian was running a diner and was perfectly self-sufficient before I met her. "Sorry." I hand her a spreadsheet. It shows a scattered pattern of dots and a line traveling through them like a wave.

"What are the dots?" she asks.

"Hospital deaths where the cause of death could have been something similar to a digoxin overdose. Ones where the patient didn't die in the middle of a procedure, on the same day as admittance, and a few other factors."

Jillian squints as she stares at the dots. "Am I supposed to see something here?"

"The goal is to not imagine something there. Thousands of people die in hospitals every day. That's the problem."

"I'll say," she replies.

"Yes . . . oh . . . right. That is a problem. But what I meant is that it's too noisy. There's no way to look at that and say, 'Hey, these dots are because of a serial killer.' I had to figure out another approach and make some assumptions."

"Didn't that get you into trouble before?" she asks.

"Well, yes. Because I didn't know I was making an assumption. That's the difference. Now I'm assuming that there were at least two serial killers at that hospital operating at least briefly at the same time." I hand Jillian another graph. This one shows a red and blue line. "The red one is N1, who I believe is Sergio Filman. It's the longest one there. The blue one is N2. She or he was only there for a short period of time. Notice that there's a period to N1's killings? They're never closer than three days. They also never happen on days he has off. N2's are more spread out, and they don't cluster like N1's."

Jillian nods in agreement. She's spent enough time with me to understand my train of thought. She's also not one to bullshit me if she doesn't get it.

"All right, so my assumptions are: one, that N2 operated out of Southern Star facilities at least once; and two, N2 only kills in the same area during an interval—meaning that she's not responsible for killing people in Seattle and Miami at the same time, for example. She's not in two places at once. Those are the only things that I'm fairly certain about. Unfortunately, I have to make some more fuzzy assumptions to find a signal. So, I'm assuming that N2 tends toward hospitals that are more like Southern Star—lower pay, poorer patients, higher death rates. At first, I looked within the state of Louisiana, but then I realized that if she'd been licensed in a different state that's part of the nursing-license compact, she could move around much more easily. She could plan ahead and get certified before moving on."

"Why are you so sure it's a she?" asks Jillian.

"I'm not. The data is gender blind. Statistically it's more likely, so I'm calling N2 a she. But I don't know. I have to keep reminding myself of that."

Jillian squints at the charts. "She was only at this hospital for just over six months. Is that normal for her?"

"I don't know. I think she'd stay longer if nobody noticed. In this case, we already had N1 killing patients, which meant that N2 would probably move on."

"It's like a predator," Jillian replies. "Didn't you say that Joe Vik had a similar hunting pattern as a great white shark?"

"Yeah. The problem is, there's so much more noise in the data. I'm looking at *millions* of deaths," I explain. "So what I have to do is feed a model as many known data points as I can and then give it part of my data set and use the rest to test it."

"To predict where she's going next?" asks Jillian.

"I wish. No, I need to use a neural network just to see where she's been. That's what I'm trying to say. With Joe Vik I was looking at places with high numbers of missing persons and then looking for his burial grounds based on his past kills. I had a much smaller area to search—mathematically speaking. Places like the cave at Cougar Creek seemed a natural fit."

"I miss hiking," says Jillian.

"We usually found dead bodies," I reply.

"I don't miss that part. So where is the search for N2 now?"

I point to my computer. "It's trying to find a pattern. I didn't give it the data from Southern Star because that's my one certainty. I want to see if the model can predict that. Meaning, if it works, it'll give me a graph showing a timeline and locations."

"How much data?"

"Everything I could find." I cough. "And maybe some stuff that wasn't that well protected." I check the progress bar. "Another hour or so. What did you want to talk about?"

"Hold on." Jillian sets down her wineglass and walks into the other room, then returns. She sets a small stuffed teddy bear in front of me.

I glance at the wineglass and then at her stomach . . .

"No, Theo. I'm not pregnant," she snaps. "I didn't go unfreeze your boys, if that's what you're worried about."

"Oh." Should I mention to her that my first thought wasn't complete terror? That after Amanda's scolding me for being irrationally worried that Hyde would turn me into a kill monster, I'm maybe slightly less afraid of myself?

"Hailey and I worked on this," says Jillian.

I pick up the bear. It has big eyes and black-and-white fur like a reverse panda. "You sewed this?"

"No, you idiot. Hailey was able to have these manufactured and shipped over."

"Bears? Um, cool," I reply.

"You have no idea what I'm talking about, do you?"

I'm about to open my mouth but then remember a wise proverb about not confirming one's foolishness. Instead I simply shake my head.

"When you told me about the children getting killed when they were away from their families, that really got to me. I remember when we were in the forest with Joe Vik. I remember the terror I felt."

"I think I was the one screaming," I reply.

"My point is that I thought maybe there's something we could do. I found a company that already made teddy bears with surveillance cameras inside to be used as nanny cams. This one has a small computer—"

"Raspberry Pi?" I ask.

"Yeah. With a camera, a microphone, and a speaker. It also connects to Wi-Fi—that way Mom or whoever can see what the bear sees. Hailey wrote a program so the bear recognizes faces. Hold on." Jillian squeezes the bear then sets it back down.

"Hello, Theo!" the bear says in a slightly computerized child's voice.

"Hey, bear," I reply.

The bear just sits there.

"We haven't added a lot of features yet. But watch this. Bear bear, lights on."

A bright LED emanates from the bear's mouth.

"This is great, Jillian!"

"It'll turn off after a minute. Hailey says the bear will go a week with a charge. It'll tell the parent to plug it into a USB when it gets low."

I pick up the bear and admire it. "A camera and microphone?"

"Yeah. But only the parent can access the images."

"Interesting. It's running Python?"

"I think so. Hailey wanted you to take a look at the source code if you had a chance."

Very interesting. "Definitely. How soon can you send them out?"

"You haven't looked in the garage, have you? We're ready, but I wanted to ask you about that." She points to my computer. "When your friend there is done, maybe you could give me a list of hospitals that N2 hasn't been to? We could start there?"

"Sure." I marvel at Mr. Bear again. So many possibilities. Forget Mycroft . . . this has even more potential. "How many of these do we have?"

CHAPTER THIRTY-SIX
DARK WAVE

I take off the wall a painting of a desert landscape that I have no idea how we ever acquired. Like the furniture, it just showed up mysteriously one day—or Jillian took care of it when I was in one of my absent-minded spells. In place of the painting, I stick the printouts from my computer model to the wall with thumbtacks.

I can hear Jillian make a small sigh as I puncture the drywall. Oops, maybe I should have used some Blu Tack.

There are seven charts in all. Some of them are six sheets taped together. Others are two or three. Each displays a wave the computer picked up as a high death rate appears to move from hospital to hospital. At the top corner is a confidence score. The highest one is a 97 percent fit and consists of four pages. The second highest is 96 percent and has five sheets. The six-sheet charts are 83 percent and lower. I already threw out the ones that didn't have Southern Star at the right time.

Jillian pulls one out of the trash can and asks me what they are. "That's not N2," I tell her.

"But could it be from a different serial killer?" she asks.

"Oh! Right!" I grab the sheets and put them on the coffee table. I was a little too single-minded. Jillian brought up a very important point. Chances are, they were casual connections and I should ignore them—but I'm not really confident in my ability to decide what I should and should not ignore at this point.

"Are these dates?" asks Jillian, pointing to the bottom.

"Yes. The chart in the middle is the longest run. It ends a year ago." I indicate a shorter one. "This one has a higher confidence score but doesn't cover as long a period."

"You're looking for the longest continuous wave?" she asks.

"Yes. That's where I want to start." I point to text at the bottom of the bounding boxes that overlap the graphs. "This box is one hospital. I assumed that there was no more than a four-month gap between killings." My finger traces the wave of death from one end to the other.

I don't like the fact that the longest waves have lower scores, because I can't really know what's random and what's not. Adding to that is the frustration of not really knowing how the computer created these predictions. I could take the tensor apart frame by frame and never understand what it was really doing. All I can do is adjust my inputs and see what happens.

"Why are you frowning?" asks Jillian.

"I was hoping for one long, strong wave."

She leans in and reads the labels on the charts, then starts to move them around.

"What are you doing?"

"Putting them in chronological order," she replies. "You just stuck them to the wall like a kindergarten art show."

"They overlap," I reply.

"Not all of them." Jillian grabs two of them and places them next to each other with a gap in the middle.

"Oh crap." I realize what she's done. The two charts with the strongest confidence were from two different time periods. Jillian placed them to show what they look like with the space in between. The wave continues from one and picks up on the other.

"How does that look?"

"Good, but why did she stop? If this was a regular serial killer, we'd assume he got caught and was in jail for a period and then picked up where he left off. This . . ." I shake my head. "I don't get it."

"Illness?" asks Jillian.

"Maybe. My next step is to get a list of nurses who worked at the hospitals and see who worked at all of them."

I sit on the floor next to my laptop. "I have some partial personnel records that I . . . um, found." I write a short Python program to loop through the names in a list and compare them to hospital-employee records.

A split second after I hit "Enter," the screen shows the results: 0

"Okay. No name was at all of those hospitals," I grumble.

"How complete are your records?"

"Not very. And it's possible she used variants of her name." I shake my head and stand back up. "This blank spot bothers me. What were you doing here?" I ask the wall.

"Are there hospitals you don't have data for?" asks Jillian.

"I have every US hospital in here, as far as I know." I look at the other charts. "That could be overfitting—making my model too complicated. The answer might be in one of these."

"What about starting with the early hospitals and working through them?" asks Jillian.

"The hospitals are approximations. One out of three is probably wrong. The model looked for more of the gestalt of a pattern. If she used a different name . . ."

"Can nurses do that?" asks Jillian.

"Maybe. I can't find a consistent name match. Even if I did, I need more hard evidence." I'm missing something. I place one hand on either side of the gap. "This is the answer. This is what tells me who you are. This is the antisignal." I turn to Jillian. "If we can find out where she was, we might find out who she was."

"But she disappeared."

"Did she? Let's assume she kept killing. Why can't we see it?"

"Because she killed somewhere you don't have data."

I drop to the floor and start typing.

"What are you looking for?"

"World Health Organization data," I explain. "Hospital mortality rates. Sudden spikes. Sometimes American nurses work overseas."

CHAPTER THIRTY-SEVEN
WINDY CAY

Stoneman Hospital in Saint Lucia sits on a small ridge with a view of the town of Soufriere below and the ocean beyond. A cool afternoon breeze rolls in from the sea, passes through the palm trees, and causes the wildflowers at the edge of the green lawn to waver in the wind. The hospital itself was built on the Crispin Stoneman Estate, named for a British expat who set down roots on the island shortly after World War II and bequeathed the buildings to a charitable foundation dedicated to providing medical care to the poor children of Saint Lucia and the neighboring islands.

The Dark Pattern led me here. Ten months after N2 left the Southern Star hospital group, deaths spiked here. I tried to find a common name among the hospital directories but came up blank. There were several dozen people who went between those hospitals, but none of them were very strong candidates. For several years after Hurricane Tomas struck the island, nurses were brought in from the United States and Canada. They were usually employed on either six-month or twelve-month contracts.

Add to that the problem that many small hospitals use medical-staffing agencies and have no records, making it virtually impossible for me to get a full account of who was working there without subpoena powers or some extreme black-hat hacking—which I haven't completely ruled out. But for now, I decided to follow the wave here.

N2 could be a doctor, a nurse, an orderly, or a dozen other occupations you find in a hospital. There's also the disconcerting possibility that she (or he) is none of these. N2 could be an impostor who simply dons a uniform and walks inside a hospital and kills. It's happened before.

Stoneman Hospital has me excited because it's such a small facility. It has eighteen beds and a staff of twelve full-time employees, including eight nurses. The majority of nurses who came from the United States appear to be either young and just getting started or single older ones looking for an adventure.

"Mr. MacDonald?" someone calls out to me.

I hesitate for a moment and then remember that's the name I'm using here. Well, the name I'm implying. MacDonald was Jillian's maiden name before she married her late husband. I had her make a small donation to the hospital through their website and then asked if we could take a tour.

It's a deception, but I didn't have an alternative approach.

I turn around and greet the short, dark-skinned man wearing a light cotton dress shirt and tan slacks. He appears to be in his fifties but is probably a decade or so older.

"Mr. Stevenson?"

He shakes my hand. "So nice of you to visit."

"Thank you for offering the tour. I'm sorry, but Mrs. MacDonald was unable to make it. She's caught up with business back home. She sent me here to house hunt."

"Another time, then. Here, let me give you the tour."

Stevenson leads me into the entrance to the hospital, which used to be the foyer when it was a residence.

"Mr. Stoneman actually lived on the island prior to World War II," explains Stevenson. "He was working with British intelligence and trying to root out Nazi spies." He waves at a woman in a nurse's uniform sitting behind a wooden desk. "Hello, Ms. Donna. This is Mr. MacDonald."

I shake the woman's hand. "Ted, please. Just Ted. How long have you been here, Ms. Donna?"

"Nine years next May. Second longest next to Mr. Stevie," she replies, nodding at Stevenson.

Okay, she definitely would have met N2. I need to talk to her at some point when Stevenson isn't around. While I have no reason to assume either of them doesn't have the best of intentions, because the matter involves a rash of patient deaths, it may be a bit embarrassing. Although I doubt they even realized what was going on.

Stevenson takes me down the hallway and into the main ward. From what I've seen of pictures of other hospitals here online, this one's actually rather nice. The beds are lined up along the back wall with a view of the window and ocean. Unlike at Woodland Lake, the kids can actually see the scenery.

There are eight children either in beds or playing at a table by the window next to a television showing Nickelodeon. The child closest to me is a skinny adolescent reading a book in bed while hooked to a dialysis pump.

"This is Cedric," says Stevenson. "This is Mr. MacDonald."

Cedric covers his mouth with his book and mock whispers, "Get me out of here. Mrs. Shine beats me."

A woman reading a magazine at a desk at the far end of the ward replies without looking up, "I heard that, and I can make it true."

Stevenson lets out a laugh. "Cedric's nickname around here is Mischief."

"I'm wrongfully accused," Cedric replies.

"I know the feeling." I glance over at the book he's reading—*Wild Seed* by Octavia Butler. "Science-fiction fan," I ask.

Cedric nods to Mrs. Shine. "She is. That's all she brings me."

"If you don't like my reading material, maybe you should try the library, then, Mr. Hamilton?"

"How long have you been here?" I ask Mrs. Shine.

"Almost two years," she replies.

That puts her here right after N2. Maybe she's heard something. I'll have to figure out a way to talk to her as well.

"This way. Let me introduce you to Dr. Cannon," says Stevenson, leading me down the ward to a small office.

A man a few years younger than me sits at his desk, working at his computer. He's wearing a maroon polo shirt over a muscular build.

"Hello," he says, giving me a firm handshake. "Taking the tour?"

"It's an amazing place," I reply.

"I know. My office is down in Canaries at the hospital there, but I prefer to do my work up here."

"Is there a physician here full-time?" I ask.

"Dr. Cannon and Dr. Solvay are on call." Mr. Stevenson points to a small cottage at the edge of the property. "One of them overnights there."

"And the nurses?"

"We have six right now. They live elsewhere, but there are usually at least three here in the day. Two at night."

I say goodbye to Dr. Cannon and follow Stevenson as he gives the rest of the tour, including small guest bungalows that have been converted into exam rooms.

Outside, two children sit in wheelchairs on the grass while another floats in a pool as a woman in a bathing suit carefully keeps her above water.

"This is a beautiful place," says Stevenson, admiring the resort-like atmosphere.

"It certainly is," I reply, almost asking out loud why so many children died here—but the answer is obvious. This place looks nice only on the surface.

CHAPTER THIRTY-EIGHT
BAD LUCK

In 1906, a well-to-do New York family hired a sanitation engineer named George Soper to help them find the source of an illness that had stricken their household. Several family members had come down with life-threatening *Salmonella Typhi* infections. Soper discovered that there had been a member of the staff who'd only worked for a short while for the family and left shortly before they became seriously ill.

When he spoke to other affluent New York families that had also become ill, in some cases fatally, they also described a similar woman who had worked for them briefly before moving on. Because she changed positions so quickly, tracking her down was difficult until Soper heard about an active breakout in a Park Avenue penthouse.

It was there that he encountered a female Irish cook who matched the description of all the other breakouts. Her name was Mary Mallon, soon after known as Typhoid Mary.

She was an asymptomatic carrier of *Salmonella Typhi*, and because she didn't believe in washing her hands, she spread the bacteria to others. Even after informed that she was a carrier, she refused to stop working as a cook and often used aliases to gain employment. She was briefly confined and agreed to never work as a cook again upon release, but she soon returned to her old job and continued to infect people until she was eventually placed in lifelong quarantine.

By the time her last major outbreak occurred at the Sloane Maternity Hospital, where twenty-five people were infected and two died, hundreds, possibly thousands, had been made ill by her spread of the disease. Some estimates say that at least fifty cases proved fatal.

I can sympathize with Soper. Much like my quarry, Mary Mallon had a keen sense of when to move on and avoid suspicion.

However, unlike with Mallon, all my victims were killed, and the living witnesses—at least the hospital staffers—may not care or even understand what happened. Even if they did, it would arguably be in their best interests to pretend that it never had.

Approaching Mr. Stevenson about the case is a challenge. While there was one article in a Caribbean newspaper about a high number of deaths at the clinic during N2's turn there, the tone was more sympathetic than accusatory. The slant of the article was that Caribbean medical facilities needed more public support. Not a single hint of something nefarious going on. That said, it doesn't mean that Stevenson and others didn't suspect anything was amiss. That's why I have to approach them with some subterfuge.

"Anything else I can show you?" asks Stevenson after showing me several empty cottages and expressing his hopes to add more medical equipment—which was an indirect plea for more financial support.

"Actually, an odd question. The whole reason we found out about you was because a friend of ours asked us to look you up for a favor."

If you were to ask me what my darkest secret was, I'd be torn between who really killed Joe Vik, my jumping the gun on John Christian, Butcher Creek, and what I did three nights a week for eight weeks a year ago. But that's a secret between me and the Austin Improv Comedy and Acting School—which I paid in cash under an alias.

It made me a slightly less reluctant liar, but it's debatable if I'm any better at it.

"Mr. Stevenson, about two years ago, my wife's sister was visiting the island and was at a restaurant and nearly choked to death. A woman gave her the Heimlich and left before my sister-in-law could thank her. Someone told her that the woman was a nurse who worked here. Would it be at all possible to find out who that woman was?"

I'm making several assumptions in this lie. The first is that N2 is a nurse and the second that N2 is female. If I'm incorrect on either of those, I'll find myself at a dead end shortly.

"When was this?" asks Stevenson.

Curious. He asked when first.

"March, I believe—2016." I chose this date because it falls right in the middle of N2's murder spree.

Stevenson pauses. Does that time period make him uncomfortable? "Do you know what she looked like?"

I shake my head. "No. My sister-in-law was a bit distracted. Do you by chance have a list of nurses who were working here at the time? I'd be happy to email them."

"So many faces. It's hard to remember them all. I'll see what I can find." He doesn't exactly sound eager.

"Thank you. Another question: the resort I'm staying at is a bit touristy for my taste. Do you know if there are any houses for rent around here?"

What I want to know is where the nurses stayed. The people nearby might know something.

"For how long?" he asks.

"A few weeks."

"No. Maybe try the Airbnb? Lotsa people put their places there."

I've never met a person who lived on an island and didn't have a friend with a rental. Did my questioning make him suspicious?

"No worries. Thank you."

Stevenson shakes my hand and heads toward a cottage at the other end of the property. I walk back to the front of the estate and then make a beeline for the entrance.

"Hello, Mr. Ted," says Ms. Donna as I enter.

"Hi. Two questions: Can you recommend a place to stay around here and maybe a bar? Something slightly less touristy?"

"Bar? The Crab Nest. You'd like it. More Jimmy Buffett than Bob Marley, but not too touristy." I think she's telling me it's where the local whites hang out, but I can't be sure. "Are you looking for a cottage?"

"Yes, for a few weeks."

"And Mr. Stevenson didn't try to get you to rent one of his Cherry Lane ones?" she asks.

"Um, no. I should have asked. Thank you."

Apparently, I also should have taken the advanced course at the Austin Improv Comedy School, because I still can't lie to save my life.

"One more thing?"

Her phone rings. "Sure, one moment." She takes the call, glances at me, then seems to pull back slightly. Without saying anything further to the person on the other end, she hangs up and says, "I'm sorry, I can't talk right now."

She pushes her chair back from the desk, gets up, and walks away, leaving me alone in the foyer and the front of the hospital unmanned.

Theo's magnetic charm wins again.

CHAPTER THIRTY-NINE
SIDEWAYS

I walk down the road that leads to the clinic and contemplate the completely inarticulate way I handled the situation. Instead of getting information, I seem to have put everyone on guard. Hopefully that's just me being overly worried. This place is my single best opportunity to find out more about N2. I don't want to screw it up . . . more.

I take out my phone and look for a map to get my bearings. It strikes me that N2 walked down this path nearly every day for half a year. What I'm seeing is almost exactly what she saw—or *he*. I have to avoid getting stuck in my own assumptions.

The island is both beautiful and fascinating. The sharp green volcano-forged peaks and tall mountains are unique for a Caribbean island. It reminds me of something I'd see in the South Pacific.

The town of Soufriere is more like an extended neighborhood, with a soccer field right in the middle. It's relatively self-contained like the other towns on the island, with its own schools, markets, and pizzerias. It makes me wonder how N2 felt when she came here. On one hand, it must have been liberating to be away from the specter of suspicions back in the United States, but did she worry about being caught here?

From my regression analysis, it appears that she waited almost a month before killing at Stoneman. Was Saint Lucia meant to be a new start? Or did it take that long for her to feel comfortable enough to pick up where she left off?

My phone rings.

"Hello?"

"Hey, how's it going?" asks Jillian.

"We'll see. Nobody has warmed up to my charm."

"I see. Goldman called. He left a number for an attorney."

"An attorney? I thought he was an attorney."

There's a moment of silence. "This is a criminal attorney. Goldman says the DA's office is going to subpoena you."

Not good. The last subpoena was for Filman's civil lawsuit. This one implies that the Baton Rouge DA is looking into criminal charges for me.

Not good at all.

"Okay. Text me the number."

Five minutes later, I'm sitting on a rock that's been painted with the name of a street, Cherry Lane, on the phone with Helen Donada, a criminal-defense attorney.

"How soon can you be in Baton Rouge?" she asks.

"I can leave here tomorrow. How serious is this?"

"I think it's a fishing expedition. They're getting pressure from Southern Star to do something. I'd like to take a counterintuitive approach and be extremely proactive. Southern Star is the crook here. Let's volunteer to go in to the DA sooner than later," she explains.

"How does that help us?"

"They don't know what to ask you right now. Maybe Southern Star wants to charge you for stealing records, but that's going to be hard if they can't claim what you stole. Also, they'll be very nervous about discovery. At this point they might want to just score points by making you the target of an investigation."

"And what if they have something more? What if it backfires?"

"That's the risk. If there's something on you and the DA's really out to get you, I have to tell you, this could all go south and they arrest you."

"This sounds sketchy."

"If they want to put you into cuffs, they're going to do that. I think strategically going in now is better than waiting. But it's your call."

I realize that I'm staring at one of Mr. Stevenson's rental cottages. "Okay. Can we make it the day after?" I have no idea when I'll be able to come back to Saint Lucia—if ever.

"Sure. So, you want me to call the DA and tell them we're coming in?"

"Tell them I'm ready to talk," I reply.

I stand and walk around the gravel in front of a cottage. It's secluded behind rows of palm trees and a green berm covered in gladiolus that haven't been attended to in a while. The flowers are still young, maybe two seasons old at most. They were probably planted then and forgotten.

Twenty meters past this cottage is another identical one and one after that. None appears occupied. They look to have been built at the same time as the estate that became the hospital. It's possible these were caretaker residences and eventually sold off or possibly bequeathed to Mr. Stevenson.

A rusty bicycle leans against the side of one. The other has an open shade revealing an empty interior.

There's nobody here to ask questions, so I move on down the hill. I pass a small house that's been converted into a pizza shop. The rest of the buildings are private homes with an occasional sign in the window proclaiming it a business. I see two nail salons and one tax preparer. As I pass by, I can smell food cooking in one of the salons.

Everybody knows everything about everyone here. Forget the physical size of the island—the interconnectedness here is a world away from the anonymity of a large hospital like Southern Star, let alone an entire city where you can hop onto a freeway and go thousands of miles.

At first it had to be appealing to N2, the sense of being able to know a place completely, but that couldn't have lasted. Eventually it must have become stifling. *Was it stifling enough to kill? Or did it become claustrophobic after you killed and realized the real currency here was rumor?*

The hillside levels off, and I come to a ridge that extends to a small tavern near a bluff that overlooks the southern part of the town. A sign says "Crab's Nest," but the establishment is closed. I've learned that business hours are flexible here, determined more by mood than rigid timetables. I make a note to come back later and walk to my resort on the hillside at the north side of town.

N2's presence is all around me, yet invisible. Her nail clippings could be wedged into a floorboard back in the salon. A follicle of her hair could be in a ceiling fan at the pizza place. The rocks crunching under my feet could have been kicked by her bare toes.

The clerk in the market at the corner could have seen her face a hundred times.

Almost everyone here has seen her.

Mr. Stevenson knows her—but probably doesn't *know* her.

Yet she remains invisible.

The part of me that doesn't understand concepts like logic or cause and effect wants to scream, *Didn't you all realize you had a killer in your midst?*

But they must have, eventually, like a herd that twitches at the sound of a breaking twig and runs to safer ground. The cottages that Stevenson rents out are empty. All the faces at the hospital appeared to belong to locals.

They knew something was wrong. Changes were made.

The herd surrounded their young and expelled the outside threat—possibly without uttering a single word. They may not have known, but deep down, they *knew*.

Now if I can only get those two parts to talk and tell me something.

CHAPTER FORTY
BARRISTER

I spend the rest of the afternoon contacting different Saint Lucia authorities to find out anything about the nurses who'd worked here while N2 was on the island. When you're dealing with a country whose entire population could fit into Disney World and have it be a slow day at the park, you soon realize that many of the governmental offices you're calling are probably cubicles in the same room.

At one point, I called the board of professional licenses and heard in the background the voice of the woman I'd just spoken to about travel visas to the island. I half jokingly wonder if the smarter strategy would be to show up at the building and just flat out ask if anyone remembers an odd American nurse living in Soufriere two years prior.

Then I realize that's probably *exactly* how things are done here. I'm used to a nation of 330 million strangers. I need to think of Saint Lucia as a small town.

I check my watch. I can be at the capital in an hour and a half. Things shouldn't be closed by then. At least it's a better use of my time than getting rebuffed on the phone.

I leave my room and cross the lobby of the Emerald Garden Resort. A middle-aged man in a business suit stands and says, "Mr. MacDonald?"

I take two more steps, then stop, realizing he's talking to me. "Yes?"

His suit looks more business than casual. Something about him says lawyer or government official. It could be both.

"My name is Mr. Junqué. May we speak over here?"

He directs me to an empty lounge overlooking the trees and the bay beyond.

"Okay," I reply, following him over to two wicker chairs by the balcony.

He straightens the crease on his slacks. "You're checked in under Theodore MacDonald."

"Yes," I reply, unsure how guarded I need to be.

"Immigration has nobody under that name arriving in the last week. Are you here under a false name?"

Okay. This got interesting. "I'm sorry, who are you?"

"Please, just answer the question."

I've been intimidated by the best. This guy's game could use a little work. I stand and start to walk away.

"One moment," he says.

I turn around and do my best to look bored.

"I'm an attorney for Stoneman Estate. Either you gave a false name when you visited there or you're in our country illegally."

I sit back down. "I simply made a donation. Mr. Stevenson was kind enough to give me a tour."

"Are you an attorney?" he asks.

That's an odd question . . . unless . . . Oh, I see now. I think.

Stevenson probably called Junqué after I left because he was worried that I was there to sue them for wrongful death. Perhaps he thinks one of the families of the dead hired an off-island attorney?

There has to be some way I can use this to my advantage. Right now, he doesn't know what's important to me or what I know. What I want is a list of nurses that were working here. That's something that would likely be revealed in a courtroom's discovery process . . .

Wait . . . Were they sued before? Those records could be sitting in a filing cabinet north of here in Castries.

"No, Mr. Junqué, I'm not an attorney."

"And you're not employed by the Clyborne family?"

Okay, now I know what to look for the case under. "No. I'm not. Who are they?"

He studies me for a moment, trying to see if I'll flinch or blurt out that I'm lying under the pressure.

"They're not important," he replies.

"Should I be concerned about making an additional donation? Is the hospital involved in some kind of litigation?"

Let him think he might've just screwed his clients out of a larger donation.

He shakes his head. "Normal problems. What kind of donation did you have in mind?"

"I haven't discussed that with my wife," I reply. "I'd made a request to Mr. Stevenson. I've yet to hear from him."

"Unfortunately, we no longer have those records."

"I didn't ask for records. I just wanted some names."

"Yes. And we still don't know *your* name, do we? Perhaps an exchange?"

I have a feeling no matter what I say, things are about to get less cordial for me here. Junqué is no idiot. He knows I'm not the friendly potential expat trying to ingratiate myself into the local community.

I glance at my watch. I can still make it to the Castries courthouse before it closes if I leave now.

"I'll consider it," I reply. I have no idea if he'll tell me anything once he realizes who I really am. My reputation with hospitals isn't the best at the moment.

I give him a nod, then head out the lobby to my rental car. As I drive away, Junqué still hasn't left the building. I'd bet anything he's asking the front desk about the man who checked in as Ted MacDonald.

Right now, a clock is ticking to find out whatever this island can tell me before I find myself entirely unwelcome. Junqué didn't say he represented the hospital, he said the estate. Estate implies money. Money implies something to protect. If Junqué and his partners are the custodians of the Stoneman Estate, it means that they're the ones handling the trust, and any threat to them is a threat to the fees they make every year as managers of that fund.

He seemed extremely concerned about potential litigation from a wrongful death. I'm not sure how he'd feel if he realized I was there to investigate twenty potential wrongful deaths.

I step on the accelerator and take the windy road up the island, hoping I can outrun my name.

CHAPTER FORTY-ONE
LOCAL MATTER

The red-and-blue funnel of a Carnival Cruise Line ship is visible over the roof of the commercial division of the High Court of Justice—a striking visual reminder of how much of the island's business is tourism related. The interior of the building is a cheerful azure that would feel more in place at a family seafood restaurant.

Behind a mahogany door with a sign next to it declaring this is the civil court division, I find more azure walls and a large glass-windowed section that makes the office feel like an empty fish tank.

I wait behind two women and try to not be obvious as I listen in on their conversations with the clerks inside the tank.

One woman is trying to find out about the status of a court date over an eviction notice. The other one is trying to get the right documents for some kind of title search.

Finally, it's my turn. I greet the woman behind the counter with my best attempt at a sincere smile. "Hello, I'm trying to find records concerning a lawsuit. I think it would be *Clyborne versus Stoneman Hospital?*"

"Did you try online?" she asks.

"Online?"

She hands me a slip of paper with a URL for the Eastern Caribbean Courts website. "You can do a search here."

Huh. I could have done this back in the hotel. I hadn't expected them to be so . . . modern. "Oh, thank you. Could you do a quick search for me?"

"Clyborne and Stoneman?" Purple-painted fingernails tap away on the keyboard. "Mmm. Nothing."

"Nothing? Could you do a search for Stoneman Hospital? Anything between 2016 and now?"

"Sure," she replies, being too polite to tell me to go do it myself. "Nope."

Interesting. Either the Clybornes never filed or the case disappeared. I fold the slip of paper up and put it in my pocket. "Thank you."

I get back into my car and head to Soufriere. The records were a complete dead end . . . or were they? Junqué made it sound like there had been some kind of litigation, but as far as the woman could tell from the online records, there was no history of any. Maybe the Clyborne family had only threatened legal action but never gone through with the case? An out-of-court settlement? Or they might have found it hard to get an attorney if Junqué and his friends applied pressure.

I take the road back out to Millennium Highway and see police lights flashing in my rearview mirror. I panic for a moment, afraid that I'd been driving on the wrong side of the road. Nope. Right . . . um, left side.

Like the law-abiding tourist I'm supposed to be, I pull smoothly off the road and into a parking lot across from the port where cargo containers are stacked higher than the buildings of Castries.

My pulse starts climbing as I remember some of my research into the island. Nine years ago, reports had surfaced that the police department here had a death list and killed over a dozen criminals when the crime got too high and started to scare away tourists.

While I'm not a known criminal in Saint Lucia, I could be a threat to the tourism industry. No tourism board likes to hear the phrase *suspect serial killer.*

"May I see your license and registration, sir?" says the exceedingly formal police officer at my window.

"Yes, sir." I hand him the car rental and fumble my license out of my pocket.

"Thank you." He takes them back to his SUV behind me.

In the rearview mirror, I watch the man take a photo with his cell phone of my documents, then place a call on the same phone.

This doesn't seem like standard procedure. More like a favor for a friend. A moment later, he returns to my window and hands me my license and rental papers back.

"Thank you, Mr. Cray, have a lovely stay."

And that's that. Mr. Junqué now knows who I am. I take my phone from my pocket and call Stoneman Hospital.

Ms. Donna picks up. "Stoneman clinic, how may I help you?"

"I'd like to speak with Mr. Stevenson," I reply.

"Are you the gentleman that came by earlier?" she asks.

I hesitate. "Yes."

"I've been told to refer you to Mr. Junqué. Thank you, have a nice day."

Okay. So there goes that avenue. Stevenson won't even take my calls. If I set foot back at the hospital, Junqué won't hesitate to have one of his friends in uniform escort me off the property.

This island has shut me down in the most cordial way. However, I have a feeling if I push much more, it's going to get a lot less polite real fast.

I take the highway back to Soufriere and consider my options. If this were the United States, I'd consider a little cloak-and-dagger and sneak into the clinic for a peek at their records. But given that this island is rumored to have a police death squad, that might not be the smartest move.

Perhaps a better option would be to try an electronic approach. I have a Wi-Fi sniffer app on my phone. I could probably get access to the network here and then hack into it from the safety of my home in Austin.

I reach Soufriere after dark and take the road back up to Stoneman Hospital. As I reach the front of the estate, I see Mr. Stevenson on foot walking into the entrance.

I start the app up and hop out of my car. "Mr. Stevenson," I call out to him.

He turns around at the front door and glares at me. "You are not welcome here, Mr. Cray."

"All I want are some names," I reply, not bothering to deny my identity. I take my phone out, pretend to use it as a note app. "Just tell me who was working here." My app is still searching the hospital's networks.

"Leave the premises," he demands.

"One of them is a killer. She's still out there."

Stevenson is completely unfazed by this, which surprises me to some extent. Did he know?

"I'm calling the police, Mr. Cray."

My phone is looking up IP addresses and keeping track of the IP addresses of all the other computers around here. "That's not necessary."

Seriously. I don't want to meet them. I check my phone. I have the wireless network's IP address. It's on an older frequency, which implies an ancient router that's probably pretty easy to hack.

I head back to my car while Stevenson watches me depart, his gaze following all the way to the end of the driveway. I head back to the hotel but turn at the last minute when I see the lights are on at the Crab's Nest tavern.

Maybe the island hasn't shut me out completely just yet.

CHAPTER FORTY-TWO
PITON

The Crab's Nest is a small wooden building that's more of a shanty. Painted plywood shutters are raised to reveal a small interior illuminated with Christmas lights and junk all over the walls, ranging from outboard motors to the rusty hood of a Volkswagen Beetle. String lights cover the patio where an older couple sips at Coronas. Inside, a bartender with a Florida Marlins baseball cap over his dreads is emptying bottles from a crate onto his shelves. Two women sit at the far end, drinking fruity cocktails.

"What can I get you, friend?"

"A Red Stripe," I reply, then immediately feel stupid for asking for the most touristy choice of beer on a Caribbean island. "Better yet, you decide."

He nods, reaches down into an ice chest and places a Piton on the counter. "You 'ad it yet?" he asks.

"No."

He pops the cap off and sets it in front of me. "If you don't like it, get out. I'm just kidding."

I examine the label. It's brewed locally. It tastes kind of like Corona. I'm really not that picky when it comes to beer, so it's fine by me.

As he stocks the shelves, I look at all the bric-a-brac decorating the interior. There are postcards, sandals nailed to the wall, and thousands of photographs. The other customers here seem subdued. They don't have the giddy energy or sunburned and drunk malaise of tourists.

"I'm Donnie. What brings you here?" asks the bartender.

"Theo. I'm looking for a woman, I think."

"You think? A man your age, you should know by now. Shouldn't you?"

"A nurse."

"Ah, you should have come here in the good old days." He folds his arms and leans against the back counter. "Young ones. Old ones. We'd get them in like clockwork every six months. And they only wanted one thing." Donnie grins and looks off at the lights near the sea.

"To help the sick?"

"Right. Right. They were mad about helping the sick."

Curious. Or maybe it shouldn't be. So, Stoneman Hospital nurses had a reputation for coming here and hooking up with the locals.

I mean, I guess it makes sense. In fact, I feel kind of silly for not thinking about that in the first place. Maybe Stevenson's connection to them was more than professional? If he had a relationship with one of the women and the deaths started piling up, how would that affect him?

"I'm trying to track one down that would have been working at the hospital about two years ago."

"You a detective?" he asks.

"No. Doing a favor for a friend. You remember them? Names, faces?"

Donnie's face breaks into a huge grin. "Lots of faces. The name part . . . I've never been so good at."

All right, this isn't going anywhere. "Were all the nurses . . . um . . . here to party?"

"Some more than others. But they all ended up here."

Of course they did. N2 probably sat on this very stool. Did she hook up with the local talent? Is Donnie her type? Does she have a type?

"Did you stay in contact with any of the nurses from then?"

He stares at me and blinks. "Like pen pals and shit?"

"Never mind."

"What did this woman do? Someone come home with a black baby and you're trying to find the daddy?"

"Well, the baby did have dreads and a Marlins cap," I reply.

Donnie lets out a laugh and holds up his hands. "It wasn't me. Nah, seriously. Who you looking for?"

"Just somebody I need to ask questions. That's all."

"That's all? There's never a 'that's all.' Especially a man like you. I can tell it's never that simple."

I make more small talk with Donnie and find out that he studied in Florida and his parents were originally from New York. He came back to the island because, as he put it, he liked to keep the complicated all in one place.

I try asking him more about the nurses, but he's been running this bar for more than a decade and all the faces have sort of blended together. I'm about to ask about credit card receipts when I notice that his cash register is a rock to put bills under and a bucket for the change.

Realizing this is a fuzzy dead end, I turn to the cocktail-drinking women to my left.

"How's it going?"

"Wonderful," says a woman a few years older than me with short auburn hair. "Visiting?"

"My wife and I are thinking about moving here," I reply. "How about you?"

She nods to the woman next her. "We bought a place here last year."

Our conversation fades away as we realize neither one of us has anything more to say. I sip the rest of my beer, afraid to order another and get pulled over on the way back to the resort.

Donnie glides around the bar, laughing, making people laugh and keeping up the good vibes as a handful of people start to fill up the tiny bar.

I've run out of questions except the most urgent one—"You have a bathroom?"

Donnie points to a door at the other side of the bar that's almost completely covered in nets, tackle, and bottle caps.

I squeeze into the bathroom and turn on the light. A split second later, my brain almost explodes from sensory overload.

CHAPTER FORTY-THREE
COLLAGE

The bathroom is filled with photographs—Polaroids, glossies, and home printouts. Birthday party photos at the bar, New Year's Eve, Saint Patrick's Day, general parties. Many of them feature women in nursing uniforms, and I quickly spot the same women in other photos wearing more casual attire.

The photos go back decades. I start to examine them one by one, then think of a better approach, step back, and use my phone's camera to capture every part of the wall. At some point someone knocks, but I ignore them.

N2's face is here somewhere. It's just a matter of figuring out in which of the hundreds of photos. It's too bad most of them don't have date stamps . . . or do they?

Some of the photos show New Year's Eve celebrations and the year. Others have birthday cakes with candles. The style of clothing also says something, but not enough to me.

There might be some way I could build an image-recognition system to go through them all and create some kind of timeline. I could also use Mycroft to identify some of the faces. That would be a big help.

It's too bad I can't just look at a photo and know, or see a date stamp like when they came back from the photo processers.

I stare at a Polaroid of a group of women smiling at the camera and wonder if there's some way I can date their Denver Broncos football jerseys . . .

I rip the photo off the wall and kick open the door, almost knocking over the woman I'd been speaking to earlier.

"Sorry! Donnie!" I yell across the bar, getting the attention of just about everyone in the hut.

"Yeah?" he says, looking concerned.

I show him the photo. "Who took this?"

"You can't go ripping things off the wall."

"Who *took* this?" I demand.

"I did. Settle down." He grabs the photo and stares at it. "Oh yeah. Super Bowl party."

Super Bowl 50. February 7, 2016. Now I have faces of people from when N2 was here. Some of them potentially identifiable.

"Are these nurses? Did they work at Stoneman?"

There are at least sixteen people in the photo. Mr. Stevenson lurks at the edge of the frame. There are eight women in the middle. Six of them are white. Three look like they're in their late forties. All appear drunk. I can't tell which one could be N2, but I know enough not to make impulsive judgments.

"Yes. They worked up at Stoneman. There's Mr. Stevie himself. You can go ask them."

"What are their names?"

My manic mode is getting attention from other people. I don't care. I'm holding N2 in my hand.

"What are their names?" I push the photo into Donnie's face.

"Relax, man," a male voice says from behind me as he grabs my shoulder.

I lurch around, fist clenched, and glare at the man. It takes every effort in my body not to punch him. "Back. Off."

I think it's the murderous look in my eyes that makes him step away. I turn back to Donnie.

Donnie rolls his eyes. "Catherine, Margot—um, shit, man. I don't remember."

"Last names. Give me a last name. It's important. Really important!"

He points to a redheaded woman in the photo. "Tanya Luger. I remember her. Funny last name. Like the wrestler."

Tanya has a neutral expression. Is this N2?

"Any others?"

Donnie shakes his head. "You're making me angry, man."

I back off. "I'm sorry. I'm sorry." I glance around and notice that everyone is staring at me while some pop-reggae song from the 1980s plays in the background. "Sorry."

I go over to the corner of the bar overlooking the moonlit bay and stare at the photograph, almost caressing it. If these are all American nurses, then one of them is N2.

The image is faded and slightly out of focus, but I scrutinize every grain. I examine every iris, every smile, every detail of every face. Somewhere in the back of my brain an inner voice is telling me, *You've seen her. You've seen the killer.*

I take out my phone and snap a photograph of the Polaroid and send it to Mycroft. A fraction of a second later, my computer server in Austin wakes up, loads the photo, sends it through an image-recognition system, and begins to process the data.

I type in a series of keywords designed to help it narrow the search: "Saint Lucia, Nurse, Super Bowl, Crab's Nest, Island, Catherine, Margot, and Tanya Luger."

Eight seconds later Mycroft sends me a report identifying three women in the photograph—Tanya Luger, Catherine Ross, and Margot Flaherty.

I have names. Even if none of them is N2, they should know who she is.

I'm getting close. So close.

CHAPTER FORTY-FOUR
ADVOCATE

Helen Donada doesn't exactly lean over and grab me by the lapels and tell me to keep my mouth shut, but that's the emotional reaction I get from our quick-and-to-the-point conference before the DAs enter the room. A sturdy woman in her fifties with curly dark hair and the presence of a drill instructor, she's made it perfectly clear to me that she's in charge. Not the district attorneys, not any investigators, not the judge. When it comes to Theo Cray and his brain and his mouth, they answer to Donada.

I can understand why she's got a good reputation as a defense attorney—she knows the weakest link is her clients, even those who think they're innocent, which I'm not sure applies to me.

An assistant pokes his head into the conference room and says, "It'll be about five more minutes."

Donada gives him a polite get-the-hell-out-of-here smile, then returns her fiery gaze to me. I want to ask her if she had a weak father figure she needs to compensate for, but I'm afraid of being slapped. Not quite, but almost.

"Right now, they're figuring out what the fuck to ask you. They'll come in here with something all typed up, but we'll be able to tell from the typos how fast they put it together."

"Why did they agree to meet so early?" I ask.

"Because they're afraid I'd ask for a delay if we waited for them to come to us. Oh, and what did I say about keeping your mouth shut?"

I nod.

"You only answer their questions after I tell you it's okay. That includes follow-ups. Got it?"

I nod again.

"Know who my worst clients are? It's okay to answer."

"People who've never been in this position?" I reply.

"Nope. People like you who have spent a ton of time in rooms like this and never been convicted of anything. You start to think you know the system. You start to think you know how to only tell them what you want. That's how you get tricked. It's how politicians and CEOs get tripped up. They're so used to being in courtrooms spinning their version of things that they start to think the lawyers are a bunch of dumb asses. The problem is, it's like going to the zoo and thinking you know what it's like to be inside the lion's cage. You don't. Got it?"

This is the most expensive emasculation of my life. As condescending as Donada is, she's not wrong.

Ella Bailey and Mark Versant, the DAs I spoke to before, enter the room along with an older man a head taller than either of them and sporting a gray cop mustache. This must be their boss, Oliver Capstone.

Introductions are quick. Mark Versant gets right to the point with the questions. There's a recorder on the table, and I agree to the interview after Donada gives me a nod. The first few minutes cover background: who I am and who I work for. Even though it's rote, I look to Donada before every single response. Even my name.

This does not go unnoticed by Capstone, who makes no effort to hide his impatience. While this might intimidate mere mortals, I get the feeling that Donada is just waiting for him to say something.

"Dr. Cray, on September 16, were you at 400 Red Terrace at approximately 11:00 p.m.?" asks Versant.

I think that may be the address for Woodland Lake, but I say nothing. I wait for Donada.

"Could you be more specific?" she asks.

"I'm sorry? It's an easy question. Does your client want to tell us if he was there or not?"

"Does driving by count? Does sitting at a restaurant down the block count? You just gave us an address without specifying what this is. Is this an apartment complex? A mixed-use building?"

"Woodland Lake," replies Versant. "Was your client there?"

"You have to be more specific. I believe Woodland Lake ceased to operate two years ago. They may have relocated," she replies.

Capstone interrupts. "Let's simplify this. Was your client on Southern Star property located at 400 Red Terrace at 11:00 p.m.?"

I brace myself for Donada to have me decline to answer that question. Instead she surprises me. "No. My client was not on a Southern Star property located at 400 Red Terrace at 11:00 p.m."

This takes everyone aback. Most of all me. I was at Woodland Lake at that time. What the hell is Donada doing?

"Can we have your client state clearly that he was not there?" asks Versant.

She leans over and whispers into my ear so quietly that I can barely pick up the words myself.

I glance down and say into the microphone, "I was not on a Southern Star property located at 400 Red Terrace at 11:00 p.m. on September 16."

Versant and Bailey exchange knowing looks. Since this isn't a trial, they don't have to reveal all their cards unless the goal is to show me it's so hopeless I should admit my guilt and make a deal.

Capstone speaks again. "We have two eyewitnesses that have positively identified Mr. Cray at 400 Red Terrace on that night. Would he perhaps like to correct his statement?"

"May I see their statements?" asks Donada.

Bailey hands her a document. She reads it over, then slides it to me and points a red fingernail at the critical part of the eyewitnesses' testimony: Southern Star.

"Were these statements made under oath?"

"It says it right there. One police officer and one security guard," replies Capstone.

"Okay," she replies.

"Okay, your client wishes to change his statement?"

"Oh no. My client stands by his statement," says Donada.

Capstone and his attorneys look at each other. "You understand the penalty for perjury, even in a deposition?" he asks me.

"My client is well aware," Donada replies. "Were the witnesses who made this statement aware of this as well?"

"Yes," says Capstone.

"And am I to also understand that Southern Star is the one that initiated a complaint about trespass and theft of property?"

"That is correct," says Capstone.

"I see," says Donada in a slightly drawn-out manner. "You may have a problem. It's our understanding that there is no Southern Star property at 400 Red Terrace. Therefore, it would be impossible for him to have been there, meaning your witnesses perjured themselves."

"What?" blurts Versant.

I can see the wheels turning in Capstone's head. He realizes their mistake and how their whole case has just been undermined. Southern

Star doesn't legally own Woodland Lake. They passed it to a subsidiary that's supposed to be a totally separate company This was part of their scheme to raise the property-rental prices on their own nonprofit, and it just backfired.

They can't accuse me of trespassing on a property they don't own. That would require the real owners of the property to step forward— which would reveal that it was Anderson and his partners after all.

Capstone is probably perfectly aware of Southern Star's machinations. For all I know, he may have helped them come up with the scheme. He seems daunted for a moment, then regains his composure.

"Let's table the trespassing charge for the moment," he says.

"Or you can explain to me who the owners are and we can handle it right now," replies Donada.

Capstone ignores her. "Mr. Versant, next question."

Versant frantically flips through his notes. "Dr. Cray, did you remove property from the premises at 400 Red Terrace?"

Capstone interjects, "There is no need to establish who the owners of the facility are. Southern Star has made it clear that the property in question, three hard drives, belongs to them. Did you take them, Mr. Cray?"

I keep my mouth shut and pray that Donada has another trick up her sleeve.

"Can you clarify?" asks Donada.

"I think it's pretty simple. Three hard drives owned by Southern Star," says Capstone.

"I understand it may be simple to you. But as we've seen, nothing you've said so far has been simple. How would one know the difference between these hard drives and three other hard drives?"

I try not to crack a smile. I think I know exactly where she's heading.

"Mr. Versant, can you read the description of the hard drives?" asks Capstone.

Versant reads from his document. "One or more computer hard drives containing confidential patient records belonging to Southern Star Hospital Group."

This is the trap they're laying for me. If I deny being there, they have two witnesses who can refute me, and then the prosecution can make their case that I stole the hard drives. Donada warned me that what they really wanted to charge me with was violating patient record confidentiality laws, which is a felony and could get me up to ten years in jail for each infraction.

Proving I had the records would be hard, but not impossible—something I have to keep in mind. Donada made it clear that Southern Star plays dirty, and it wouldn't be beneath them to have somebody plant evidence—like three hard drives—on my property.

Donada reads the charge. "Okay, so you're asking my client if he stole hard drives with patient records from the 400 Red Terrace property, which is not owned by Southern Star?"

"Correct," says Capstone.

"And we're to understand that possessing these records without explicit permission from the patients would be a violation of the Health Insurance Portability and Accountability Act?" she asks.

"That is correct," replies Capstone.

"Okay. Then simplify things for me with an answer to a question: Are the owners of the 400 Red Terrace property licensed and authorized to store confidential medical records? In particular, ones that belong to Southern Star? If not, is Southern Star or are the 400 Red Terrace property owners violating HIPAA rules for proper storage of confidential medical records?"

Versant looks like he's about to sweat through his jacket. Bailey seems annoyed and perhaps a little amused. She might have some animosity for Capstone, who just stepped on his own dick.

"Did your client steal the hard drives or didn't he?" asks Capstone.

"I'm not sure we can even agree to what the word 'steal' means right now. You've accused him of trespassing on a property the alleged victims don't own on the basis of witnesses who have apparently perjured themselves. And now you're asking him if he removed property that was either illegally left there or illegally possessed by another." She slowly shakes her head. "Let's see, that's false statement of ownership by Southern Star. Felony. You have one Southern Star contractor who perjured himself. Felony. You have a police officer who perjured himself. Felony. And you have god knows how many individual HIPAA violations on those hard disks for whoever wants to lay claim to them. That's a whole bunch of felonies right there." Donada picks up the witness statements. "I see signatures from Southern Stars' attorneys right here. I have to say, we're thrilled we could come in here and help you with your investigation. I think any judge would agree that you have Southern Star by the balls. Let us know when you take Southern Star to court—we'd love to be there. Anything else we can help you with?"

"We're done," says Capstone. He gets up and slams open the door, leaving Versant and Bailey behind. Versant hastily collects the tape recorder and the papers on the table and exits.

Bailey gets up after he's gone and says in a low voice. "Well played. Well played."

"Wait until Theo sees my bill. He'll wish he fell into your trap and plea-bargained."

I laugh, but only half-heartedly.

"Don't worry, Theo. If Southern Star is smart, they'll offer you a settlement for making false statements."

"I don't care about any of that," I reply. "Ms. Bailey, what about Filman? I know I made a couple of mistakes in my accusation. But he's bad, and someone even worse was working there as well."

Bailey glances over her shoulder to make sure the door is closed. "You might be right, Dr. Cray. But you can bet that after this, Capstone won't let us anywhere near Filman. Your best bet is trying to get someone on the federal level to take it up. You have to excuse me. Versant and I are about to get chewed out." She leaves us alone in the conference room.

"Holy cow," I say to Donada.

"See what happens when you keep your mouth shut?"

"I could have used you two weeks ago," I reply.

"Don't get cocky and start acting stupid, thinking you have a lawyer that can get you out of anything. I can't. The only reason this ended like this is because Southern Star is so crooked they'll do anything to not set foot in court—even if they're the victim. Capstone knew he had a flimsy hand. But somebody pressured him to play it. Now he's pissed at them. He's pissed at you."

"And Filman?" I ask.

Donada shrugs. "If you get him, don't send him my way unless you want to see him back out on the streets in an hour. I'll play him against Southern Star. And I know who has the higher body count."

CHAPTER FORTY-FIVE
Invasive Species

All of Donada's admonishments that I not do anything stupid lasted exactly six hours. That's how long it took me to remember that tonight is Sergio Filman's pizza night with the girlfriend and her daughter and that his house will be empty.

Just to be sure, I drove past his girlfriend's place and made sure that Sergio's Kia was parked in the driveway. I didn't bother to wait and see if it was going to be Domino's or Pizza Hut tonight. Instead, I hightailed it back to his neighborhood, parked one street over, and scaled the small fence into his backyard.

I land and give the yard the sniff test, making sure that he doesn't have a dog. If he does, it's not a large one, and it doesn't care that I'm in its territory right now.

I walk up to the sliding glass door. A porch light with a motion sensor makes a click sound, but it doesn't turn on because of the burned-out lightbulb.

Picking a sliding glass door is fairly easy. Older ones like this can be opened by grabbing either end of the door and tilting it slightly.

I hear the latch unfasten and slide the door open enough to squeeze through.

I've given a disturbing amount of thought to whether I should leave my point of entry open or closed after I break in. I lean toward open because it makes it easier to make a quick exit—which is critical when dealing with murderers.

Sergio's kitchen/dining room is clean and orderly. The table and chairs are something better than what you'd find at Walmart. His kitchen's well stocked and the living room is a little unkempt, with laundry baskets and fishing magazines, but otherwise not a mess.

My killers tend to be tidier than most people. I think that's why they're hard to catch. They're more likely to wash their hands or make sure they don't have something inconvenient like a bloodstain on their clothes.

At some point I should do a survey and find out if extremely organized serial killers prefer the same detergents because of their stain-fighting capabilities. Ditto extra-strength garbage bags and easy-to-clean floor mats.

I only half jest. There could be patterns we haven't even thought about when it comes to organized serial killers.

Right now, I'm looking for patterns in Filman's home. I don't know what they would be. Since he does all of his killing at the hospital, there might be no clues to be found here.

Yet I wonder . . . When Joe Vik started out, he stashed his bodies in one place. After that became untenable, he placed them in locations he could easily find again, but I doubt he did. Vik was merely a killing animal, not a nostalgist who wanted to lie in the dirt and pretend he was some big butterfly about to be reborn.

John Christian, on the other hand, being a magic-obsessed cannibal, liked keeping trophies. His residences were littered with bones. That's how I was able to catch him.

Forrester was an odd beast. His mementos were the things he stole from crime scenes and the scientific samples he stole from his victims. He wanted to know everything there was about death.

But Filman . . . what *is* Filman?

I walk through his house with the lights off so the neighbors don't get suspicious. I have night-vision goggles in my backpack, but the wash of light from the street and neighboring houses is enough to help me make my way around the house.

His bedroom doesn't look all that different from mine before I met Jillian.

Jillian . . . I was supposed to call her. In a moment.

The adjoining bathroom is clean. There's a hamper overflowing with hospital uniforms. Other than that, the place is neat enough that Filman might have a maid.

Okay, Theo. If he has a maid, that would suggest he doesn't have any secrets here.

I check the second bedroom and find a couch in front of a large television with three game consoles. On the far wall are several framed photographs. I see the same one that appeared in the newspaper, showing him in Iraq at the same time I'd accused him of killing people here. The fact that a simple Google search would have told me as much makes it sting that much more.

I open up the closet and see boxes with clothes, taxes, books, military gear, and the other debris we accumulate in life. I walk back into the hall a bit disappointed. I wasn't expecting a sex dungeon filled with corpses, but I was at least hoping for something weird.

Filman seems like a regular guy. His place is like a million other bachelor pads.

A bachelor pad?

I go back into the bathroom and open the cabinet. Shaving cream, cologne, razors, mouthwash, and toothpaste.

I check under the sink. Toilet paper, towels, and cleaning supplies.

I run my hand along the back of the toilet tank and bring up a gob of dust and hair but no strands more than an inch long.

I go to his bedroom and run a piece of tape across the floor. Hair, pubic follicles, and dust.

I go into the game den and try the same thing inside the crevice of the crouch. Same.

Sergio Filman's girlfriend and her daughter have never *been* in his house—at least not long enough to leave any trace.

Filman likes his privacy. I love mine, but a week after I started dating Jillian, you could find traces of her everywhere. Filman's girlfriend is nowhere to be seen here.

Between the two of them, he lives in the nicer place. You'd think they'd want to spend time here. But they don't. And that's probably the way he prefers it.

This place is sacred to him. Maybe he'd let a maid in here, but a maid has certain boundaries. An exploring child doesn't. A curious girlfriend doesn't, either.

I sit on the floor and think. What are Filman's boundaries? Are they merely mental? Or is he hiding something here?

It's a small house. I think I'd notice a secret room.

Wait a second. It doesn't have to be a secret room, just part of the house that's off-limits. In the north, that would be a basement. But there aren't too many of those in Louisiana.

I turn my attention upward. It's right there. I walked under it a dozen times in the last few minutes.

Sergio Filman has an attic. And it's locked.

CHAPTER FORTY-SIX
CRAWL SPACE

I use a chair from the kitchen to reach the padlock. It's not terribly difficult to pick. The lock is the kind you buy because it looks big and strong and can take a hit from a bullet. Unfortunately for Filman, a bump key is far more effective and cheaper than a bullet.

I pull the door down and unfold the ladder after returning the chair to its spot in the dining room. The first step makes a loud creak, but I keep going since nobody is home. Pizza night started less than an hour ago. Filman's probably still dipping his crust in marinara sauce.

At the top of the ladder, I turn on my flashlight and illuminate the interior of the attic. It's . . . boxes. Boxes of Christmas decorations. Boxes of clothing. Boxes of lightbulbs. Boxes of antique silverware. It's the world's most boring garage sale.

The attic is barely tall enough for me to crouch. I do a frog crawl to the farthest box and open the flaps. It's an old Nintendo game console.

I move another box and find a rat stuck in a glue trap. Inside the box I find some military packs and clothing. I move to the other side of the attic and find another rat stuck in a trap and a box filled with medical textbooks.

Maybe Filman locked the attic so the souls of all the dead rats wouldn't come down to haunt him?

I sit back against the edge of the attic and try to figure out what I'm missing.

It takes me probably five seconds to realize the most urgent thing I missed is the sound of a car in the driveway.

I poke my head out of the attic and hear the sound of a key in the lock of the front door.

Damn.

I could leap down and try to make it out the back door, but Filman would definitely see me as he enters. Did I close the sliding door or leave it open? Damn it, Theo. You had a philosophical discussion about it but forgot to remember your conclusion?

As the front door opens, I grab the stairs and pull them up into the attic, praying that the door's sound covered my sound.

I lie flat and listen to someone entering the house.

Door shuts. Lock engages. Footsteps. Keys on a table. I remember scuff marks on the dining room table. That means he's looking at the back door . . .

Fast footsteps. Glass door is pushed open. Several-second pause. Is he looking into the backyard?

Footsteps into the house. Frantic ones. Front door opened? Is he checking the street?

Car door? Car door closed. Front door closed. Footsteps below me.

Sound of door pushed open. Game room. Door opens. Bathroom. Door opens. Bedroom. Closet door slid open. Footsteps. Hallway.

Hallway . . .

He's right below me.

He's looking at the attic.

He notices the lock is gone.

The lock that's in my pocket.

Footsteps to the kitchen.

Chair sliding on tile.

Filman is sitting. He's trying to think of what to do now.

A sane man would call the cops. But he's not calling them. Filman isn't sane.

That must mean that there's something up here. Something he doesn't want anybody to see.

Did I check the boxes as thoroughly as I should have? Is he embarrassed about all the Christmas tinsel? Did I overlook a box of XXL women's lingerie?

The only signs of murder I see up here is the dead rats slowly decaying. Nearly every glue trap found has a victim.

Nearly.

I did notice one empty glue trap, at the back end of the attic. It was the farthest away yet was the only trap that didn't have a permanent resident.

I slide my body toward the back wall. I don't make a sound but, unfortunately, the attic boards do. A loud *creak* fills the air.

Damn it. He knows I'm up here.

Okay. So what if he does? He's not about to call the cops, is he? We have a stalemate. I might as well use the opportunity to find out what his secret is.

I slide my body toward the back wall again, this time unconcerned by sound.

Footsteps below. He's following me.

Are you getting nervous? Afraid I'm going to find your secret?

I reach the far wall. At first inspection, it's just bare plywood, but then I notice scuff marks on the floor and the complete absence of dust near the middle section. I find a screw sticking out of the wood and pull it.

The hidden door panel begins to swing open.

BANG!

The attic is filled with a deafening echo.

Five inches from my face, there's an eruption of splinters from the floorboard.

Sergio has a gun.

My chest convulses, and I realize that I haven't breathed in a minute. I quietly allow myself to gasp for air. I can't make another sound.

My guess is that he's trying to decide if he hit me or not. He can't make up his mind if he should fire the gun again. The first shot woke the neighbors. The second will bring the cops. Maybe.

The second one could be the one that kills me.

It's like a deadly version of the game Battleship, but he's the only one that gets to shoot.

You know what? If he won't call the cops, I will. Or rather, I'll send a text message to Jillian telling her to call.

When I pull up iMessage, I realize I already have an unread message from her.

> I asked a friend at DoD to look into Filman. Wanted to tell you over the phone. They said there were several suspicious deaths in his military medical unit. They may be taking another look.

Now you're telling me? I type a message, trying not to drop my phone and get a bullet in my spine.

> Great. I'm trapped in his attic. He has a gun. Call cops to the following address saying you heard gunshots

She doesn't even send a response asking for more information. Jillian is smart enough to not hesitate.

Okay, I have a minute or so to hatch an escape plan. If Sergio hears sirens, his course of action might be to fire into the attic again, kill me, and then answer the door and talk his way out of it or fail to. It doesn't really matter at that point, BECAUSE I'D BE DEAD.

I need a smart strategy so I can survive his dumb strategy.

All right. I have a horrible plan.

Just in time. I hear sirens. So does he.

He must be trying to figure out if they're coming here.

Footsteps.

Now.

I kick a cardboard box filled with clothing onto the attic door. It begins to creak from the weight and starts to lower.

Bang! Bang! Bang!

As Sergio fires at the attic door and his heavy box of clothes, I push the box of textbooks across the floor with my feet.

The sirens are getting louder. He has to be panicked now. What if the cops want to have a look around?

More footsteps.

I kick at the box of books until it slides over the attic door and falls. Four years of nursing college education lands on his head.

"Fuck!"

There's the sound of a body hitting the floor and a clatter. The clatter of a gun on tile? No time to guess.

I jump into the breach and plummet like a cannonball. My feet hit the back of Sergio's shoulders, and his forehead smashes into the lowered steps, breaking one of them like a shopping-mall tae kwon do demonstration.

I fall backward and land on my ass in the most ungraceful position. It doesn't matter. I have to get up. Fortunately, Sergio's slower than I am to regain his footing. Before he can turn around, I throw an arm around his neck and choke him. Off guard, he can only flail his arms at me, but I tuck my head so he can't get at my eyes. Moments later, he passes out and goes slack as the blood to his brain is cut off.

The sirens are close now.

Where's the gun? Forget the gun. Find out what's in the attic.

I scramble back up the ladder, stepping on Filman, and scrabble toward the back of the crawl space. When I pry open the hidden panel, I'm completely confused.

Why would he shoot me over a bunch of boxes of stuffed animals and toys? Is he hiding the fact that he had a childhood? I reach into a box and pull out an old pair of dentures. Okay, a weird childhood. Why would a kid collect these things?

I put the glass holding the dentures back and pick up a blue elephant.

I've seen it before.

You idiot.

Of course you saw it before. It was in a photo of Cooper lying in his hospital bed.

Oh lord.

Filman does have mementos.

He does have trophies.

He steals from his victims.

Toys. Stuffed animals. An old man's glasses. The dentures.

There are boxes and boxes of these objects.

This is what he's hiding.

The sirens are deafening now.

I drag the boxes out of the hidden space, down the ladder—clocking Filman in the head again to keep him out of the action—and set them on the floor by the front door. I take a picture, then open the door.

I'm running out the back as the police pull up.

If they don't know what those objects are, they will soon enough. I'll make sure of it.

I'll make damn sure that nobody can ignore what Sergio Filman has done.

CHAPTER FORTY-SEVEN
TEAM PANDA

Jillian shakes me awake, which is a bit startling because I got only three hours of sleep after driving back from Baton Rouge. "I need to go feed the pandas," she says.

"Pandas? What are you feeding them?" The tiny part of my brain that's awake is trying to work out what she's telling me. Is Jillian going to the zoo?

"Cupcakes. Want to come?"

"They allow that?" I reply.

Jillian puts her face an inch in front of mine. "My baseball team. The one you and I sponsor through the bakery. It's Saturday." She's already dressed.

My mind is focused on her scent, so it takes me a moment to process what she's saying. "Oh, the team!"

I quickly put on my clothes and hop into her car. Up until now, my mind has been concerned with whether I did enough to separate myself from what happened at Sergio Filman's home.

After I had left the DA's office, I made a point to drive past the traffic cameras covering the roads to the interstate heading west. When

I circled back to Filman's girlfriend's house and then his, I tried to avoid all the traffic cameras I could.

This wasn't to give me an alibi—who knows how many private cameras caught sight of me?—it was to rule me out quickly in a brief investigation.

When I get that inevitable call from Baton Rouge police asking what I did after leaving the DA, and I tell them I drove home, they'll find confirming evidence when they check the cameras at the parking garage and will be able to follow my path out to the interstate.

If they dig more deeply, I'm sure they can find someplace where I slipped up. I didn't plan my infiltration as well as I should have. Hopefully they won't ask too many questions, now that they can legitimately focus on Filman and the items he stole from patients.

I check the Baton Rouge news on my phone and see an item about police answering a call concerning shots fired and a break-in at Filman's home. Well, that's a start. I find no mention of the boxes I placed by the door.

"So, care to tell me what happened last night?" asks Jillian.

She was already asleep when I got home. I'd texted her after I got away, assuring her I was okay and suggesting she get some shut-eye.

"Uh, sorry. I think we got him. I found a bunch of toys and things belonging to patients he killed."

"So that's why you were in his attic. Got it."

I can't tell if she's upset. She wanted me to go after Filman. What could be bothering her?

"You know, I don't tell you everything, because when I screw up, I don't want it affecting you," I explain.

She pulls into the parking lot for the bakery and turns to me. "How could it not affect me?"

"I mean jail and all that."

"Oh. Because having you in jail wouldn't affect me? Got it. What if you got killed in that attic? Would that not affect me?"

"That's not what I mean," I reply. "I just don't want you criminally involved. I have to resort to all kinds of . . . well, criminal behavior to catch these criminals."

She locks eyes with me. "You don't think I don't know that? Who pulled the trigger on Joe Vik?"

"I mean . . ."

"Theo, I know you have to do some illegal things to get these people. But that doesn't mean you have to be stupid about it. I could have been there. I could have been your lookout."

"I'm just trying to keep you out of all that."

"Out of that? Or out of that part of your life?"

"You're helping find N2," I tell her.

I'd given Jillian everything I'd found on the women in the photographs at the tavern in Saint Lucia. Yesterday, she'd reached out to any nurses she could find by those names with innocuous emails asking about working in the Caribbean. As far as I know, there hasn't been a response yet, but I shouldn't be surprised: it's been less than a day since they went out.

"I won't get a lot of satisfaction out of finding her if it means losing you," she replies.

There are times like this when I've realized there's only one appropriate answer, even if I disagree or feel it's more complicated. "You're right. I understand."

We go inside the bakery and start setting up for the ensuing raid of rabid pandas. Jillian hands me a list of cupcakes and a small tube of frosting. "Write the numbers of the players on the corresponding cupcakes. Think you can handle that?"

"I'll tell you my Erdős number if you tell me yours," I reply.

"I don't even know or care what that means."

Cars begin to pull into the parking lot, and tiny versions of people wearing black-and-white uniforms begin to invade the bakery. They look more like baby killer whales than pandas, but I keep my observation to myself. Jillian didn't like it when I complained about a Texas baseball team calling themselves Pandas. What was wrong with Rattlesnakes or Red Wolves? Heck, I'd even settle for Tigers. There were more of those in the state than pandas. Jillian told me I was a Neanderthal fixated on macho symbolism. I then had to remind her that her army unit's unofficial mascot was a Viking holding a bloody battle-ax. I know this because she wears that as a sleep shirt. Some nights, that image is the last thing I see before I go to sleep.

I start handing out cupcakes to nine-year-olds, some of whom I can only tell are there by the baseball caps and grimy hands rising above the counter. Jillian can see me twitching when a little girl reaches for a cookies-and-cream with fingernails that have bits of grass sticking out. Did she crawl her way to second base?

Jillian plants a bottle of hand sanitizer on the counter and says, "Robin, clean your hands first."

I don't comment on the fact that all that sanitizer will do is redistribute the bacteria and other pathogens more evenly across her hands. Not that sanitizer is useless—it's just not useful for that amount of dirt.

I hand numbers thirty-two and eleven their cupcakes and deal with a minor crisis when eighteen declares that strawberries are no longer her favorite, replacing hers with a chocolate mint.

My phone buzzes, and I retreat to the back of the bakery to take the call.

"This is Theo."

"Dr. Cray? It's Bailey from the Baton Rouge DA's office."

Here it comes. Get ready to speed-dial Donada. Although I'm almost more afraid of a scolding from her than what the DA's going to do to me.

"How may I help you?" I ask.

"This call didn't happen. Understand?"

"Okay . . ." Is she warning me?

"Police investigated a disturbance at Sergio Filman's house last night."

"Okay." I only answer because I'm afraid saying nothing would implicate me.

"He'd fired his gun multiple times but wouldn't explain why. The police found several boxes of toys and other items by the front door. Filman wouldn't say who they belonged to. They only issued a citation for the gun discharge but took the boxes. Right now, they're sitting in evidence, and we got a call from his attorney asking that we return them."

Filman panicked initially and was afraid to say they belonged to him. He probably now realizes that, regardless of who was in possession of the items, they have traces of him all over them.

"Okay," I say again.

"Right. So, here's my question. Capstone's told me to return them. Would it be worth my while to push back? Maybe even leak something to the boys over at the *Trumpet*?"

I wasn't expecting this. Still, I have to be careful. I could be walking into a trap. On the other hand, I think Bailey is a straight shooter. She wants to know if this is worth risking her career for.

"Do you have a photo of the items?" I ask.

"I'm actually looking at the boxes right now," she replies.

"Well, Cooper Hennison had a blue elephant in his hospital photos. The family never found it after he died."

There's a long silence. At first I think she's looking through the boxes; then I hear a sad gasp.

"Filman . . . that evil fucker. Capstone can go screw himself. We're going to nail this asshole. I'll make goddamn sure of it."

"Good," I reply. "There's just one other thing."

"What's that?"

"Filman wasn't the only one."

She lets out an exasperated groan. "You're killing me, Cray. One psychopath at a time. Is this other one still at Southern Star?"

"I don't think so."

"Baton Rouge?"

"Probably not even in Louisiana," I reply.

"Then *you* worry about that one for now. Let me nail Filman."

I glance out into the bakery and see kids sitting at stools, leaning on counters, and devouring their cupcakes. In my head I start multiplying the number of children until I get to how many teams' worth N2 has probably killed. At least ten. She kills a school bus full of children and adults every two years.

"This one's worse than Filman. Far worse."

I can tell she feels conflicted. "Let me know when you have something I can take action on. Right now, it's going to take everything I have to get Filman."

There's nothing else I can say. "You're right. I understand."

CHAPTER FORTY-EIGHT
GOOD TIMES

Sitting across the table from me in a Memphis Starbucks, Tanya Luger isn't as tan as she appeared in the photo I tore from the Crab's Nest wall, but she has the healthy glow of someone who takes care of herself. We're watching each other warily, and I'm fairly certain she's not N2 for two reasons. The first is that the Dark Pattern didn't follow her to Hillcrest Community Hospital. The second is that she agreed to meet without me giving her any false pretense.

That was Jillian's idea. She'd read Luger's Facebook page, followed her social media, and thought the woman came across as a considerate and deeply religious person whom I should approach directly.

This was a radical approach for me. I'd concocted all kinds of plans for hacking her phone and online accounts to try to get more information; instead, all it seemed to take was a politely worded email.

I begin with the basic questions. "Tell me about Stoneman."

She glances out the window into the parking lot and makes a small sigh. "They had sixty beds at that point, but they really weren't equipped for more than twenty patients. Tops. But the clinic was getting some kind of outside funding per head. They were patient stacking."

"Sixty," I reply. "It was mostly empty when I was there."

"Well, yeah. After . . . after things got bad, they started sending patients elsewhere."

"What do you mean, 'got bad'?"

"We started losing people that we shouldn't have been losing." She gestures out the window. "Patients that never would have died at Hillcrest or anywhere else, for that matter. At first you might attribute it to the limited resources in a place like Saint Lucia, or any other hospital in a poor country, but then you start to realize something's up. About a month before I arrived, they brought in Dr. Farnós."

"Farnós? Who is he?"

"Farnós wasn't there when you visited. Interesting." She smirks. "Farnós used to run hospitals in Cuba. He was the one that would go clean up clinics for visiting foreign politicians and news crews. He made sure that the hospitals looked good on camera, the medicine cabinets were full, that kind of thing. Anyway, he defected and started working with other hospitals that needed to clean up their act in a hurry. Stoneman needed that. The locals were starting to get suspicious."

"What was going on there?" I ask.

"Farnós took us each aside and confided in us that one of the local nurses may have been using poor sterilization procedures and that we might have had some kind of respiratory infection that could cause sudden heart failure. But he implored us to keep it quiet.

"I didn't say anything, because I knew that was baloney. Our local nurses were thorough. They didn't have as much training as some of us outsiders, but those ladies were more hygienic than some of my peers here. And when I asked for specifics on this so-called respiratory infection, he wouldn't provide any.

"I also heard that he told the local nurses that one of us was spreading the infection. He set us against each other. It didn't make sense until I realized that he had no idea what to tell anyone and was probably just trying to contain the problem."

"And what do you think the problem was?" I ask.

"There were over thirty people working there. Maybe we had a bad apple."

"Someone was killing patients?"

Her eyes go to her hands, which are twisting a napkin. "Yes."

"How?"

"Overdosing. Tainted blood. Poisoning. It didn't matter. There was no proper determination of cause of death in any case there. Generally, if the patient was being treated for something potentially fatal, then the cause of death would be attributed to that," she explains.

I decide to level with her. "I found World Health Organization surveys that appeared doctored. I looked for anomalies and used fraud-detection algorithms to find a pattern similar to other problem hospitals. I'm pretty sure there was someone killing patients there. Did you talk about this with any of the other nurses?"

"By the end we'd divided up into our own little cliques. Catherine—Catherine Ross—and I kept to ourselves. We shared shifts and just didn't spend much time with the others. So no, we didn't really talk about it much."

She's open enough that I feel I can ask her the key question. "Who do you think was doing it?"

"I don't know."

"You don't know? Or you won't say?"

Her eyes flare at me. "If I knew, I would have told someone."

"I'm sorry. But I have to ask."

She glances over her shoulder, then lowers her voice. "Can I tell you something?" She hesitates. "First, are you recording this?"

"No." I probably should be, but it would be a breach of the trust she put in me.

"You ever work in the medical field?"

"I was a paramedic for a while."

"You ever have a bad day? Ever have a bad week? You ever have a patient who is so difficult with you, that makes your life a living hell?

Imagine being a nurse and dealing with that person day in and day out. If you can tell me you'd never even fantasized about the possibility of just putting something in their IV drip or altering a prescription, you're a better person than I am. Now, I'd never, ever hurt someone. But there are times when a difficult patient is hollering for help and maybe you don't have as much spring in your step because an hour earlier they threw their food at you and called you a horrible name.

"Doing a slow walk isn't the same as killing someone. Sometimes it is, maybe. But at the end of the day it's all one slippery slope.

"So if you're asking me which one of my coworkers at Stoneman could have thought about committing murder? You can start with me."

Tanya Luger has eloquently described a feeling that I have to admit I understand all too well. Her remarkable empathy extends from her patients even to the people who may wish them harm.

But it doesn't help me.

"Who was closer to the edge than the others?" I ask. "Who do you suspect?"

"I'm not playing that game."

"Did you see anyone do anything suspicious?" I ask.

"You'll have to narrow it down. We all had the chance to do suspicious things."

"What about someone getting caught taking medications from supplies?"

She makes a small laugh. "How much do you know about Stoneman? Did you meet Mr. Junqué?"

"Yes. He shut me out."

"Did you know one of his law firm's biggest clients was accused of selling opioids in the Caribbean? Care to guess which hospital was ordering way more than its fair share?"

Oh man. Stoneman wasn't just a bad hospital—it was a criminal front like Southern Star. I hadn't even thought about that. Junqué wasn't only worried about me finding out about excess patient deaths, he was also afraid I'd uncover something about their illegal drug peddling.

I place the photo from the bar on the table. "Okay. Can you at least give me names and any contact information on the other nurses?"

"Sure. But I don't even follow half of them on Facebook."

"Would the others know them?"

"Maybe. Like I said before, we kind of had our own group. A few of them spent more time with nurses from the other hospital. But yes, I'll tell you what I know. I'll even give you all the photos I have, if it will help."

CHAPTER FORTY-NINE
ENDS THAT ARE DEAD

I'm sitting in front of my monster displays for Mycroft, wondering where the hell I went off the rails. I've got a clear-as-day pattern showing the dark wave at Woodland Lake, Stoneman, and several other hospitals, up until the wave ended fourteen months ago. That's where the data stops. That was when the CDC ended the surveys and data collection that made it possible for me to gather even this much information. I've been trying to figure out a way to get more current information, even including a massive hack, but there has to be a better approach. I kept hoping this problem would present a solution. But it hasn't. N2 still ends where the CDC data set stops.

Tanya Luger was extremely helpful. I've been able to get names and records on the other nurses in the photo. The problem is that none of them show up in any other hospitals in the Dark Pattern.

Either N2 isn't one of them or she went to Saint Lucia under a false name. If that's the case, I think I know the name she used: Grace Duset. After Saint Lucia, Ms. Duset vanishes.

She also vanished *before* Saint Lucia. Or, rather, she simply didn't exist. I don't think it would have been hard for N2 to use an alias or a slightly altered name to get work at Stoneman.

But that's what's driving me crazy. I was hoping that narrowing her down to one small hospital would give me everything I need. It hasn't.

It *has* given me a face. The problem with that is that it's a rather average face with large glasses that have Mycroft turning up thousands of false positives.

N2 doesn't Instagram, Facebook, or spend much time with anyone who does.

I know she has an average build. She's white or Hispanic and is probably in her late forties or early fifties—which narrows it down to about seven hundred thousand nurses in the United States.

When I called Tanya Luger and asked about Duset, I got the response I expected: "She was quiet and kept to herself."

I've asked Mycroft to create a much higher-resolution image of her face by taking all of the images and doing a 3-D map. That should give me enough features to make a positive ID if I see her in person.

I also have one other use for that composite: I could send it to my mysterious hacker pen pals who helped with the airliner crash. But they might well refuse. This isn't a national security issue.

I'm stuck staring at monitors trying to figure something out. Other than placing N2, aka Grace Duset, at Stoneman, I have no other witnesses.

I also sent the photo to families who lost a child at Woodland Lake, but nobody could remember any details about a woman that looked like that. My next step in that direction will be to email employees at the different hospitals where the Dark Pattern's present and hope somebody has something useful.

The problem with that will be all the false information it yields. What I need is to talk to someone who knew her other than Luger. Someone who was suspicious of her.

At the back of my mind, a little voice is whispering a name—someone who may have a crystal-clear idea of who N2 was and what she was up to, or at least a strong suspicion.

The problem is, that person is Sergio Filman.

If I call Ella Bailey and tell her I want to talk to Filman, she'll blow a gasket. Right now she's trying to build a case against him. The last thing she wants is another serial killer clouding the issue. If I tell Filman about N2, that's the same as giving his defense a viable suspect to deflect attention from him.

However, if Filman knows about N2, then I wouldn't really be *telling* him anything about her that he doesn't already know, would I?

It's a horrible choice. Do I try to access Filman and ask him about N2, possibly reminding him of a potential alibi? Or should I leave things be and wait for his defense team to throw that out there?

Ugh. N2 is out there. I have to stop her. If Bailey can't make a case against Filman with me asking a couple of questions, I'm the least of her problems.

I slide my burner phone off the desk and call Filman.

My mind was already made up when I programmed this phone to spoof the number for his attorneys, the Lowry and Summer law firm.

Serial killer–hunter tip: Want to make sure a suspect picks up your call? Make caller ID show it as coming from their lawyer.

"Filman," he says into the receiver. His voice is a little distant, like he's high. It could be painkillers from the injuries I inflicted.

I figure the best approach is to start with a question and skip the introduction. "We need to know something. Was there ever anyone suspicious at Southern Star either before or after you got back from overseas? A woman?"

"Suspicious? What do you mean?" he asks.

"Hold on. Let me send you a photo."

Serial killer–hunter tip number two: If you want your suspect to see a photo, but you don't want them to be able to use that photo later? Send it as an HTML-embedded image in an email with a spoofed address. Which is what I just did.

"Check your email. Did you get the photo?"

"One second. Oh shit. This cunt. Yeah. She was up in my shit like you wouldn't believe. I kept finding her watching me."

"And why was that?"

Filman wants to say because she suspected what he was up to. But he won't say this, because he and his attorneys are still pretending he's innocent. "I don't know. Maybe she had a thing for me."

"Okay. We need to track her down before they do. Anything else you can tell us about her? A name? Something unusual?"

"Uh, let me see. I talked to her once. What was her name . . . ? Cynthia? Cindy? Definitely one or the other."

I type the name into Mycroft and three hits: Cynthia Posset and Cynthia Bludge were both employed by Southern Star during that time. Cynthia Bludge's tenure came at exactly the right point. But I can't find a record of her at another hospital in the Dark Pattern.

"Anything else you remember about her? Did she have any friends?"

"Not that I know. We worked different floors. You know, actually, I think I saw her get into a car with another nurse once," he replies.

"From Southern Star?"

"Nah. I think she worked elsewhere. To be honest, I thought she might be a . . . um, lesbian. Some of the older single ones pair up like that. I mean no disrespect."

"Did you get that vibe?"

"I didn't get any vibe. She was just, I don't know. Quiet. Except when she talked to me. But she didn't really talk. Anyway, she was a weirdo. So, do we know what's happening? Are we getting the stuff from my house back?"

I should get off the phone now. But I can't.

"I don't handle that end. Between you and me, I'd call up the DA and make my own deal before I'd let Lowry and Summer screw me again."

"Wait? Who is this?"

Click.

Let him think that one over.

Meanwhile, he has me thinking. I realize that I overlooked something big back in Saint Lucia. I was literally standing on top of what might have cracked the whole thing open, but there's no way in hell I can know for sure unless I go back there—and that means putting myself in Mr. Junqué's crosshairs.

CHAPTER FIFTY
FULL BLOOM

I caught Joe Vik because of a quirk in the way he buried his victims. You could spot one of his graves by the topography he chose and the frequency of certain weeds and plants that were fighting over that particular location. I could walk into a wooded area and pinpoint within a foot any body he'd left there.

I noticed this because my area of expertise was modeling how different systems stake out and create their own ecosystems. I use the term *system* because sometimes it's a confluence of organisms working together—in their own interests—yet yielding a mutual benefit. The shape of a thing isn't always the thing.

Perhaps my most useful contribution to forensics has been the papers I've written on the subject. Yet, somewhere along the way, I seem to have ignored my own advice about stepping back and examining the entire system and looking for things that may seem irrelevant but are actually significant.

The moon is only a crescent, but there's enough light to see the knee-high gladiolus jutting out of the grassy berm behind the farthermost of Mr. Stevenson's rental cottages.

The property dead-ends on a rocky hill with a thin layer of grass and weeds clinging to the volcanic rock.

A few days ago, I looked right at this grass, these rocks, this berm, and even these gladiolus and barely paid them any attention. The biologist part of my mind was asleep. Had he been awake, he might have screamed for me to notice what's plainly obvious:

Something is buried here.

More precisely, something was buried here around the time that N2 vanished from Saint Lucia.

I'm reasonably certain it's not N2. Her dark pattern picked up a few weeks later. But the appearance of this suspicious mound during her stay here is too much to ignore.

When I called Luger, she confirmed what I already suspected: the woman known as Grace Duset lived in this cottage. Luger recalls her being alone, which raises the question: If I'm right about there being a body here, whose body is it?

Normally I'd call the local police and ask them to investigate the scene, or the FBI if there was an active task force, but since my last encounter with local law enforcement was at the direction of Mr. Junqué, I'm not terribly eager to contact them.

Calling Mr. Stevenson is out of the question. If there is a body here, I'm certain he'll make sure that it disappears before anyone else can see it.

I check the ground one last time and feel the stalks of the weeds that are trying to soak up the nutrients the gladiolus are laying claim to. Their texture is moist and waxy. When I bring some soil to my nostrils, I can smell a faint sweet smell. It's the smell of decay.

I place several vials of the dirt into my pocket. The soil atop this crime scene is a little like a box of baking soda in the refrigerator—it may only look like powder, but it actually contains a record of all the scents and free-floating molecules that it covered.

After I get my samples, I push my shovel into the dirt and start making a pile on the plastic sheet I've spread out on the grass. I take my time, not wanting to put the edge of the tool into the soft bridge of a decaying nose and collapse the skull, making facial reconstruction even more difficult.

I'm two feet down when I find a layer of black plastic garbage bags wrapped around something . . .

I've pulled too many corpses out of the ground to feel any kind of elation at this point. What I really want to know is who this body was.

Having found the body, it's time to use my glove-covered hands. I spread the dirt away from the plastic until it's outlined like a mummy in a dirt sarcophagus.

The plastic bags are fastened tightly with duct tape. So much so that I'm afraid to open them and expose the body to further decomposition.

This is the ethical dilemma: Do I take a peek? Or do I call the local authorities and run the risk of this vanishing?

Of course, I look. Even if the police are acting in good faith, the first thing they're going to do is open the plastic and expose the corpse anyway.

I use my knife to cut through the plastic and tape around the head. When I peel it open, the smell makes its way through the gap between my face mask and the bridge of my nose.

Before my eyes register what I'm looking at, my nose tells me that this smells about right for how long ago she was buried.

She.

There's still enough tissue below the skin to make out facial features. The blonde hair is down to her neck. I inspect it more closely and see gray roots. If I had to estimate, midforties.

I slice the rest of the bag open and find that she's only wearing a T-shirt and boxers—the kind you sleep in. The sealed bag has left the body remarkably well preserved.

I inspect the neck and find bruises.

Best guess: this woman was strangled in her sleep.

I inspect her arms for tattoos. She has one on her left shoulder: a dolphin-moon yin-yang.

Okay, but who is she?

I take a glove off and pull out my phone. Tanya Luger picks up after the third ring.

"Hello?"

"It's Theo Cray. Sorry to bother you. Did—" I almost say *N2*. "Did Grace Duset have a friend about her age? Blonde hair? Dolphin-moon tattoo on her shoulder?"

"Hmm. No. Actually, maybe she did. I mean, I saw the two of them together a few times. Sophie? I think that was her name."

"Was she a nurse, too?"

"I think so. She was one of the ones over at Providence Hospital on the other side of the island."

I send a text message to Mycroft. A second later, he replies with an answer.

"Does the name Sophie Dixon sound right?"

"Yes! Do you think she knows where Grace is?" asks Tanya.

"I doubt it. Did anyone else know Sophie?"

"I think we talked a couple of times at events and such. But nobody I can think of. I'm sure you can call Providence and track her down."

Tracking her down isn't the problem. I know exactly where Sophie Dixon is right now. I also know where someone going by that name showed up next: Mountain View Hospital in North Carolina.

That's the next place the Dark Pattern showed up after Saint Lucia.

N2 isn't forging documents or slightly altering her name. She's killing other nurses and assuming their identities.

She came to Saint Lucia as Grace Duset. She met another nurse named Sophie Dixon and profiled her. Probably because Dixon had no close relations, N2 assumed her identity and took whatever job was waiting for her next. Maybe she's even befriended her victims and convinced them to go to some new city and some other broken hospital.

This revelation excites me and frightens me. It means that when I trace N2 to Mountain View Hospital where she worked as Sophie Dixon, the trail will end.

Dixon isn't listed anywhere as a missing person. Nor will the next identity that N2 assumes. She finds lonely, single women with no family, becomes their friend, and then steals their identities so she can keep on going. And killing.

I thank Tanya, then call Jillian.

"I found a body."

"Of course you did. Are the police there?"

"No. It's tricky. They might not be happy."

"Then leave it and call them anonymously," she replies.

"They might make it vanish."

"I told you to take me with you," she replies.

"Somebody has to be able to post bail." I say it as a joke, then realize it's the truth.

"Okay, Theo. Let's try a different approach. How's your internet connection?"

By the time my latest YouTube video has finished uploading, the lights of the Royal Saint Lucia Police Force are visible at the bottom of the hill leading up to the cottages.

While posting a rather gory video of my discovery may prevent the body from vanishing, I'm not so sure what it will do for me. This island has a knack for making problems go away.

CHAPTER FIFTY-ONE
NORA: VISITING HOURS

The Night Lady keeps staring at me, Nora realized. Normally the woman only looked into her room for a moment before moving on.

Not tonight.

Why tonight?

Nora had her big surgery today. Her arms still felt like they're made of bricks, and her head was woozy. She tried to beg for her mommy to stay, but the words came out all mushy.

"We'll read a book tomorrow, baby," her mommy said before kissing her on the forehead and leaving.

Nora tried to say, "But the Night Lady!" Except it sounded more like, "Bum might maidey."

Mommy left, and then the nurses turned down the lights so the children could sleep.

Nora knew the Night Lady was coming. But it didn't seem fair that she'd go into her room tonight. That meant going to the place where you don't take your shoes.

The Night Lady lingered at the door, then took a step forward. Nora tried to turn her head, but she couldn't. She could barely open her eyes to see the Night Lady.

Does she know I'm awake?

The Night Lady leaned over and looked into Nora's face.

It was strange . . . even this close the Night Lady's face was blank and without expression. She didn't feel like a real person. It was like looking at someone's shadow.

"You're awake, aren't you?" said the Night Lady.

The voice was the whisper of a snake.

Nora tried to speak, but she couldn't. All she could do was whimper.

The Night Lady pressed her cold hand on Nora's stomach and let it rise and fall as Nora breathed. This brought the tiniest glimmer of satisfaction to her face.

"Don't worry, little one. It'll soon be over."

She smiled, but to Nora it was a wrong smile.

The Night Lady reached into her pocket and pulled out a syringe. Nora thought the smile on the woman's face was like looking at a shadow pretending to be a smile.

Nora tried to sit up. Tried to scream. But all she did was push aside her teddy bear and fall back down.

The woman placed her cold hand on her tummy and pressed her down. She put her nose right to Nora's. The wrong smile was gone. Everything was gone, her face blank again and without expression.

And then it happened.

CHAPTER FIFTY-TWO
DETAINED

My cell is slightly larger than the closet Jillian and I share back in Austin. I'm at the end of a corridor facing a concrete wall with suspicious stains. The bed is a thin mattress on a metal frame and my toilet has no privacy, but it's not all that bad.

At least I'm not in the cell next door, where three men are stacked up together. One or more of whom was displaced so that I could be in here alone. From the occasional taunts that come from that direction, they're not too happy about it.

I suspect that the police are worried about me getting hurt before they have a chance to figure out what to do with me. My neighbors have what sound like French accents, so perhaps they're from a neighboring island like Martinique. This might be the international wing of the police station.

I've been in custody for a total of eight hours. It's not my longest period of incarceration. In fact, up until Mr. Stevenson showed up at his cottage and started yelling at the police, I wasn't actually under arrest.

When the police seemed reluctant to arrest me, Stevenson made a call, presumably to Mr. Junqué, and I was shortly thereafter placed into handcuffs. They were so unsure what to do with me that an hour later

I was sitting handcuffed in front of the local police commander with at least three lockpicks on my body, two hidden knives, and an even better-hidden, hard-to-find tool of my own design that I'm now in the habit of carrying with me everywhere.

Captain Lowther was an excellent listener and only had a few questions for me. One of his sergeants made notes as I spoke, and the entire conversation ended within a half hour.

I was then taken to this cell, where I still have all of the tools and weapons I started with. However, if I'm sent to the Bordelais Correctional Facility on the other side of the island, I'm pretty sure they'll be a little more thorough.

While I should be concerned that they never let me make a phone call or speak to an attorney, I'm more preoccupied with the fact that N2 may have gotten away. Finding Dixon's body has chilled me to the core. Normally finding a body is an instructive step, but here it's the opposite. I already knew who the killer was. The cause of death was almost irrelevant. Discovering the grave only confirmed my fear that capturing N2 could be next to impossible.

My bumbling actions have now made it that much harder. What I hadn't even considered until I sat down in here with a moment to reflect is that by calling attention to Filman, N2, an alumna of Southern Star, would be on alert that the phrase *serial-killer nurse* is being bandied about in a place of her previous employment.

While she may feel reasonably secure in her latest job due to her identity-switching trick, posting a video of myself finding a corpse at the cottage she stayed at in Saint Lucia will likely send her running.

I screwed up. Technically, it was Jillian's idea, but I acted on it. I didn't think it through.

Up until now, I'd been hoping that some kind of data search would show me where she's working, but all she needs to do is go somewhere else and take a murder break for a while.

If she can.

I've been contemplating what goes on inside her head, which is better than thinking about what goes on inside mine. She kills with such regularity that it's like a mission for her.

Filman was bad, but he was more like someone with a compulsion let loose in a place where nobody was watching. If he'd been at a hospital that was properly run, I don't think he would have killed nearly as many. N2 would simply seek out better killing grounds.

In biology, there's an idea known as Foster's rule, informally known as the island effect. Basically it states that when a species is trapped on an island, it either gets smaller or larger depending upon available food or predators.

Mammoths isolated by rising sea levels in what are now the Channel Islands off the coast of California adapted into a species of pygmy mammoths 10 percent of the size of their ancestors when grasslands were gradually reduced. This would be like adult humans adapting into a form the size of kindergartners—which is something that actually happened on Flores Island.

Other animals get larger, like the giant lizards that evolved on Flores when there were no predators to keep their sizes small.

When N2 was introduced to the island of Saint Lucia, she could have scaled down her kill rate; instead she continued like a rapacious predator. And this is what caused problems. Her killing was too much for Stoneman or the island to absorb. It was noticed. The hospital operators reacted by bringing in someone to fix the problem, and whether or not they knew who was directly responsible, when the current group of foreign nurses left, so did the problem. But so much damage was done to the reputational ecosystem, the hospital's still trying to recover.

This is why I believe that N2 can't stop herself. She had to have foreseen what would happen at Stoneman, but she kept going. And while she might adapt and change her tactics once she realizes I'm on to her, I don't think the killing will stop. She'll find new victims, and they'll be lost in the noise of the thousands of unsolved murders that happen every year.

I'm beginning to think Mycroft isn't enough. My pattern-matching software can only take me so far. Ultimately, I face the problem every data scientist deals with—too much noise, not enough data to find a signal.

MAAT, Predox, and Mycroft are incremental improvements on a way of thinking. What I need is a new way of thinking. That's why I've been toying with Moriarty—an artificial intelligence that thinks like a killer. Moriarty would see things from the inside out—not just uncover patterns, but invent new ones.

Footsteps approach, and a police officer arrives at my cell door. "Your lawyer is here."

He has me stick my hands between the bars to be cuffed, then escorts me to a small room at the other side of the jail. I keep asking myself, how did Jillian get me an attorney so quickly? And how the hell did he find me?

CHAPTER FIFTY-THREE
Exchange

When I'm brought into the conference room, my questions are quickly answered. My "attorney" is one Mr. Junqué. Well, this will be curious. I'm pretty sure he doesn't have my best interests in mind.

"Dr. Cray, you are a pain in the ass," he says as I sit down.

"I'd say that's a fair assessment."

"You're a problem that I wanted to go away, and now here you are, with a dead body, no less."

"I'm sure even the local forensics expert will tell you she died long before I got here," I reply.

"No doubt. I read your statement. You didn't hold anything back. Of course, you admitted to trespassing. Also, arguably, you were tampering with a crime scene. There's also interfering with a dead body. All of these are serious crimes," he explains.

"I don't doubt any of that."

"Yet you stood around and let them arrest you, as if you were somehow invulnerable. This part I don't understand. Are you under the illusion that they're going to just let you walk out of here?"

"It seems like the prudent decision," I reply.

"Because you think the people of Saint Lucia are afraid to arrest an American? Maybe you should take a look at some of the people in our jails. Maybe you should also take a look at relations between our two countries in the last few years. We've been accused of being lawless. What could be more law-and-order than giving you due process?"

That's an alternative I hadn't considered. Saint Lucian authorities could charge me with those crimes and hold me for a very long time before I go to trial.

Mr. Junqué's presence tells me that's not what he wants. What's his angle? What *does* he want?

He wants to protect his criminal interests.

What's the biggest threat to them?

I don't know anything, so it can't be me . . .

But he doesn't know that. I showed up asking suspicious questions. A week later I come back and pull a dead body out of the ground. He's terrified that it might connect to their little pill clinic, or god knows what else they're up to.

The door opens behind me, and a man I think is one of the guards from earlier enters and stands in the corner. He's wearing a T-shirt and dark pants—no uniform. He's also extremely well built.

So, this is how it's going to go down. Junqué gets him to rough me up to see what I know. If the bruising is too bad, they'll keep me long enough to heal or I'll have a permanent accident.

If Jillian or anyone makes a fuss, the response will be that I'm being held until trial. I could tell the first person I can that I've been treated unfairly, but that would probably only bring on a beatdown from a cellmate.

So, what do I do? Let Mr. Junqué have his friend kick the shit out of me until he's satisfied I've told them everything?

Do I think of something really clever to say?

Do I wait for him to throw a punch and then fight back?

Why let him have the advantage?

Both of these men think I've been searched. I've been cornered too many times to let that go to waste.

"Why are you here, Dr. Cray? Who are you working with?"

I visualize the distance between myself and the man behind me. I wait for the creaking sound of his leather boot taking a step.

I jump up and kick my chair backward into his knees.

The man lets out a groan.

I reach forward and grab the handle of Junqué's metal briefcase and swing it around and into the side of the guard's head. There's a loud crack as the case slams into his skull and sends him flying. The man bounces into the wall and crumples to the floor.

Junqué just sits there, unsure how to react. His right hand is flat on the table, like he was going to reach for something. I look over on the floor and see a gun sticking out from inside his broken briefcase.

I lunge for it before he can get around the table.

"Back in your chair," I say softly as I point the gun in his direction.

Once he's sitting, I pop the magazine out, spill the bullets onto the floor, and take the gun apart, tossing the pieces onto the ground.

Mr. Junqué can't make heads or tails of what I'm doing. Me, either. I'm kind of in improv mode. If only the Austin school had taught me to do interrogation scenes.

I nod to the gun parts on the floor. "I could still kill you."

For all I know, Junqué could be some kind of specially trained commando, but I utter the words with such certainty, there's not much point in a debate.

Junqué stares at his unconscious goon, then back at me. "What do you want?"

"I just want to go home. At this point I don't even care about the body. I'd like to see that her next of kin is notified. Other than that,

I don't care." I nod to the unconscious man on the floor. "He was unnecessary. If I want to, I could sever an artery so deep inside your rib cage the only way to keep it from bleeding out between here and the hospital would be for me to use my own fingers to clamp it shut. If I wanted to escape, I'd simply jump out of the ambulance on the way. I'd be free and you'd be dead. But that's not what I want. And I'm certain you don't want that, either.

"Instead, let's just walk out of here together. I get my things. I check out of my hotel and I go to the airport. And if one of your other friends on the police force tries to stop me like last time, keep in mind that making me disappear is only going to bring more outsiders and more questions."

He weighs this for a moment. "There's still the trespassing and interfering-with-a-crime-scene charges."

"That's why I have a good lawyer." I extend my hand.

Junqué hesitates. He's trying to measure me and decide what the best course of action is. "Okay, Dr. Cray. As your attorney, I think I can get them to drop all charges on the condition you never come back."

We shake hands, each of us wondering if this is really the last of the matter. It would be stupid for him to try to threaten me or make me vanish, but if there were no stupidity in the world, we'd all be riding around in flying cars and colonizing Proxima Centauri.

I collect my phone and backpack from the officer at the front desk, take a seat on a bench outside the police station, and check my messages.

Jillian's last message was to tell me that she was on the way to the airport. I try reaching her but get voice mail. I text her back to let her know everything is fine.

I scan through my texts and see one from an unknown sender. I almost ignore it, thinking that it's spam. I check the text body itself, and my brain skips a beat when I process the message.

MCRFT: UNSUB_1 spotted at 39°57'13"N 75°10'33"W @ 02:22
AM EST

The message is from Mycroft. He's telling me he found something.
He thinks he's found N2.

I catch the first cab I see and tell the driver to get me to the airport
as fast as he can.

CHAPTER FIFTY-FOUR
BEAR_GROWL()

Hailey is standing by the visitor's entrance to Mercy Hospital just under the awning and out of the pouring rain. Her flight must have arrived shortly before my connection landed. She's every bit as tall as I remember, and just as youthful—but the look on her face is quite mature.

"What's going on, Theo?"

We'd only exchanged a few text messages back and forth since I left the Saint Lucia police station. I'd told her I was heading to Philadelphia, but I didn't say where. She probably figured out the rest for herself.

I hand her a lanyard with a badge showing her face and a bar code. She glances at it and realizes that it's a forged hospital ID. I made it with a portable printer I bought at the airport.

"Follow me," I reply, holding open the door.

She takes the opposite one and glares at me. "What did you do?"

"I'll explain." I go up to the security guard at the desk. "Is there a head nursing station?"

He points down a hallway. I walk briskly in that direction, but not too fast that he stops us.

Over my shoulder, I explain to Hailey, "I tried calling the hospital, but I couldn't get through to anybody who could tell me anything. I just hope . . ." A senior-looking nurse is walking toward us. I pull out my phone and show her a photo on it. "Excuse me, could you help us out? We're trying to find this nurse. Have you seen her?"

"I think I've seen her on the third floor. What's this about?" she asks.

"I don't know," I reply, then make for the elevators.

I press the button, but nothing happens. Hailey presses another button and points to the "Out of Order" sign on the elevator I'm still standing in front of. I haven't slept since . . . the last time I slept.

"My code, Theo. What did you do?" she asks as we step inside.

"I couldn't tell you," I reply.

"Because you were breaking half a dozen privacy laws? Because it's creepy?"

"It's not. I covered my tracks."

"I found you. I literally found you here," she explains.

"I wasn't trying to hide from you . . ."

The doors open, and I jog to the nearest nursing station. "Have you seen this nurse?"

The woman behind the counter examines the image, then Hailey's and mine. "What's this about?"

"If you know who she is, we need you to call security," I reply.

"She definitely works here. I've seen her on the sixth sometimes."

"Sixth?" I turn around, and Hailey's already at the elevator. She's looking at the plastic signs that denote each department.

"Oh no," she says when she reads the one for the sixth floor.

PEDIATRICS

"Theo," she murmurs.

We take the elevator up three floors. The doors open, and I trip over a teenager in a wheelchair waiting to enter. Hailey picks me up as the orderly yells at me to watch where I'm going.

We ignore him and head to the nurses' station. An older woman is on the phone behind a computer. I shove my phone with N2's photo in her face.

"Where is she?"

The woman is about to snap at me for interrupting; then she sees the image. Her demeanor changes in an instant. "I'll call you back," she says, hanging up. "We haven't seen her since last night."

Her gaze drifts down the hall to an open door and an empty bed. I walk toward the door, my stomach sinking.

"What happened last night?" Hailey asks.

My lungs feel like they're trying to breathe water. Each step's heavier than the last. I try to remember all the alterations I made to the code.

Jillian and Hailey's teddy bears seemed like too good an idea to pass up. When I looked at the code, I realized there was already an image recognizer built in. All I had to do was add the ability to secretly upload other images.

Every time the bear connected to a Wi-Fi network, it would ping one of my servers, which would then upload an image of someone I was looking for to the bear. If that person had been seen by the bear, its little onboard computer would ping another server with a URL containing the location of the bear based upon known Wi-Fi networks.

Last night, a teddy bear in this hospital saw N2. It told Mycroft. Mycroft alerted me.

But that wasn't the most controversial part of what I added to the code.

As I near the room, I mentally review the code I added to the bear. I did it late at night and remember being reasonably positive that I would get an alert if the image recognizer had 99.7 percent certainty. I remember testing the system against a database of images in Mycroft. It was really, really good.

```
def bear_alarm(image_file):

    for image in uploaded_unsubs:

        if recognizer(image_file) > 99.7:

            message = beargGPS(image.id)

            p r o t e c t _ s u m m e r .
            mycroftMessage(message)

            #bear_growl()

        bear_alarm(image_file)
```

How certain was I? Did I comment out the last string of code or let it run? Despite my confidence in the image recognizer, a false positive posed a huge risk.

I wrestled with what would happen if the bear thought it saw N2 and made a mistake. It could jeopardize Jillian and Hailey's entire project. The damage I could do to Hailey's company could bankrupt it.

But if I *didn't* let the code run . . . the damage could be immediate. It could be personal.

I reach the doorway and stare at the empty bed. The little bear was in here last night. The bear saw N2.

And now . . .

A child's giggle startles me. I look to the other side of the room and see a girl with an IV drip sitting in her mother's lap on a couch as they read a book.

Mr. Bear is sitting in the girl's lap, and she's pointing out words to the bear, teaching him to read.

"Oh, hello," says the mother, realizing that I'm watching.

"Sorry to bother you."

"Do you work here?" she asks.

"We made that bear," says Hailey, pointing to Mr. Bear.

Mom's eyes light up. "It's wonderful. You get so worried when you have to leave your child alone." She taps her phone. "It's nice to be able to keep an eye out for her. Not that I don't trust them here."

I'm about to explain to the mother why she shouldn't, but her child realizes what we're talking about and speaks up. "You made Robert?"

"Yes," replies Hailey.

"He growled at the lady last night. And she ran away."

"What lady?" asks the mother.

"The Night Lady. The one I keep telling you about. She was in my room last night next to my ivy. That's when Robert growled. Real loud. So loud the nurses came."

I can see the color draining from Hailey's face. In a barely audible voice, she whispers to me, "I understand now."

"Why did you name your bear Robert?" asks Hailey.

"I named him for the boy next door. The Night Lady used to visit his room, and then he went away."

The tears in the corner of the mother's eyes tell me what "went away" means. I'm fairly certain the girl knows, too.

Hailey pulls away from the doorway and leans against the wall, out of sight from the mother and daughter. She's experiencing everything I've been feeling more than a year, but in a matter of seconds—fear, elation, and then the painful realization that you didn't do enough.

I'm dealing with the turmoil of emotions over the choice I made. That tiny little line of code is why the girl's alive right now. It's also why I may never catch N2.

The message Robert sent to N2 was unmistakable. The moment the bear's software recognized her face, he let out a loud growl and yelled in a gruff voice . . . *my* voice, "YOU'VE BEEN RECOGNIZED. STAY AWAY FROM THIS CHILD!"

And so she ran.

CHAPTER FIFTY-FIVE
CITIZEN RESPONSE

Detective Sherman is talking to the head nurse for the floor in an exam room down the hall from the pediatric ward. He's an older man with curly, silver-tinged black hair and a careful, calm demeanor. He would have been a great doctor. When I explained to him that I came here because I was investigating the high death rate and staff recognized the photo of N2, he didn't treat me like a crackpot—at least not to my face. He has an almost fatherly quality that makes you want to tell him everything. Hailey and I avoid that.

He's letting us listen in as he talks to a nurse named Lydia Cebrià while another detective is interviewing two hospital administrators in another room. From what I gather, they're trying to track down N2, aka Miranda Parley, the identity she used here.

"How many times did you see her on this floor?" asks Sherman.

"Once or twice," Cebrià replies.

"During the whole time she was here?"

"No. Maybe more than that. She was always going from one place to the other."

"Did you ever see her go into the rooms in the pediatric ward?" he asks.

"Probably." The woman is clearly stressed out by the questioning. Nobody has explicitly said what's going on, but they all suspect. The pediatric ward alone has lost four children in the last two months to similar conditions. Another detective is pulling all the records for patients who died, trying to make an official assessment.

"But she doesn't work on this floor?"

"No. But it's not unusual for us to fill in for others. We do it all the time."

"So, somebody assigned to work with old people could come up here and just walk into a child's room and nobody would say anything?"

"As long as they're a nurse."

Sherman points at me. "So, if this man was in a nurse's outfit, he could just walk into any room?"

"No. No. We'd recognize that he didn't work here."

"How many nurses work here?"

"Three hundred, I think."

"And you know all their faces?" he asks.

"No. I mean, you become familiar with them."

I turn to Hailey. "Let's go."

"Where?" she asks.

"We need to find her. While they're talking to the clueless here, N2's out there. She's getting away."

Hailey tilts her head at the detective talking to the administrators. "They're trying to track her down."

"Yes, and she's way ahead of them."

"I overheard one of the nurses telling a detective they dropped her off once at some place called Valley Avenue." She thinks something over. "Damn it. I should have put a logger in the bear to track all the nearby Wi-Fi networks. We could have got a MAC address for her phone and used that to pinpoint her."

"She's probably long gone. Not every answer is technology."

I pull up a map of Philadelphia and find North Valley Avenue. There're at least a hundred houses in that area before it turns into commercial property. Two people going door-to-door . . . we could canvass that in a few hours.

Hailey sees my phone and starts typing away on hers. "Never say never."

"What are you doing?"

"I'm hiring some Wombats to go door-to-door and conduct a survey," she answers without looking up from her keyboard.

"Wombats?"

"Work Wombats? Kind of like TaskRabbit? On-demand workers. College students. Bored people looking to make extra money."

"You realize that you're asking them to potentially knock on the door of the most prolific serial killer I've ever encountered," I reply.

"Oh shit. I didn't think about that. Should I cancel it?"

"Let's hold off for now. Did you rent a car?"

"Yeah, it's in the parking garage."

"Let's try it on foot and then bring in the Wombats. Okay?"

We leave without asking for permission. Sherman's careful approach is too slow for what the situation calls for. If he wants to talk to us, we're not hard to find.

Hailey keeps tapping away on her phone as we get into the elevator. I glance at the screen to make sure she's not about to send out her gig-economy army. She catches me watching.

"Don't worry. I get it. I get it. Man, do I get it." She snaps her fingers. "When I saw that little girl, I understood the choices you face. Where do you stop, right? What are the limits?"

We exit the elevator and take the walkway to the parking garage. Hailey is still tapping away on her phone. I catch a glimpse of Google Street View. She's looking at North Valley Avenue, scrolling house by house.

"I doubt you'll see her standing there," I say.

"I know. I know." She looks up and realizes we're in the garage. "Crap. What did I rent?" She pulls out a key fob, and we hear a distant beep from a floor above.

"That way."

She hands me her phone when she gets into the driver's seat. "Is there any other clue you could find looking at the street?"

"It's not that easy. It won't be her house. It's probably some other nurse that she befriended and lived with so she could assume her iden-tity. There won't be anything relating to N2 herself, here. It'll just be—hold on." I zoom in to an image of a car. The license plate is blurred out, but the windshield isn't.

"What is it?" Hailey asks.

"Eight oh one North Valley Avenue."

Hailey's already racing down the ramp toward the exit. "What did you see?"

"A parking sticker for Riverside Hospital."

"Another nurse," says Hailey.

"Possibly another nurse."

By the time we get to the house, I've already pulled up the property records. The rain-soaked two-story brick house belongs to an Audrey Mavis. When I called Riverside Hospital, they told me that Audrey hasn't shown up for work yet.

Hailey comes to a stop in front of the house. The car in Street View isn't out front, but a "For Sale" sign stands in the front yard.

This is something I hadn't thought about. N2's MO might be to convince her friends to sell their assets before she kills them. She might have amassed a nice little fortune doing that.

The "For Sale" sign also means we probably caught her before she was ready to run. The implication of this sinks in, and I burst out of the car and run to the front door.

Hailey catches up with me as I'm pounding on it. "Ms. Mavis? Ms. Mavis?"

No answer.

"What do we do now? Call the cops?" asks Hailey, glancing at the street.

"Fine by me. But I know what I'm going to do." I step back and kick the door right above the doorknob. The frame snaps, and the door swings inward.

"Okay, there's that approach," says Hailey.

I burst inside and immediately smell smoke from the fireplace. "Put that out!"

As she races to the kitchen, I start running through the house, looking for Ms. Mavis. "Audrey? Audrey?"

I check every room, the closets, under the bed, and even peek inside the attic. There's no sign of her. But in one of the bedrooms, I see clothes all over the floor and open dresser drawers. It looks like someone packed in a hurry.

"I checked the garage," says Hailey. "No car."

"Okay. We need to tell the police that. But I'm sure she's switched plates by now."

"Why? There's nothing to connect her to here, is there?"

"Audrey Mavis?" I go back downstairs and into the backyard. It's all green grass—no suspicious mound.

"Hey, Theo," says Hailey from inside.

I leave the rain and enter. She's sitting by the fireplace looking at the ashes. In the middle there's a piece of melted plastic and a sparking battery.

"Cell phone?" I ask.

"Yep." She points to several small round metal disks. "But what are those?"

I get a closer look. "Magnets."

"Magnets?"

I put on my rubber gloves. "Refrigerator magnets. The kind you use to stick photos to the door."

I push the ashes around and see the edges of burned photographs. "Can you take pictures of those? The cops will definitely want them, but I don't want to lose them." I get up and walk to the sliding glass door.

"What are you doing?" asks Hailey.

I stand in the middle of the lawn and inspect the tiny backyard. I hope not finding Audrey Mavis means she's out running errands. But I'm afraid the "For Sale" sign out front portends an outcome that I'd rather not accept.

My little bear code not only allowed N2 to escape—it led to the death of Audrey Mavis. Although no body means that may not be the case.

I turn around and examine the exterior of the house. A tiny plastic storage shed stands to the left, but its door is ajar and I can see there's no body inside. All the tools are pushed to the side as well.

I get a closer look to make sure that there's no body under the rakes and shovels. Nope. But why are the tools piled up on one end? Did she store something here that she took with her? A go bag?

You idiot. All the tools are pushed to one side because that's where they fell when she pushed the flimsy shed on its side . . .

I reach down and pull on one of the planks the shed is resting on. It doesn't take any more force than Jillian or Hailey would be capable of to lift it away . . . and reveal the hole dug underneath and the naked body of Audrey Mavis.

CHAPTER FIFTY-SIX
CURBED

The rain has soaked all the way through my blazer, and my skin is beginning to feel the pinpricks of the freezing wind. From the curb outside Audrey Mavis's house, I watch as the blue police lights bounce off puddles and windows around the neighborhood, announcing something bad has happened here.

I happened.

Up until now, my worst fear was that the Hyde virus would go active in my body and I'd wake up a murderer. Guess what? It didn't take an engineered version of rabies to do that. I did it all on my own.

Hailey is walking up to me. I can already play out both sides of one hypothetical conversation. Me: "I killed her." Hailey: "You saved that little girl." Me: "We don't know that N2 was going to kill her then." Hailey: "You didn't. But you chose to protect that girl."

She sits down next to me. "It's raining, Theo."

"Yeah." I look up at the sky and get splashed by drops the size of my thumb.

"It's a screwed-up choice," she replies.

"Yep. I'd kind of buried the memory of the first two people I got killed. They were a couple of meth heads who tried to roll me. I convinced them to help me find the body of a friend of theirs instead. That was the last I saw of them."

"Joe Vik?" asks Hailey.

"Yep. Joe Vik." A police forensics van pulls up, and two people get out. "You try to tell yourself there was nothing you could do. They were doomed to begin with. Then you start to realize the corners you cut, the mistakes you made, and all the times you put other people in danger. Everybody who died the night Joe Vik went berserk died because I lit the fuse. I don't know what else I could have done. Same with Audrey Mavis. It was a fucked-up choice. But a choice, nonetheless."

"You saved that—"

"Little girl," I reply.

"Yeah." She wraps her arms around her knees. "I guess you've had all sides of that conversation in your head."

"N2 . . ."

"I hate that name," says Hailey. "It makes her sound like a math problem."

"Well, I don't have a name, and she is kind of a math problem."

"How about That Bitch?" she replies.

"She's going to kill again and again. They're not going to find her."

"They have her face. They'll probably get some forensics. She'll make the most-wanted list. Hospitals will be alerted."

"Maybe. But she's smart. She's anonymous. And she's been expecting this. That's the problem. She can change her hair color, get a new nose, and she'll be somebody else."

"Are you going to answer that?" asks Hailey.

I realize she's talking about my buzzing phone. It's Jillian. We haven't talked since I was in Saint Lucia. Which was technically yesterday, but it feels like ancient history.

"Hey," I say into the phone.

"She's gone."

"I know."

"I'm sorry, Theo. I know she meant a lot to you," says Jillian.

My brain tries to connect what she just said. "Hold on."

I wipe the water off my screen as I try to do a search. For some reason, I don't want Jillian to say the words. It's a magical belief. If she doesn't speak her name and Google doesn't show the result I don't want to see, it never happened. She's still alive. She's still back on her ranch, looking up at the stars with Orion at her feet.

But she's not.

She's dead.

Amanda Paulson died yesterday.

She's gone.

"You okay?" asks Hailey.

I hand my phone to her. Not for any good reason . . . I just don't want to deal with the world right now. "Tell Jillian I'll call her back. I need to go for a walk."

I get up and walk and don't stop.

The Dark Pattern is out there, somewhere, and I'm afraid that I've just realized the only way I'm going to catch her.

CHAPTER FIFTY-SEVEN
DETROIT: THREE WEEKS

A nurse steps through the back door and lights up a cigarette. She talks to the orderly, who's smoking a vape pen, and they exchange a small laugh. I make my way toward them, head down, pretending that I belong here.

"Can we help you?" asks the nurse, acting territorially about their smoking spot.

I pull the flyer from my pocket. It's a better image of N2 than the one the FBI is using. "I was wondering if you'd seen this woman."

"Oh, you're that guy," she replies.

That guy . . .

This is my new name, because she's seen me here before, handing out the same flyer.

The orderly takes one from me. "I saw this in the break room. They pay you to hand them out?"

"No. I'm Theo Cray. I'm trying to find her."

"Uh, good luck, Theo," he replies with a smirk.

"She's killed at least 172 people. Is that funny to you?"

He wads up the flyer and drops it to the ground. "I heard about this. But they don't have any proof, do they? You're just some guy out there saying she did it."

"Would you like to see a picture of a body?" I reach for my phone. "Her name is Audrey Mavis. I found her under a shed in her own backyard. Her best friend was this woman. Until she killed her."

The orderly backs away. "Easy, man."

I put my phone back and take another flyer from my pocket. "Remember this face. Maybe she doesn't work here, but she might be friends with somebody who does."

"Okay, Theo. I think it's time for you to leave," says the nurse.

I turn around and head back toward my car. The evening shift is starting at Township Community Hospital on the other side of town. These are the two worst hospitals in the city. They're exactly the kind of place where N2 would work.

But I thought the same about Raleigh, Syracuse, Richmond, and Baltimore. She wasn't there.

I know she's working somewhere, because she has to kill. The same day she killed Audrey Mavis, a woman matching N2's description was seen at a gas station near Youngstown, where authorities subsequently found Mavis's car. Two days later, a road crew found the body of a college student in a ditch near Interstate 77. That same day, they found the student's car in Charlottesville. The last place she was seen alive was at the same gas station where N2 was spotted.

The girl's body had more than a hundred puncture wounds. N2 only needed her car, but her rage had to have an outlet.

When I found out what happened, I sent Jillian a long email and checked out of my hotel in Pittsburgh. I left everything behind.

The data I collected can't show me what I need. I can't see into the shadows. That's where she lives. That's where I have to be.

I pull up to the backstreet behind Township Community Hospital. There's a line of tents and cardboard boxes against the fence. This is where skid row starts. Homeless people are sitting in broken chairs and on the curb, carrying on whatever conversations they have out here at this time of night.

This hospital is on my new list. The last one was a prediction made by Mycroft based upon the kinds of hospitals N2 liked best. This one was made in a public library when I did a nationwide search for hospitals that were hiring immediately and offered markedly low pay compared to others in the area.

My theory is that a hospital in financial difficulty might look the other way if an applicant's staffing licenses aren't completely up to date.

I turn the corner and park in a fire zone near where employees get picked up by friends. Cars pull up and people hop out. Sometimes they're Ubers; other times they're personal cars driven by spouses. I look for anyone that could be N2.

I've already asked several people who work at the hospital if they'd seen her. They all unequivocally said no. But most of them didn't even look at the flyer. This is the kind of place that will hire you if you have a criminal record. They're that desperate.

My phone buzzes. Jillian, texting me.

She does the same thing around this time every night.

A week ago, the message was Please call me.

Now it's Come home.

I can't.

I've tried talking to her. Every phone call ends in tears. Hers and mine.

N2 has killed two people since Philadelphia that I know of for certain. I hoped those would be the last, but at this point I can reasonably expect her to have found a new job.

She's either using her old identity or a new one—possibly borrowed from a living nurse. That's until she decides it's time to move again. I have a feeling she won't wait long.

The cars stop coming as the shift begins. I have one more hospital to stake out before it's time to move on.

CHAPTER FIFTY-EIGHT
Madison: Six Weeks

My car wouldn't start this morning. I think the cold snap froze the fuel line. It was a bad one. I left the window cracked and woke up shivering even though my sleeping bag is filled with down.

I've got five hospitals and a nursing home to check out before I move to the next city, but I have to think about what I'm going to do about the car.

I transferred everything I owned to Jillian weeks ago. When she told me that process servers were stopping by the house with subpoenas on an almost daily basis, there was not much else I could do.

I can't have any contact with her until I find N2.

I have about fourteen thousand dollars in cash cards. I keep some hidden in the car, the others in a waist wallet.

I can afford to fix the car, but it won't be cheap.

I get out and walk to the nearest clinic on the list. Businesspeople move out of the way when they see me, afraid I'm going to ask them for money or harass them on their way to work.

Healing Hands Hospital has one hundred beds and takes more Medicaid patients than insured. Two weeks before N2 fled Philly, there was a big write-up about the hospital failing state inspections.

At first, I thought this would be an unlikely destination for her, given all the attention, but the hospital fails those inspections almost every other year.

I walk up to the security guard standing at the door and hand him a flyer. "Have you seen her?"

He looks at me funny. "Have you seen yourself?"

I catch a glimpse in the glass door behind him. The face that looks back isn't mine. I haven't shaved in . . . one week? Two? I'm a little thinner, but the dark circles make it worse. My overcoat is a bit scruffy, but I bought it for warmth, not looks.

"She's a killer," I explain.

"So's your breath."

Shit. I forgot to use mouthwash this morning.

"Sorry. Sorry." I back away. "Please contact that number if you see her."

I move on to the next hospital.

The bad news is, there are more than six thousand of them in the United States. The good news is that only three thousand of them are below average.

I giggle at my dumb joke and watch my laughter turn into a cloud of ice.

CHAPTER FIFTY-NINE
Columbus: Fifteen Weeks

The car is no longer a problem. First, someone broke the window and stole my sleeping bag. Two weeks later, someone stole the whole car. This was after I paid a grand to have the fuel line fixed.

On the upside, if you buy a cup of coffee and don't ask the other customers for change, the manager of this McDonald's won't kick you out.

I guess they had a problem a couple of years ago when a man froze to death by their dumpster after getting kicked out in a cold spell.

I lost half my fortune when the car was stolen. Now, every penny is precious to me. I ration my money based on how many calories I need and what it'll cost to keep buying minutes for my phone.

I only turn the phone on when I have free Wi-Fi and sometimes at night to see if Jillian is still texting me.

She is.

But the message is no longer **Come home.**

It's **Get help.**

N2 has killed between eleven and thirteen people by now, based on her average kill rate of almost one per week.

That's how I measure time now—by her kills.

If I could spare the money, I'd tattoo one *X* into my arm for every lost soul. Instead I keep repeating the total count: 185.

It could be more; it could be less. But each week I add another victim.

When Jillian tells me to get help, I instead try to imagine who will be next.

Statistically speaking, it will be someone between fifty-three and seventy-eight. The children were outliers for her, but I suspect she'd kill more if she could. It's just that they're harder to kill. You can get lucky and find a place like Stoneman or Mercy Hospital only so often.

Does fatally injecting a heart patient suffering from dementia give her the same thrill as watching a seven-year-old take her last gasp?

I can't think that it does.

Sometimes when I sit on a bus bench or the steps near a hospital and watch people enter, I fantasize about what N2 feels when she kills.

Filman was a passive-aggressive sociopath who killed out of anger and then fetishized his murders by taking trophies. For N2, the killing is the thing. She doesn't need to take anything from it for the same reason that we don't take souvenirs from our last sexual experience. Well, most of us.

When I saw Filman's box of trophies, I suspected he'd confess. Which, apparently, he did, according to the news.

N2 won't.

She needs to see that glow of life fade away from rosy cheeks. That gasping rattle of someone realizing they're dying. That's what drives her.

It's her power.

It's her everything.

She's my everything.

I lean heavily against the window, my hands still wrapped around the coffee. I'm exhausted. I'm a customer. Don't kick me out.

A cold breeze wakes me as a woman walks into the McDonald's and turns toward the seating area. She wears a thick parka and black-rimmed glasses. She doesn't order anything. She starts to walk back outside, then stops at the door and looks to the back of the restaurant where I'm sitting.

She steps closer.

Her lips part. "Theo?"

That's my name, but I think I'm dreaming.

"Theo, is that you?"

She's a meter away. I glance up at the face.

"Hello, Hailey."

We stare at each other for a moment. I don't know how long I was asleep before she walked inside. I think I'm awake now.

"Theo?" she says again.

I've stopped looking at my reflection. I just gave in and let the beard win. The fact that my belt fits around me like a comically long noose tells me enough about my weight.

"What the fuck?" she asks, then leans closer to study my eyes and complexion.

I grin so she can see that I'm not a meth mouth. "I'm still me," I manage.

"Like hell. I've been looking all over for you. Jillian . . . she's been worried sick."

I don't have a response. I only nod.

"You're going through some kind of PTSD. We need you to get help."

"Are they going to tell me that N2 isn't real?"

"Fuck her, Theo. This is bad."

"One eighty-five, Hailey. That's the count. In two more days, it'll be 186. Will it be another old-timer this time or some child like Cooper or Nora?"

"And you're going to catch her? Like this? Have you looked at yourself? Theo, I say this as a friend. You're insane. You're certifiable."

"The photos," I reply.

"What?"

"The photos from the fireplace. Did you find anything?"

"They were almost all gone. Just a few edges of buildings. Nothing. There's no leads, Theo. There's nothing to do now but get better and think of a new strategy."

"N2's out there killing children."

"So's leukemia! Why don't you go back to your lab and work on that, asshole!"

"I don't have a lab anymore."

"I'll buy you a new lab if it'll get your ass off the street."

"I can't find her in a lab," I explain. "That's not the way the Dark Pattern works. Sometimes you can see it. Other times you just have to be it."

"The Dark Pattern? Do you even listen to yourself?"

"I'm sorry, Jillian. It's the only way that makes sense."

"Hailey. You're talking to Hailey," she replies.

Damn it.

I check my watch. "I'm sorry. I have to go. The bus will be here. I'm sure N2 uses public transportation to get around when she's in a new city."

"Theo!" she calls after me.

I wave goodbye and step out into the snow.

As the snowflakes dance around me, I try to imagine the underlying mathematics of a snowstorm. I open my mouth and capture one on my tongue.

CHAPTER SIXTY
PORTLAND: THIRTY-ONE WEEKS

From down here by the base of the bridge at night, the Oregon Health and Science University Hospital looks like a shining, futuristic city on the mountainside. They actually have an aerial tram to take you from down here to up there. Normally it costs $4.90 per round trip, but I can ride it as many times as I want with my bus pass.

A monthly bus pass is a hundred bucks, but if you're an "honored citizen" it's only twenty-eight dollars. "Honored citizen" is Portland's polite way of referring to the homeless, the elderly, and the disabled.

I've been wandering around the city trying to find N2.

I realized what my problem had been all along after I walked into the blizzard and started trying to understand the patterns in the snowflakes.

I'd completely rejected mathematics in my quest for the Dark Pattern and embraced first-person subjective experience.

What I needed was to synthesize the two. The bad data sets weren't going to help, but that didn't mean there was no meaningful data set out there that could reveal her location.

This was my arrogance.

This is what Ken taught me.

I don't know if Ken is his real name, but that's what I started calling him.

I found Ken after I woke up on the sidewalk near Boulder Medical Center. I remember leaving a 7-Eleven. And I think I remember some people watching me from the back of the store the night before, when I paid for my coffee and banana with a prepaid debit card I had tucked into my waistband.

I think those people were waiting for me when I left. Well, one of them. I saw one of them.

I think the other one hit me from behind with something. I don't have too much recollection of what happened until I woke up in a pool of frozen pink saliva.

My phone was gone. So were most of my prepaid cards. I was sitting on a bench, curling my toes in my boots to warm them when I noticed Ken.

He was across the street, reaching into a garbage can near a Subway sandwich shop.

I vaguely remembered seeing Ken before. His face was weatherbeaten, but his shoes were new and he had an overcoat in better shape than mine. To be honest, Ken looked to be in much better condition than I was.

That's when I decided to follow him. If I'd been lost in a forest, following Ken would be like following some other animal with better survival instincts.

Ken was smart. If you're looking for food in a trash can, the best places are where people have to eat in a hurry: the Burger King next to the high school, the garbage can by the stadium, the movie theater next to a Starbucks.

I followed Ken to a church that had a clothing bin for the homeless. I then followed him to a library that offered coffee and doughnuts most weeknights in the various meeting rooms.

That's where I sat down and tried to talk to Ken. He didn't seem alarmed by me. I think he knew I'd been following him.

He simply nodded at me. When I asked him his name, he pointed to his mouth and shook his head.

Thanks to Ken, I realized that I didn't have to spend what money I had left on food. I could use it for bus passes and transportation once I solved the Dark Pattern.

Which I did three weeks ago in the Denver public library on the back of a brown paper bag. The Dark Pattern told me to go to Portland.

Since arriving, I've been using my bus pass and the skills Ken taught me to find N2.

OHSU is not the kind of hospital that would hire N2, but it's exactly the kind of place where she'd find her next victim.

I've been riding the tram, looking at all the women's faces, trying to figure out which one could know N2. Sometimes I follow them to see if they meet up with her.

So far none has.

The calculations are correct.

I have no doubt.

CHAPTER SIXTY-ONE
PORTLAND: THIRTY-FIVE WEEKS

I had to pull out one of my molars in the Wendy's bathroom. It had been bothering me for some time. I used a pair of pliers I keep in my pocket and then packed the socket with a piece of paper towel.

One of the employees gave me a funny look when I took my water cup and poured ten packets of salt into it. Short of a proper antibiotic, it'll do.

Of course, when I swish the water around, it knocks the paper towel loose.

They asked me to stop riding the tram last week. The security guard was polite, but he told me that I couldn't go onto OHSU property unless I had a medical issue.

I think it's because of the redheaded woman I followed. She didn't look like N2, but she seemed to be her type. Same age, same build, and I never saw her talk to anyone. A loner looking for a friend.

I followed her to the bus and took that all the way to North Portland. That's when she suspected that I had been following her. I almost got off at her stop but then decided to continue on.

It's okay. I'm not mad at her. The OHSU tram isn't the only way to find N2.

I've also been listening to ambulances and mapping which part of the city they start from and where they end. I've noticed a peculiar pattern. The longer the ambulance siren sounds, the lower the Yelp rating for the hospital.

I pay for my coffee at the McDonald's counter with my last prepaid card and step back onto the street. As I walk down Sixth Avenue, I feel a sense of déjà vu.

I turn around and see two men heading toward me. One of them is tall and extremely skinny. The other is short and stocky.

"Hey, old man. Come here. Let me ask you something," says the shorter one.

I'd walk away, but I don't want to put my back to them. I also notice the tall one is holding something close to his body.

I would be afraid, but this is part of the Dark Pattern. I've seen it coming.

The tall one raises his arm and a metal pipe.

I push the shorter one into his armpit. The short guy takes a step back, then pulls a knife from his pocket.

I used to have a lot more strength for this. I have to keep my distance.

The smaller one lunges at me. I hit the inside of his arm with my left fist and barrel into him. We both fall to the ground. He can't stab me because I'm on the inside of his knife arm.

However, his friend can hit me with the pipe.

And he does.

He cracks the metal into my back as I punch his smaller friend in the jaw.

Crack.

Punch.

Crack.
Punch.
It's a pattern.
It's a dark pattern, but not the Dark Pattern.
That's what happens next.
Crack.
Darkness.

CHAPTER SIXTY-TWO
PORTLAND: THIRTY-FIVE WEEKS, DAY TWO

I'm in the back of a police car. We're pulling into the gated part of a police station. My hands are cuffed in front of me, and my nose smells the scent of blood.

I remember leaving McDonald's.

I think this is Boulder.

Or is it Denver?

The door opens, and a police officer asks me to step outside the vehicle.

I climb out of the car and trip as the world spins around me.

His badge says "Portland."

How odd.

I'm guided/carried up a set of steps and seated in a plastic chair. There are three other men sitting there. Two look like me; the other is clean-shaven but smells of alcohol.

One of the cops who escorted me out of the car goes over to a workstation and starts typing. "What's your name?" he asks.

"Dr. Theo Cray," I reply. Of this much I am certain.

"Ooh, a doctor?" says an officer sitting at another desk. "What was this doctor doing?"

"Brawling."

"Brawling?" He looks at me. "You lucked out there, buddy. Officer Irish McIrish here can't stand brawlers."

Irish McIrish says, "Disorderly conduct in the second degree and obstructing pedestrian traffic on a public way."

The other officer turns to the second officer who was in the car with us. "Let me guess—you found him passed out on the sidewalk?"

"After he fought with a couple of other bums."

"Honored citizens," says Irish. "Hey, is that Cray with a *C*?"

"Affirmative," I reply.

"John, come take a look at this."

Officer John slides over on his swivel chair and stares at Irish's monitor. He looks up at me and then back at the screen. "Theo Cray?"

"Double affirmative."

The two of them whisper, and the third officer steps over to look at the screen. He glances up at me and shakes his head. "Holy shit. You didn't tell us you were a celebrity."

"Today is your lucky day," says Irish.

"What are you going to do?" asks John.

He rips up a report on his desk. "I've decided that I was in error. Mr. . . . Dr. Cray is free to go."

I fall off my chair when the room starts to spin. Two officers rush over and pick me up.

"Shit. He got hit bad."

"You okay?" asks one of them.

"Yes. Splendid," I say to the man with three heads.

"Take him to Samaritan?" asks one of the officers.

"Nah. They'll make him wait nine hours."

"How about the shelter?" asks another.

"They don't take them this late. And I thought you wanted him to live."

"I'm sure they will if you're insistent," says the other.

"Okay."

"Where did I set my cuffs?"

"I think you . . ."

❧

I wake up in the back of a police car. We're pulling into somewhere.

I remember leaving McDonald's.

I think this is Boulder?

Or is it Denver?

The sign says "Portland Citizens Shelter."

Two policemen politely escort me out of the car. I'm brought inside.

There is a small argument.

A man and a woman escort me to a cot in a room with many other men. It smells like coffee and sweat.

They set me down on a bed. The woman pulls back a gloved hand.

"Shit. I can't believe they deliver them like this. Get Peterson."

A man in a lab coat is flashing a light in my eyes. He's asking me questions. He has me sit up.

He says I'll be fine until Dr. Morgan gets here in the morning.

I go to sleep.

CHAPTER SIXTY-THREE
PORTLAND: THIRTY-FIVE WEEKS, DAY THREE

A man is flashing a light in my eyes. Is this Boulder? The last thing I remember is leaving a McDonald's.

He's muttering something. He's angry. Not at me, but he is handling me a little roughly.

My shirt is off, and I'm being inspected.

His fingers touch my ribs. They hurt.

There's also a gash that I'm still bleeding from.

He looks straight at me. "Are you on anything?"

"A table, I think."

He shakes his head. "Are you on any medication or drug?"

I shake my head. "I might have a dormant virus in my body that could cause a unique form of encephalitis, which would then impair some of my higher functions. Am I running a fever? If so, you should call the CDC."

"I want whatever you're having."

"It's called the Dark Pattern," I explain. "Is this Denver?"

"Jesus. This guy got knocked hard. I don't think we can handle him here. Nurse? Could you stitch him up so we can get him to an MRI before we lose another one this week?"

I realize that I have arrived at the very bottom.

I'm receiving substandard medical care in a facility for homeless men. This is where the Dark Pattern wanted me.

I turn to the nurse and smile.

Her face is blank and without expression.

"My name is Theo Cray."

I grab her wrist before she can pull away.

I put a handcuff around it before the doctor can separate us. I don't remember where I got the cuffs, but I'm glad I have them.

This is not Boulder.

This is not Denver.

I did not just walk out of a McDonald's.

This is the very bottom of the Dark Pattern.

I am exactly where I'm supposed to be.

And she's precisely the one I am after.

EPILOGUE

Myanmar: Nine Months Later

I ignore the footsteps coming toward me and study my surroundings for the thousandth time.

The wall of this cell seems to consist of layer after layer of paint. In the corner, I can see where someone has tried to peel their way to freedom, only to discover more layers.

Freedom is possible—if you're one of the cockroaches that crawls in and out of here freely. Unfortunately, I'm human-size and forced to think of some other means of getting out of here.

Six months ago, I was saying goodbye to Jillian. Neither one of us knew if it was going to be for the last time. Catching Rebecca Graham took a toll on our relationship that can never be fully repaid.

Or rather, I took a toll. Or a debit, or whatever the metaphor calls for.

When I called her from the hospital, all I could do was cry. There was sadness in her voice, but also a distance.

She had forced herself to let me go after I'd shut her out completely. I gave her no choice.

On one level, Jillian understands that I had to do it. In order to catch Rebecca, I needed to crawl into the same pit she had. There was method to my madness. Not that I can make any sense now of what I'd scrawled on that shopping bag . . . But she'd been in Denver. She'd been to Cleveland.

We were in the same cities at the same time on at least three occasions.

It took bottoming out in Portland for us finally to meet. But she almost got away there. I wasn't the most credible witness, after all. However, Dr. Morgan had had a suspicion.

They'd all had a suspicion.

But none of the other health-care workers who suspected Rebecca of murdering patients had someone screaming at the top of their lungs so loudly that the allegation couldn't be ignored.

I didn't want to scream anymore.

When I got home after the hospital, there was a present waiting for me from Professor Amanda Paulson. It was her backpack, sent to me by her daughter, Jewel.

The subtext was apparent: finish what she started.

And here I am in Myanmar, awaiting my fate.

I might have started another civil war.

Things got bad.

I did things.

I didn't scream.

I didn't run.

But things got bad.

Commander Zaw is at the door of my cell.

I like him the most. He punches the softest.

He unlocks the door and motions for me to follow. His English is heavily accented, so he doesn't like to speak in front of me.

He leads me down the hallway. We pass the small skylight I keep thinking about using as a means of escape.

But if I do that, it'll have to be when I hear a motorcycle go by so I won't have to flee on foot.

He takes me right instead of left. *Curious.* This hall leads to the front of the police station. Not the back.

Hmm. No questions today?

Zaw takes me all the way to the front desk, where a man is stamping papers. This would be one of the clerks.

"Dr. Cray. You have been bailed out."

"Bailed?" A minute ago, I thought I was going to be tried for war crimes. "By whom?" I ask.

"The lady over there."

He points behind me. I turn around, expecting to see Jillian or Hailey. It's neither. The face is somewhat familiar, but I can't quite place it. It's attractive but even more so intelligent.

The dark-haired woman gets up from a bench and walks over to me. She holds out her hand. "Dr. Cray? My name is Jessica Blackwood. We need to talk."

ABOUT THE AUTHOR

Andrew Mayne is the *Wall Street Journal* bestselling author of *The Naturalist* and *Looking Glass*, an Edgar Award nominee for *Black Fall*, and the star of A&E's *Don't Trust Andrew Mayne* and a Discovery Channel *Shark Week* special. He is also a magician who started his first world tour as an illusionist when he was a teenager and went on to work behind the scenes for Penn & Teller, David Blaine, and David Copperfield. Ranked as the fifth bestselling independent author of the year by Amazon UK, Andrew currently hosts the *Weird Things* podcast. For more on him and his work, visit www.AndrewMayne.com.